SAMHAIN

MIDSUMMER
BOOK TWO

JENA DOYLE

DIRTY WORDS PUBLISHING LLC

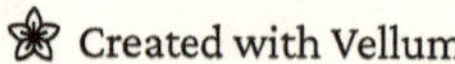 Created with Vellum

For Hel ... Thank you.
Also for Loki...don't fuck this up for me, you little shit. Love you and
thank you.

PROLOGUE
CARTER

NOW

It was a sham marriage.

I knew that. They'd both told me. We'd promised each other honesty, and I believed them. That didn't stop the throbbing ache in my chest. I used to have a heart there, once upon a time. Now, I only had a hole and a leaking sieve.

I should be there.

I sipped my scotch. It went down smooth and sweet, burning my stomach with enough agony to remind me I was alive, even after everything that's happened.

"It's the wedding event of the season, Mark," said the talking head on the TV, her blond hair bouncing as she stood in front of the Washington estate. "Any moment, Alexei Fairfax will take his place in front of the altar. We're told five minutes after that, Ivy will walk down the aisle. I was fortunate enough to get a glimpse of her wedding dress, and it is *to die* for."

What a way to put it. I snorted as I took another drink.

How long had I loved her? How many times had I held her in my arms while she fell apart? Being here, watching it on TV instead of in person, well…I didn't know which was worse. I had endured this and much more for them, but publicly holding my tongue while they made vows to each other they'd already made to Miri and me took an act of God.

I'm not worthy. Not yet.

"You know, René Calvert designed this dress himself," said the other presenter, Mark. "It took over two million dollars in diamonds."

Jesus.

I bet Ivy hated it. She'd rather get married in hot garbage than walk down the aisle in some pretentious sparkling number that weighed a thousand pounds.

I took another drink and winced against my breaking heart, now racing at the mention of a countdown. Lex and Ivy would soon make legal what we had made symbolic in the woods four years ago, and like an itch that wouldn't go away, my fingers went to the scars on my right palm.

Matching scars, ones we all shared.

Until the end.

We'd promised a lot of things that night. Even more in the nights after it. So many promises we shattered to pieces. And despite that, I never suspected we'd end up here. Spread to the farthest parts of the earth. Drowning our sorrows in liquor and hopelessness and existential dread.

I thought of Miri. What was she doing to ease the pain of today?

Christ, we'd been dreading it for so long now that a part of me was relieved to finally stare it down.

My phone rang, my eldest sister calling for the hundredth time. My family knew how I felt about Ivy, how much today would wreck me despite the years between us. I couldn't bring myself to talk to them. I couldn't bring myself to talk to anyone. I let it go to voicemail. Again. It didn't surprise me when I got a nasty text message after that threatening to leak embarrassing baby pictures of me if I didn't answer.

Go ahead.

I didn't care. I didn't care about much anymore—not since it happened. Not since this ridiculous curse brought us together and tore us apart.

As long as she was leaving me shitty voicemails, she was safe. They were all safe.

My phone buzzed one more time, but the name on the screen made my dead heart give half a thump.

Juliet.

"Hey, you," I said when I answered.

She greeted me with a sigh. "Hello, Romeo."

I smiled at the nickname. "I'm glad you called. Where are you?"

"Oh, you know. Locked in my ivory tower."

Code for her family was around. "Are you watching?"

"Of course." Another dramatic sigh. Typical Miri. "I'm sure she looks bloody amazing. And he probably looks like my prince of darkness. It's absolutely horrid."

"Did you talk to her?" No sense in elaborating. There could only be one *her* between Miri and me.

"No," she said, followed by a pause. "Have you?"

"No. Neither of them."

"I suppose we deserve this. You and me, for our sins."

"Don't do that to yourself." I knew what sins she meant, and of the three of us, I was the only one who knew what Miri had kept to herself. "We're in this together. All of us."

"All of us," she said with a sarcastic laugh. "Christ, we're pathetic."

"Have you rethought my proposal?" I asked again. "Do I need to show up on my valiant steed for you to finally listen to me?"

"I can't, Romeo," she said before another long pause and a much lower, "It's not safe."

"None of this is safe; that's the point. You know what's about to happen. You know we need to be together."

"That doesn't change anything."

"Juliet," I said. "Marry me. I can come get you in twenty minutes." I was still in London. I could still put the plan into action.

She let out a sad chuckle. "Now, there's a silly idea."

"I'm serious."

"Ivy would kill me," she said. "She would kill you, too."

"They have each other. All we have is us."

She made another sigh. "I have to go. They're always listening. I wanted to make sure you were okay."

I almost begged her to come to me, to spend this night, the worst night of our lives, together like we used to. Like the good old days. That was how we could be safe. We were stronger together, the four of us. But it wouldn't do any good.

Her family had sequestered her away from the public eye. Freedom would mean goodbye forever, and Miri didn't know who she was if she wasn't part of her family.

"Be well, Juliet."

"You too, Romeo. I love you."

"I love you." I meant the words with every fiber in my being. The love I shared with Miri wasn't the same as what I felt for Ivy, nor would it match the intensity with which I burned for Lex. But it was there all the same, vibrant and everlasting.

"Wait, what's this?" the talking head said, catching my attention as I hung up. "I'm being told now that Ivy and Lex are missing. No one can find them in the marital suites."

I shot to my feet, alarm ricocheting down my spine.

Son of a bitch.

My phone rang again.

ACT I

*If then true lovers have been ever crossed,
It stands as an edict in destiny.
-Hermia, Act I, Scene I*

I

CARTER
AGE SIXTEEN

I learned at a young age that getting people to like me usually afforded me whatever I wanted. It was something about my face, the innocence in my eyes perhaps, or the dimples in my cheeks. It softened people's resolve, and once I had them laughing, most turned to putty in my hands. Growing up as the oldest of four children in a latchkey house with two working parents made this even more useful. Acted out in class and got detention? One grin and a flimsy excuse later, I was off.

Of the Scott kids, I was the one who had to keep my shit together. I was the one who had to make something of myself, the one setting the example for the rest.

"Did Charlotte do her homework tonight?" my mother asked, sorting through the mail and flexing her hosed feet on the yellow laminate kitchen floor. In the morning, she ran her own yoga studio, but after that, she worked the second shift at a call center to make ends meet.

"Yes," I said, scribbling in my math notebook.

"And Sophia took a shower before bed?" Her blue eyes wandered over a bill, and she ran a hand through her sunshine-blond hair, brushing it back from her face before opening another envelope.

"Of course." My reply came absently, my mind too focused on my homework. I wasn't sure my calculations were right. I'd have to ask someone to compare notes in the morning. Math had never been my strong suit.

"Carter," my mother snapped. "Are you listening?"

I cleared my throat and looked up at her. "Yes."

"What about Lizzie?"

"Everyone is bathed and sound asleep," I said. "Can I finish my homework now?"

Her features dropped, and she sank into the chair next to me. "I'm sorry. I know it's difficult asking you to take care of your sisters."

Especially when it should be her and our father.

"When's he coming home?" I asked.

She'd confided in me a few weeks ago that they were considering divorce. He'd rented an apartment closer to his job with a flimsy excuse about a shorter commute, but none of us bought it. We all suspected what was really going on.

"I don't know." She reached across the table to grab my hand. I tugged it away from her.

"I have something to tell you." I swallowed the lump in my throat and grabbed the acceptance letter from my book bag, sliding it across the table to her. "Some theater groups from around the world came to my school a few weeks ago. I auditioned and got an invitation from the Royal Theater Company to study with them for a year."

Her mouth hung open, and her indigo eyes, replicas of my own, fell to the letter. The faint glow from the retro overhead light illuminated her confusion as she read through it. This would be an amazing opportunity for me, one that would help me get into Thomas Washington University. One that would help me after graduation. The connections I'd make there would network me into what I'd always wanted.

"A year?" She blew the word out like it had been squeezed from her chest.

"I know you need help with my sisters. But this is important to me."

She covered her mouth and tears brimmed in the corners of her eyes. "Jesus, Carter."

"If there's any way we can make it work...I'll do double shifts at the video store. I'll eat Spam and macaroni for the next five years. I just—" I had to go. I needed to go. I wanted it with everything in my body, like something greater than myself was pulling me there.

"Of course, we'll make it work," she said. "This is—Wow." She stood and walked over to me, wrapping her arms around my shoulders before pulling me into a tight hug. "I'm so proud of you. My baby boy."

I snorted. "Not a baby anymore."

"Oh, you're my first." She wiped at her cheeks. "You'll always be my baby."

"Thanks, Mom."

"You'll have to tell your father."

"Ah." I let out a breath. "I was hoping..."

She pursed her lips. "Okay. Let me talk to him. It'll soften the blow."

My father thought my acting dreams were just that. Dreams. Fantasies. Nothing would ever come from them. Sure, the hobby gave me valuable life experience, but my time would be better spent studying business or dentistry like him. Something with a guaranteed return on investment.

But that sounded like a corporate hellhole, and I wanted the glitz and the glamour of fame. There was a downside to it, sure, but I loved the stage, and I was good at it.

"Carter?" came the small voice from the entry to the dining room.

My youngest sister, Lizzie, stood in the doorway, clutching at a raggedy teddy bear with one hand. Her messy blond hair stuck out in odd directions, but her chubby red cheeks indicated she'd been crying. "I had a nightmare."

At six, she'd been the *last-chance-to-save-a-dying-marriage* child my parents hadn't expected but had been delighted to bring into the world. In the end, it didn't save their relationship, and the ten-year age difference between me and Lizzie made it easier for my parents to lean on me for help raising her.

Charlotte and Sophia were closer to each other than to either of us. But Lizzie? Well, she'd had me wrapped around her finger since the day she was born.

"Aww, Lizzie-Bizzie." I scooped her up and wrapped my arms around her tiny body, my heart melting when she rested her head on my shoulder and let out one final whimper before she relaxed. "It's okay. It's only a bad dream."

"Will you stay with me?" she asked when I put her back in her bed.

"Always."

"Pwomise?" It came out as a muffled sigh, her eyes fighting sleep but ultimately losing.

"Promise."

But six months later, I was on a plane to London with my life packed in two suitcases, and a year after that, I met a guy who would change it altogether.

LONDON

AGE EIGHTEEN

I STOOD backstage at the King's Royal Theater, my crown in one hand, my phone in the other. It had been a week since I'd met Lex, and I still hadn't gotten the balls to text him and ask if he planned to come see the play.

I set aside a ticket at the box office for him every night, but so far, he hadn't taken me up on it.

Not that I really expected him to. What could someone like him want with someone like me? It's just...I believed in the power of firsts. First kisses. First fucks. First loves. Not necessarily in that order.

The first girl I ever slept with was Stephanie Hoppenheimer in the treehouse my father built in the backyard. We were fifteen and I came in less than two minutes, so I spent the rest of the night going down on her to make up for it. She didn't know I was a virgin. Ever since that day, I'd locked a piece of my heart away for her. She got that spot in my life no one else would ever have.

Sentimental, yes, but I was a sentimental shit, and that would never change.

I fucked around with a lot of girls in high school. Who didn't? I was tall and beautiful and athletic. People liked that, but it meant little to me. I couldn't afford to fall in love. I had dreams. Hollywood. My name in bright lights. So I purposely kept myself guarded. I couldn't lose my head over someone who would keep me in Chicago for the rest of my life.

I was meant for greater things.

"Hey," came the voice from my right. My director, Anthony Michaels, walked closer. He'd been a screenwriter for a couple of different television shows on the BBC and had a résumé a mile long. A tall, thin man with wiry hair and thick tortoise-shell glasses, he liked to joke that he'd been roped into teaching at the RTC for a semester by losing a bet to an old colleague. Most importantly, he'd taken a liking to me and put me under his wing like a mentor. "You ready for tonight?"

"Yeah." I smiled and shoved my phone in my back pocket, determined not to think about Lex anymore. "I'm always ready."

He laughed and clapped me on the shoulder. "I know. That's what makes you such a lucky little wanker."

I narrowed my eyes on him.

"Your talent? All natural. It's rare. You should cherish it."

One side of my mouth pulled into a smile. Luck. Natural talent. I knew what he was trying to say, but he didn't see the years I'd spent busting my ass for this—pleading and scraping just to be right here.

"You need to keep your head on straight. No distractions."

"I understand," I said. And I did, even as my heart ached for a beautiful boy who had promised to show up but never did. "College. Then Hollywood."

"Exactly. I'm writing a screenplay now. It's called *Fractured Crowns*. I think you'd be great for one of the parts."

"Really?" I raised my eyebrows in surprise. "Are you offering me a job?"

He laughed and held up his hands. "Let's not get ahead of ourselves. I said I'm *writing* the screenplay. I still have to finish it and sell it. But stay in touch, yeah?"

"Yeah," I said, making a mental note to ensure I did.

But I was eighteen, and I'd just sucked a dick for the first time, so my mind was a million miles away. Like I said, I believed in the power of firsts. Lex Fairfax had rocked my world. Yeah, I knew who he was when I met him. I'd seen him on the cover of magazines my whole life.

But in person? Man, those hazel eyes hit differently, like they could peel you apart, layer by layer until they saw all the deep, dark shit you were made of. Matched with the cheekbones, the pouty lips, and the tattoos? The dude was a work of art.

My mother would have called it a meeting of souls and said Lex and I had been lovers in a past life. He looked at me like I lit up the sky at night, and no *guy* had ever looked at me like that before. Or if they had, I didn't notice because I was too busy chasing pussy.

I *noticed* Lex.

Up until this point, I'd never considered the possibility that I might be bisexual. I liked girls a lot. But now? Shit, I'd give it all up for another night with him.

Was it his smile that made my heart beat faster than anyone before him? Was it how he rolled his eyes when he thought I was being facetious? Or maybe it was because he made me feel like I could be all he'd ever need?

I didn't know, but I liked it, and I wanted to believe I was special, that he didn't hook up with many guys, that I was somehow unique. Lex was a first for me in a multitude of ways.

Sentimental, remember?

I put my heart into that last performance of *Henry V*, praying the entire time that Lex was in the audience, watching with that hazel stare, waiting for his night with the king.

When I got off the stage and realized he hadn't shown, the horrible truth settled in my gut. The experience had been eye-opening for me. Earth-shattering. Revelatory. But I'd been just another fuck to Lex Fairfax.

I DIDN'T THINK I'd see him again. Thomas Washington University had more than 300,000 students. Odds were, he'd go about his merry rich boy life, and I'd keep my place with the peasants. Imagine my surprise when I walked into the cafeteria the second day of being on campus and there he was. His hair was a little longer, and he had his arm around a brunette, but it was undeniably him. I bit back my reaction, my eyes shifting to the person in the seat beside him.

Princess Miriam.

I understood the situation immediately. Lex hadn't called because he and Miriam were together. That made more sense than his interest in me. Who else could have a prince but an equally powerful princess? Why would he call piddly me when he had majestic *her*?

My focus drifted across the table, and my heart came to a standstill.

Ivy Washington.

The atmosphere changed, grew static and charged. Anticipation built in my chest, like magic had tried to tell me then, at this first meeting of the four of us, that we were destined for *more*. That we would weave a tale so wicked we could only experience it together.

I fell in love with her the first week of freshman term after a night spent studying in the library. It was late, just the two of us, and she'd disappeared into the 600 section some twenty minutes ago. The library announced they were closing soon, so I gathered my things and went to find her.

At that time of night, the racks had that eerie glow to them that made them spooky and haunted for how many lives were immortalized on their shelves. She stood in the last row, a copy of *Introduction to BDSM: Kink and Fetishes* in her hand. I watched her from the end of the aisle as she flipped through the pages, her cheeks pink, her focus captivated.

I should have let her have her moment, perhaps given her privacy. But the thought of Ivy and that book together made my blood heat, and I couldn't stop myself.

"Hey, what's that?" I said, going to stand next to her.

She startled and snapped it closed, hiding it behind her back like she'd been caught with her hand in the candy bin.

Adorable.

"Nothing," she said. "Just some reading. What's up?"

"Some reading?" I raised an eyebrow and smiled, taking a few steps closer. "Whatcha reading, Weeds?"

Ivy let out her nervous giggle and forced a smile, clearing her throat as she put the book back on its shelf.

"Oh," I said. "A new interest or a refresher?"

She balked. "What?"

I snorted and shook my head. "You know, if you need someone to tie you up and turn your ass pink, all you have to do is ask."

I thought I had her speechless, perhaps flustered and embarrassed. Then she shocked the fuck out of me and said, "Bold of you to assume I'm not the one tying the knots."

She gave me that classic Washington stare and walked back toward our stuff.

The visual that went through my mind was downright despicable. Me, on my knees in front of her, a collar around my throat, my mouth open and ready to service her. Ivy, a crop in her hand, thigh-high leather boots, all that red hair in a mane around her head.

Good lord.

I'd never been one to let something like that go. If it were any other girl, I'd march my ass up to her and demand she put her money where my mouth was, but Weeds? Well...

She was millions of miles out of my league, and even if I became the richest man on the planet, she always would be. It wasn't only that I was intimidated by her. I didn't deserve her, and I couldn't have her, so I kept my distance.

I forced myself to go home with random chicks, and I closed my eyes when I slid inside them, picturing the way Ivy's mouth fell open into that perfect pouty O, or the way her hair looked in the sunshine, or the way her skin turned that delectable shade of rose when she got flustered.

When I *finally* got her alone in my dorm, we matched in every way. There was nothing—I do mean *nothing*—that Ivy wouldn't do as long as it was with me.

Like I said, I believe in firsts. I may not have been the first person to be intimate with Ivy Washington, but I was the first person with a cock she let inside her body, the first guy she trusted with her privacy and soul.

My love with Ivy was unmatched by anything I'd ever known. It was the deep down inside kinda love, the stuff that kept me up at night wondering if I was making the right choices. Would I be able to leave her when the time came? Would I really be able to walk away from this? From her?

I had four years to figure it out, and in those four years, I tried not to worry about it.

But you know what they say about the best laid plans...

And in my case, my downfall started with a flight to Ireland and a severely fucked-up trip through the woods.

2

MIRI
AGE EIGHTEEN

I almost died when I was fourteen.

Or perhaps I did die and rebuilt myself from the ashes like a phoenix, hell-bent on seeking revenge for those who had been taken from me.

I didn't remember much from that day, the worst day of my life, and many therapists would say my brain intentionally blocked it out. I was in the back seat, ducking down on the ground to keep the photographers from taking pictures of me. I didn't like seeing myself in the magazines. I didn't like it when they said things about me.

"Drive faster," my father shouted.

"Gerald," my mother said. "We're already going too fast."

"We can lose them," he replied. I sank down farther, my hands over my ears, terror in my chest. I hated the people who chased us. Why couldn't they leave us alone?

The sound of the wreck haunted my nightmares, the sickening crunch of metal on metal as the car hit something hard and impenetrable. The world went topsy-turvy, and much of what happened after that was darkness.

When I came to, I lay in the grass ten yards away, staring into the lifeless gaze of my mother, hanging upside down in the car, her head bent at a wrong angle.

I wanted to cry.

I wanted to scream.

I wanted to yank them from the twisted cage and pray to a cruel, merciless God to bring them back to life. Just bring them back. Unconsciousness took me again, and the next thing I remembered, I blinked awake in a hospital bed. I had minor injuries and a concussion, but other than that, I was relatively fine.

"How'd you get out of the vehicle?" a policeman asked.

"Were there witnesses, Princess?" another person added.

I didn't know. I didn't remember. The *beep-beep-beep* of my heart rate monitor went faster, and I took a deep breath, my vision murky with tears.

This must be a dream.

Any second now, I told myself. Any second, I'd wake up in my bed at Kensington, realizing I'd watched too many soap operas the day before. That never happened, and when my Uncle McCormick walked through the door next, that stoic look on his squirmy face, I knew I was screwed.

My grandmother, the queen of England, had sent him to check on me. My grandparents planned to adopt me, to bring me into their household, which, at first, brought great relief. The situation quickly became stifling as my grandmother raised me like the daughter she'd never had.

It should have been little surprise I rebelled after that.

I did the whole London club scene. I woke up in strangers' beds, words of regret and an NDA on my lips. I stumbled out of buildings, unsure of where I was, only to have the cameras flash in my face, capturing the worst parts of my adolescent meltdown. I understood it wasn't a great look, that it painted my family in a manner they didn't particularly enjoy.

"This isn't how young ladies are supposed to conduct themselves," my grandmother said at brunch one morning, sipping her tea. Her white hair sparkled in the morning light, curled to perfection in the same hairstyle she'd had for decades. "You know what gossip like this does to our image." She pointed to the headline.

Princess Miriam working her way through London's nightlife. What would her father think? The Royal family declines to comment.

I swallowed the lump in my throat and glanced to the floor between us, refusing to meet that unscrupulous glare.

"I'm sorry, Gran," I said.

She raised an eyebrow. "You'll have to do better than that."

Acting out like this would hurt me in the end, but I didn't care what the newspapers wrote. I didn't care about the reputation of the royal family. I didn't care about any of it. No one understood what it was like to stand up in front of the world, missing your heart, and pretend to smile pretty for the cameras. To know you survived something that killed everyone else that ever loved you.

Was it so shocking that I'd become lonely? That I wanted companionship?

"Your grandfather and I have agreed that it would be best for you to get some breathing room," she said.

My hackles rose, but I knew better than to question the queen.

"There is a boarding school in America. The president sends her children there. It will do you some good, darling."

The last thing I needed was to be away from my home, but I didn't want to disappoint her. She promised if I played along, if I followed the rules, the Stuart fortune would be mine when I turned eighteen. My grandfather would officially invite me to court, give me my father's title, and make me a duchess. Finally. All I'd ever wanted.

So I went, and I told myself on the flight over that I'd start again. This would be a new life for me, a chance to reinvent myself.

And then I met Ivy.

She had a hard time making friends, and I thought it was perfect because I didn't have any to speak of. That became the basis of our relationship. I warmed her, she hardened me, and together, we ruled Mount Oberon our senior year. Her bright-eyed reason and calculated hesitation made me want to shake her and laugh at her.

I loved the way she blinked awake first thing in the morning, immediately looking to see if I was still there. We could sit in silence for hours, saying nothing and everything in that blissful peace. Being in her company balanced me out, and she needed me in ways she'd never admit. I grew too attached to her, knowing I'd have to leave her in the end, and the thought nearly killed me.

We couldn't go public with a relationship. Just imagining the look on my grandmother's face made me wince. An American? A progressive? Utter nonsense. She wouldn't have it.

Because of this, I kept my desires to myself until the last day of school, when we'd gotten drunk together and stumbled back to our room, giddy with teenage disillusionment. The way she'd looked at me. The way she'd brushed hair out of my face.

How could I not?

How could I not?

I took her in every way I'd fantasized about. I made her moan and twist her fingers in my hair, and the next morning, when she woke up panicked about what it meant, I pretended it didn't hurt to see relief in her eyes at my casual nonchalance. I brushed it under the rug as I always did when it came to her.

I acted like Ivy's eager acceptance to get over it didn't mean a damn thing. In truth, it had scarred me more deeply than anyone else ever could. But fate had other plans for me. The very next day, I met my soul mate.

Lex Fairfax.

We matched. Our jagged edges had always fit together like yin and yang. The media hadn't been kind to either of us in our youth. He was the drugged-out American fuckup, and I was the slutty British disappointment.

Together? Well, there was a reason we'd made it through four years of college, despite the ups and downs. I'd fallen in love with him instantly at Kensington, when he'd shown up at my gran's dinner and gotten stoned with me, eating snacks until well in the morning.

I'd just made love to Ivy Washington and acted like it meant nothing when it had meant everything. I had to pretend like everything was okay. I had to put on the pretty dress and force a smile on my face and go to dinner like nothing was wrong...*again.*

Lex and I reveled in the joke of the charade—these maniacal villains with their violent delights that would lead to violent ends. They plotted to take over the world while we plotted to escape it forever.

Was it because he reminded me of Ivy that I became so enraptured with him? Or was I looking for a life raft to cling to? Someone to replace the steady force she'd become?

I feared the answer to all of it was simply...*yes.*

My feelings for Lex were always so twisted with my feelings for Ivy; it was damn near impossible to separate the two.

I thought Ivy would be pissed. I thought she'd be jealous, and if she was, she held on to it only until she met Carter. Beautiful, sweet Carter with a heart the size of a planet and a smile just as wide. I loved him, but only the way I loved any other close friend.

Perhaps, at the beginning, there had been casual flirtation, but we immediately shut that down because Ivy was taken with him from the start. If I hadn't been so emotional both my best friend and my boyfriend, I might have paid him more mind.

He quickly fell in love with his *Weeds* and rekindled his friendship with Lex, and on life went.

Even though I had Lex and I loved him dearly, a small part of me died when Ivy and Carter made it official. I envied Carter for being able to crawl into her bed at night and kiss her the way I once had, to take her as often or as frequently as she deserved.

But there were moments when Ivy's gaze caught mine from across the room and her smile widened, and I'd feel that heartbeat in my soul again, the one that pittered just for her patter. It should have confused me, but even in its infancy, this strange relationship had always been so right.

I told myself life was too short to dwell on the things I couldn't control. I couldn't make Ivy want me the way I wanted her. I couldn't make the world be okay with a relationship between us. I couldn't change the way our families saw each other.

I had to accept it and move on.

Four years had passed since then, and I had nothing to change that perception.

I had lived with it and learned to accept it...until we went to Ireland.

AGE TWENTY-TWO
LA

THERE'S no such thing as a pleasant goodbye, especially not with a lover.

You say you'll call. You say you'll visit. You swear it's not the end. But in reality, words are only hot air and actions mean everything. Lex and Ivy could have come to California with us. They could have rebelled against their parents and postponed their law school plans, maybe held firm on their reluctance to get married.

But they didn't.

Ivy swore to fight the good fight, and Lex swore to help her, and we all swore to love each other anyway. *Swear, and swear, and swear.*

"Miriam, darling," Gran said, annoyance dripping from her tone. "I do not approve of unscheduled changes of plans."

"Of course, Gran." I forced a grin. "But this will be a good opportunity for me to network with charitable organizations on that side of the US."

I know, I know.

LA? Miri, my love, what are you thinking?

The truth was, I'd been hung over and sorely dehydrated when I agreed to go with Carter. At the time, I didn't know the secrets Lex and Ivy were hiding. I didn't know *Carter* knew the secrets they were hiding. But now that everything was out in the open, I wouldn't back down from it. Going with him seemed more important than ever.

"Hmm." She sipped at her tea, the soft noise rattling through the speaker on the phone. "The prince of Monaco has been asking about you."

I suppressed a groan, watching Carter fidget next to me in the limo. Was I cutting it close by calling her *on the way* to the airport? Certainly. But Gran didn't need to know the sordid details.

"Oh?" Hiding my disgust took work. The prince of Monaco was twenty years older than me, and even if he made a desirable financial match, I wouldn't be caught dead with that walking midlife crisis. No, thank you.

"I will allow this impromptu trip if you will agree to have dinner with him once you return."

I remained silent because I didn't want to, but Gran so rarely threw out a negotiation that if I didn't take her up on it, I would simply be commanded to come home now and have dinner with him anyway.

"Yes," I said. "Whatever you think is best, Gran."

"Delightful. Have fun in Malibu, and do try to stay out of trouble. Love you, darling."

I hung up and swallowed the impending awkwardness of having to sit through that fiasco. Oh, well. Those were tomorrow's worries. I had enough on my plate today.

"Do you have her royal blessing?" Carter grinned and winked.

I nodded. "For the time being. She'll soon grow impatient and send someone to bring me home."

He nodded, and now that we were alone for the first time since Ireland, the strangeness of this new relationship between us settled. For four years, he'd been Ivy's boyfriend. Lex's best friend. My stage partner. But now, things were different. We were running off to Hollywood together.

"I'm still surprised you agreed to this." He reached across the limo to grab my hand, giving it a tender squeeze.

"I'm surprised you asked."

The day after we blurred the lines between us during the beer pong game, the theater group had taken a bonding camping trip in the forest. Carter and I had been put in the same group, and somewhere around the waterfall, he'd wandered off alone. I went to find him, and when I did, he'd admitted to being heartbroken about leaving Ivy at the end of the trip.

"Leaving both of them is going to kill me," he'd said.

"They'll have each other, and in the end, I'll only have my garden." I had laughed, hoping to cheer him up.

He sighed. "And I'll have the lonely streets of LA." He paused before adding, "You should come with me."

I prattled on about how pissed Ivy would be, how insulted Lex would get, but then he confirmed what I'd long believed. Actions did speak louder than words. Both *could* come, and they'd chosen not to.

But I did.

I had relatives out in LA, contacts and friends that could help him. My cousin, Roxanna Stuart, had become a very successful talent agent in the last few years, and if Carter played his cards right, he could sign on with her.

"Ivy and Lex would have each other. And you and me? We could take Hollywood by storm. We could have us." He made a sad noise. "All we'll have is us."

It had hit me in the gut then and again sitting in the car next to him. "We'll be heartbroken and homesick together."

He made that same noise and shook his head. "We're not even to the airport, and I already miss them."

"Me too." I didn't know how I'd survive the next few weeks without hearing Ivy's laugh or watching Lex's eyes roll. How could I go on without listening to them bicker and complain, especially now that I knew how much adoration they'd always harbored between them?

What a strange relationship, and things between me and Carter were even stranger. I wouldn't pretend to understand what happened to us at Midsummer or the days leading up to it and after.

Did we imagine the ruins that turned out not to exist? Did we carve those words into our own palms? Did we make vows that a power higher than ourselves would hold us to keep?

I didn't know.

"Why *did* you agree to come with me?" Carter asked.

I took a deep breath and let it out on a sigh, flicking through all the replies in my head and trying to decide which was the best one. *Because I'll need you, and you'll need me. Because it would hurt too much to be alone. Because I don't know where else to go.*

I ended up with, "Because you're my friend, Romeo, and I can help you. So I'll help you."

"I'll never be able to repay you."

"Hogwash," I brushed off. "One day, you'll be a mega movie star like Marlon Brando, and then it's *me* that will need *you* on my arm."

"Pfft. I should be so lucky." He smiled, and I focused on his dimples, remembering how they'd cast a shadow in the firelight.

We'd married each other out there in those woods, too. We'd taken each other until we couldn't stand. I loved Ivy and Lex with everything in me, but in the haze of the lust and the rush and the sweat, Carter and I had unlocked a hidden sanctuary between us.

Most of it, I didn't remember. But there was this moment, when Lex and Ivy were clawing and moaning next to us, that I found myself straddling Carter's lap, his cock deep inside of me. I'd slung an arm around his neck, digging my other hand into his thigh to help me rock my hips against his pelvis. Our foreheads pressed together, his breath and mine combined, the taste of him and them hung on my lips, and the orange glow from our makeshift fire licked against his skin.

Our gazes had locked, and the world had slowed. Our heartbeats synced with each other as I cupped his jaw and he tightened his fingers on my waist, his indigo eyes bouncing back and forth between mine.

As actors who often worked together, our bodies were already familiar with one another. We'd done physical comedy. We'd played a married couple more than once. We *looked* right next to one another. But this was an intimacy we'd never experienced before. It changed the way I saw him.

Carter and I understood each other in a way Lex and Ivy never could. They'd never know what it was like to be in love with them, to be the object of their affection. They could never know what it was like to be the rival in a romance where the odds were stacked against them from the start.

Lex and Ivy could only have ended up together. That was obvious now. But that didn't mean I got *left* with Carter. It meant Carter and I got to *keep* each other.

Hardly a consolation prize, if you asked me. Six-two. Blond. Blue eyes. Gorgeous jawline. No wonder Ivy and Lex had fallen for him so hard, and if I hadn't been so blindsided by the two of them, I would have realized it sooner.

A girlish tingle twisted through my body at the thought of having Carter Scott to myself for the foreseeable future. But I pushed that down. Ivy wouldn't like it. Lex would only like it if he could watch. Were we permitted to sleep together outside of the four of us? Would I get jealous if they fucked without the two of us?

If I'd been a smarter person, perhaps a few years older, I would have called to ask. We should have put down ground rules before we left. Instead, I had only this instinct growing in the pit of my stomach like a weed.

Carter and I were meant to be more than stage partners or metamours.

But what that was, I wasn't exactly sure yet.

3

CARTER

When we landed, drivers were waiting to take us to the studio apartment I'd rented sight unseen over the internet. It was the size of the bathroom in my old digs, and the bed folded up into the wall in the middle of the space.

Miri raised an eyebrow and pursed her lips, glancing around with her arms crossed. "Cozy."

"It's not much, but it's in my price range." I dropped my bags and bit my bottom lip as I tried to figure out where to put my things.

"This is a closet, Romeo."

"There's a bed and a toilet." I shrugged, trying to see the bright side. "That's all I need."

Miri peered into the tiny room at the back and snickered. "The bathroom *is* the shower."

"Convenient," I said.

"No." She shook her head and walked toward me, her flowing pink skirt fluffing around her as she moved. "Absolutely not. We're going."

"What? Where?"

"My family owns a house in Malibu." She grabbed my hand and

nodded toward the door as if there were no arguing with her. Of course, I knew better. Princess Miriam Stuart typically got what she wanted.

In this case, the royal family had one of the most expensive properties in the area, overlooking the Pacific Ocean. At well over four thousand square feet, it housed five bedrooms, eight bathrooms, a balcony that wrapped around the building, and floor-to-ceiling windows in every room.

"Good fucking lord." I twirled around as I walked. The chandelier in the entryway likely cost more than both of my parents' houses put together. I dropped my backpack at the doorway so I could marvel at it.

"My room's the primary," she said, drawing my attention back to her. "Obviously. You can have any of the others. My cousin, Edward, likes the blue room because of the tub in the bathroom." She set her purse on the table by the door and walked through the enormous living room to the kitchen on the other side. Staff hustled around, gathering our things from the car to bring them to our rooms. Her bodyguards confirmed she was safe before heading to *their* house on the property.

The open floor plan was decorated in fresh whites and grays. The couch could *easily* seat twenty people, enough to entertain a Super Bowl party with the ninety-inch television in front of it. The kitchen had a convection stove top and one of those things where the copper-colored pans hung from a rack over the island. When I found the blue bedroom, I nearly tripped over myself at the size of the Jacuzzi tub.

"What the hell is a pleb like me doing here?" I ran a hand through my hair as I took in the view. The crystal clear ocean crashed not too far in the distance, a stark contrast to the desert-brown California landscape. *Stunning. Absolutely breathtaking.* I'd fall asleep to the sound of waves crashing every single night, and there was a part of me that couldn't believe my good fortune.

When I agreed to rent the Mount Vernon apartment with Lex, he understood I'd never be able to afford as much as him. I was at TW on a scholarship, and my parents gave me what little they could in allowance, which wasn't much compared to what came out of his trust every month. We split most of the utilities, but he paid two-thirds of the rent knowing I couldn't do half on my own. It wasn't fair, but Lex insisted and he never brought it up. Money wasn't an issue between us so long as I tried to pull my weight.

Miri and I didn't have the same relationship, and this felt too much like charity for me to accept. I went to find her bedroom to tell her so, but I caught her standing over her bed with her head in her hands, her shoulders shaking as she quietly cried.

My heart sank.

This. This is why I'm here.

It wasn't charity. It wasn't out of the kindness of her heart. She'd married me in those woods, too, and I'd married her. She was my last link to Ivy and Lex until we saw them again, and together, we weren't alone. They had each other, and all we had was us.

"Hey." I closed the distance and wrapped my arms around her to pull her in close, and she linked her hands together at the small of my back. She smelled like flowers and sunshine and coconut lotion, feminine but so different from Ivy, who had always reminded me of vanilla and coffee and sugar cookies. "It's okay, Juliet."

She took a deep breath and let it out with a sigh. "I know, Romeo. I know. Let me have some privacy, yeah?"

I couldn't leave her to cry by herself, especially not when I was agonizing over the same thing. "You don't have to be alone in this. I miss them, too." I brushed hair behind her ear, and she lifted her honey-brown eyes to meet mine.

She'd always been so beautiful. I'd never deny that. And if I didn't have such fucked-up feelings about *them*, I might have made a pass at the princess. But look at this opulence. Look at this twelve-million-dollar home in the heart of the most expensive place in the country. I could never compete with this.

I didn't deserve Lex. I didn't deserve Ivy. And I *definitely* didn't deserve Miri.

She gave my cheek a comforting pat and wiped at her eyes, taking a step away from me. She yanked her princess mask up around her emotions so quickly, I nearly got whiplash. "Tonight, we settle in. Tomorrow, we get started."

"Get started?"

"I'm not trying to be rude, darling, but if you want to get anywhere in this town, you've got to be fuckable."

I tried not to be offended. "Uh, Juliet. I'm downright smoldering. Fourteen out of ten absolutely would bang."

"Sure, in Chicago," she said. "Out here? You've got to be hot *and* look like you cost a billion dollars."

I swallowed down my pride. "That's fair."

"My cousins have some clothes in the closets upstairs. I'll dig around to see what I can find," she said. "Meanwhile, I've called my other cousin, Roxanna. She's an agent who happens to be in town this week. She's coming over for tea tomorrow evening."

"Really?" Excitement rushed through me. "Wow, Miri. That's quick."

"It's not a promise," she said. "But it's a start. We'll see what happens."

I smiled. "Thank you."

She nodded. "Until the end."

The vow we'd made in the woods. The vow we carried on our hands. I tried to put on a happy facade, even though it tore my insides to pieces when I said the words. "Until the end."

She met me with a bashful stare before changing the subject. "Now, let's call our spouses, huh? Let them know we're here."

I pulled out my phone and dialed Ivy's number, only to get an error tone.

"The number you have dialed has been disconnected."

"That's weird." I tried to send her a text, only for it to go undelivered.

Miri picked up her phone to do the same, but nothing on her end went through either.

"I'm having the same issue with Lex," she said. Sure enough, I couldn't get ahold of either one.

"Maybe it's something weird on their end," I said, ignoring the alarm blaring in the back of my mind. "They'll reach out once it's fixed."

"Yeah, you're right," she said with a frown.

Roxanna Stuart was a force onto herself. Her grandfather had been brother to the current king and moved to America in the '50s after a scandal involving a love child with another woman. Eventually, they reconciled with the royal family, but they stayed in the States. Now, Roxy was one of the most prolific agents in Hollywood. Her clients included multi-time award winners and the A-list of the A-list.

She was a short woman with pitch-black hair she kept in a professional updo. She wore slacks and a nice blouse and had this *no-bullshit* vibe about her that indicated just how long she'd been in the business. Meeting her the day after I moved to LA would not have been possible if it hadn't been for Miri.

"This is him?" Roxy asked, sipping at her tea.

Miri had found one of her cousin's suits that fit me perfectly, a decadent tailored piece made for a prince. Literally. I ignored the designer label as I slid the jacket on, preferring not to know so I didn't spend the rest of the day guessing how much it cost. It was a far cry from the jeans and T-shirt vibe I preferred, but I had to give it to Miri. It did turn this ugly duckling into a shiny new swan.

"This is him," Miri said. "He's a good friend from college. We were in theater together."

"Ahhh." Roxy raked her incinerating gaze over me, piercing and terrifying in the same blink. "Fresh meat."

"Indeed," Miri said. "I was hoping you could find him work. Maybe take him on as a client?"

Roxy raised an eyebrow and took another sip of tea. "I work with show dogs, Miri. Not pound mutts."

"Even tramps can clean up nice." Trying not to take offense, I flashed her a charming grin and a flirty wink.

She redirected her attention to me. "Have you ever done a photo-shoot before?"

"Some, when I was a kid." I'd done a commercial or two for a local broadcast.

"Well, let's get a look at you." She stood and came closer, circling me like one might size up a prize horse. "Are you in good shape?"

"Amazing," Miri answered for me. "And talented. I sent you the footage."

"I saw," Roxy said. "Still, the market is saturated, and for someone with no experience—"

"I've got experience," I argued.

"I don't mean a rinky-dink college in the middle of Virginia."

"I acted with the Royal Theater Company for a year in high school." The RTC had a reputation internationally for a reason. Many of the British greats had trained with them.

That perfectly manicured eyebrow lifted again, this time impressed.

"I told you," Miri said. "Talented."

Roxy nodded and went back to her armchair next to Miri, picking up her tea with a thoughtful glance between us. "What's your relationship?"

"We're friends," Miri said.

I licked my lips and dropped my gaze to the floor. Friends barely scratched the surface of the complexity between Miri and me. We were star-crossed lovers, bonded in brokenhearted solidarity. We were married in the soul, and we always would be.

"Right," Roxy said. "And what does Auntie think of your... friendship?"

It took me a moment to realize she meant the queen of England, the king's wife, the ruler of Miri's social calendar.

"We really are friends," I said.

Roxy's eyes narrowed on me. "Weren't you dating Ivy Washington?"

"Not for a long time," I said. "Now, we're just—"

"Friends," Roxy finished for me. "Right." She looked between us again before taking another sip of tea. I slipped my hands into my pockets and played it cool, even if I was an anxious mess on the inside. I forced my shoulders to straighten when every instinct I had wanted to curl in on myself. Insecurities ran rampant through my mind.

What if I'm not good enough? What if I'll never be good enough? What if no one likes me? No one respects me? What if I'll only ever be Chicago-good? Not Hollywood-good? What if they only ever see Ivy when they look at me?

What if I'll only ever be Ivy's ex-boyfriend?

"Listen, when I take on a client," Roxy said, "there are only two things you're allowed to put before me: your health and your immediate family. In both situations, someone better be in the hospital." She paused for effect, making sure the next part sunk in. "Love affairs are not one of those things. You can't decide not to show up to work because your girlfriend caught you sticking your dick in someone else and wants to fight you for it. You understand?"

Miri snorted.

"Miri knows this because that's how we were raised. Nothing is more important than your brand."

"I get it," I said. Almost as much as Miri did. After all, my choices were impacted by other people's images. Ivy had to marry Lex to save the Fairfax name. Because of that, I couldn't have her. Because of that, I couldn't have him. "I won't let you down."

Roxy made a sarcastic *uh-huh* noise and looked back at Miri. "We'll see."

Miri nodded in agreement, giving me a wink. "We'll see."

That night, when we still hadn't heard from Lex or Ivy, I started to worry. I tried sending a direct message on all of her socials. Hell, I even resorted to Google Messenger, making me feel like a jilted mistress desperate for any sign of my philandering boyfriend.

Nothing.

No word.

None to Miri either.

"This isn't right," I said. My gut tightened, and a weight settled on my chest. "It isn't like them. They said they'd call. They said they wouldn't let a day go by." I thought about reaching out to Ivy's younger sister, Kit, but I'd only met her twice, and I didn't know how to get in touch with her aside from the same routes I'd been trying to contact Ivy.

We sat on the balcony with whiskey in shot glasses and music playing softly in the background.

"Maybe they're busy," Miri said. "Maybe they got caught up."

Normally, I was the optimistic one, looking on the bright side of every shitty situation. But now? I didn't know. Hardly a day had gone by in four years where I didn't talk to both of them. Now I had an ache in my soul that could only be explained by something unusual.

Midsummer had opened up a connection between the four of us, tying us together by more than just shared experience. Our vows were literally etched into our hands. That meant something, and I had a sneaking suspicion this absence was the calm before the storm.

I opened my mouth to reply, but a text came through on my phone that caught my attention.

Weeds.

I slid the screen open, my eyes narrowing on her message.

Weeds: *Carter, I love you. But my mother doesn't want me in contact with you anymore. If my phone gets hacked, if we get found out—I'm finished. We said we wouldn't hold each other back. I need that now. Please don't reach out to me again.*

Shock hollowed me. My chest caved in on itself, my brain unable to comprehend the words on the screen.

"What the fuck?"

I showed the text to Miri, whose eyebrows narrowed when she got a similar one from Lex.

Lex: *Princess, I apologize for what I'm about to do. My father needs me to keep my head on straight. Don't call me anymore. Please be happy.*

No.

No.

I wouldn't accept this. I called Ivy, but it went straight to voice-mail. I called again, and the line cut off, saying the number had been disconnected. This time, I'd been blocked on all of their social media feeds. So had Miri.

Panic raced in my veins, venomous and agonizing, souring every part of my soul. It didn't make any sense. For four years, I'd loved them, both of them. I'd loved Ivy more than anything in the world. And for her to end it...*over text?*

No, I wasn't buying it. Whatever her mother had said to her, *to them,* it must have been heinous. Absolutely atrocious.

That's the only reason they'd do this. That's the only reason.

Ivy wouldn't back down. She'd fight until she couldn't fight anymore; she swore she would. Lex had no love for his father or his wishes. There were so many ways to keep our affair private, to keep it between us. They were giving up too soon.

"This is bullshit." I tried Ivy again, and when it still didn't work, I almost crushed my phone in my palm to keep from throwing it into the fucking cliffs.

"Let it be." Blinking back tears, Miri lit a cigarette and grabbed my hand to calm me, taking a long, deep inhale before reclining in her seat. "We knew this would happen. Let it be."

"Miri, she wouldn't do this." I vibrated with my helplessness, my molecules begging me to do something, *anything,* to stop this from being real. "She wouldn't be this cruel, not to us."

I swallowed down my grief because I couldn't break in front of

Miri. We needed to be strong for each other. That was why she'd come. That was why I was here.

"If it's any consolation, Romeo," Miri said, her voice cracking the slightest bit, "they're not. This has Evelyn and Kellan written all over it."

"How do we stop it?" I could barely get the words out.

"We can't," Miri said. "Lex and Ivy had a choice." She took a deep breath in, let it out slowly. "They made it."

"So, what? All of it? All we had was fucking bullshit?"

"No," she said. "It was real. It'll always be real." Another slow inhale of her cigarette had me reaching for my own. I usually didn't like to smoke, but this brand? This smell? It reminded me of Lex, and I couldn't deny myself the temptation in that awful moment.

"It was over the minute they announced their relationship; you know that." She wiped at her eyes and brought the whiskey bottle to her lips for a long, deep swallow. "Good things never last. That's what makes them so good."

I hated it. I hated everything. I wanted to jump on the first plane back to DC and show up at their apartment to make them explain themselves. Screw Roxy. Screw LA. Screw all of it.

They couldn't at least call me?

Two days ago, I'd had Lex's dick in my ass and my cock in Ivy's, and I didn't even deserve a formal breakup?

Fire raged through me.

I read her message again over and over, forcing the tears back, forcing myself to come up with an explanation for how she could take four years of *us* and smash it to hell in less than fifty words.

Ivy had asked me not to contact her. Lex had made it clear he felt the same.

I didn't know what their parents had said to them to make them run scared, but I swore, right at that moment, that I'd spend the rest of my life proving them wrong. When I swooped in and stole my lovers back from the cold clutches of these wolves in sheep's clothing, I'd make sure Evelyn and Kellan *knew* who had brought about their downfall.

4

CARTER

My mother and Lizzie flew into town a few days later. They were supposed to help me unpack and move into my studio, but when Miri sent a driver to pick them up and bring them to Malibu, the purpose of the trip changed entirely.

"This is amazing," Lizzie said, twirling around the foyer area. At twelve, she'd just finished seventh grade. Originally, my eldest sister, Charlie, was supposed to come with Mom, but Sophia had been invited on a trip with her senior high school class last minute. Charlie had gone with her to "chaperone." She'd given the ticket to Lizzie instead. "You live here?"

I laughed. "Yeah, Bizzie. Just for a little while."

She widened her eyes and leaned closer. "Where's the princess?"

For four years, she'd known about my friendship with Miri and Ivy. She'd even gotten to meet Ivy a few times on visits to TW. But something about the fact Miri was a *real* princess had mesmerized her since she was little.

"She's around here somewhere," I said, winking.

As if summoned by her title, Miri walked in from the kitchen with a big smile and her arms out wide.

"Welcome," she said. "It's so lovely to meet you." She embraced my mother, who thanked her for her hospitality and kneeled to lock eyes with my sister. "You must be Lizzie."

Lizzie's mouth hung open, her gaze focused on my friend. "You know who I am?"

"Of course." Miri smiled and held a hand out for Lizzie to shake. "I've heard so much about you."

"You have?"

"Of course, Biz," I said. "I talk about you all the time."

"C'mon," Miri said, pushing to stand again. "You can leave your things here. I'll have someone take them to your rooms. You must be tired from your trip. We can sit on the deck for lunch."

Lizzie raced after Miri, her long limbs pumping to be the first one out the door. But my mom stopped me by grabbing my wrist and peering up at me.

"How are you affording this?" she murmured.

"Miri's my friend, Mom," I said. "She's helping me."

She narrowed her gaze and nodded, but there was something else behind that expression, something she held back, something she wouldn't hold back forever.

I followed Miri and my sister outside, sitting at the table where Miri and I had spent the morning preparing lunch. We both liked to cook for ourselves. In fact, the kitchen was one of the places we'd bonded. Today, I'd made finger foods and a light salad to refresh us in the summer heat.

"What's it like to live in a castle?" Lizzie asked, hanging on Miri's every word.

"Amazing," she said, playing into her childlike wonder. "But sometimes, it's creepy."

"Really? Why?"

"They're haunted." Lizzie gasped, and I chuckled, meeting Miri's stern gaze. "You think I'm teasing, but I'm serious."

"Haunted?" I raised an eyebrow. "What do you mean?"

She shrugged. "Lots of terrible people did horrific things in those walls, Carter."

I pursed my lips. "No argument here."

"Have you ever seen any ghosts?" Lizzie widened her eyes.

Miri shook her head. "Not me. But my cousin, Edward, swears he saw Henry VIII once."

"Really?" Mom cut in as she took a drink of her water. "Where?"

"Whitehall," she said. "Edward stayed there a lot as a teenager."

"Was he as mean as everyone claimed?" I asked.

Miri laughed and took a sip of lemonade, smiling in that charming way of hers. "Worse. He walked into my aunt's room while she was showering."

That made my mother and Lizzie laugh.

"What a pervert, right?" Miri added.

Lizzie giggled, her crooked twelve-year-old grin tugging at my heartstrings. I'd missed her more than I realized, and now that she and Mom were here, I found myself grateful to be around family again. Eventually, the conversation drifted, and somehow Lizzie conned Miri out of her old clothes.

"I think I still have some boxes around here with things that will fit you."

"I wasn't serious," Lizzie cut in.

"Thank you, Miri," Mom said. "But I couldn't—"

"Oh, please. I haven't worn them in ages. I'd rather them go to someone who will use them." Miri stood and grabbed Lizzie's hand, dragging her back inside the house.

It was silent for a few moments, but I felt my mother's stare on me. When I lifted my gaze to hers, she smiled and grabbed my hand.

"I'm so proud of you," she said.

"I haven't done anything yet." I took another sip of lemonade.

"Yeah, but to have the courage to even try?" She shrugged. "I had you when I was nineteen and that was it for my Hollywood dreams."

I tilted my head to the side. "Do you regret having kids?"

"God no," she said. "Every day, you bring me such joy."

I smiled, letting her adoration warm me.

"Maybe I regret your father," she teased, and I barked out a laugh. My father and I didn't see eye to eye about my life choices, hence the reason he wasn't out here and they were. He was back in Chicago with his new family and his new son who he did everything with—who he supported no matter what.

Fuck him.

Though, I did regret not having much of a relationship with my little brother.

"But even then, you wouldn't be you without him." She squeezed my hand and leaned in close. "Are you screwing the princess?"

I gasped and lemonade shot out of my nose.

"Fuck," I said, spilling it down the front of my shirt, tears welling in my eyes. "Mom!"

"What?" she said. "I just have to know whether I should plan to share grandchildren with the king and queen of England. That's all."

"Unlikely," I said.

"Okay, fine." She paused for a moment before giving me a side-eye and muttering, "You weren't screwing Ivy Washington either."

I sighed and wiped at my shirt, pulling it away from my sticky chest.

"Ivy and I..." It hurt to think of her. It hurt to talk about her. "I don't want to talk about Ivy."

She ignored my protests. "What about Lex? Weren't the two of them—"

"I don't want to talk about Lex either." My tone was unintentionally harsh.

My mom moved closer. "It must have hurt when they got together."

They weren't together. Or at least...I didn't think they were together. *We're all together.*

"It's—It's complicated, okay?" But my voice shook, and my eyes burned, and for a brief moment, I thought I might crack right open in front of her. I took another sip of lemonade and swallowed the bitterness at the back of my throat, telling myself it was afterburn from the acid in my nostrils.

"My baby boy," she whispered. "Gods willing, you will know many great loves in your life. May you be fortunate enough to hold on to the ones who are meant for you." She nodded at the house, gesturing toward Miri. "You two have great energy together. I can feel it."

I rolled my eyes and shook my head. A certified Reiki healer, my mother believed in the power of energetic fields. If I told her what happened to us in Ireland, she'd probably have a crystal and a bag of herbs for me to chant over, proclaiming us all fated lovers from a previous life. To be fair, I didn't have much proof to argue against her.

"Did I have good energy with Ivy?" I'd meant it to mock her, but she answered me seriously anyway.

"You were born with the ability to connect with anyone, but you already know who you belong with." It was an ambiguous answer, but I got the feeling she'd meant it to be so.

All of them. All of us. We belong together.

I cleared my throat, the thought of my Weeds too much. All of this...too much. "Well, she's already spoken for so—"

Mom stood so she could hug my head into her stomach the way she used to do when I'd skinned my knee as a kid. I tried to resist the vulnerability. I was a grown-ass man, after all. But I sat my lemonade down and wrapped my arms around her body, pulling her closer, maybe hoping she could put a bandage over my broken heart and kiss it better.

This would take more than a mother's love to fix.

She put her hands on my jaw and tilted my attention up to her so she could give me a peck on the forehead.

"Remember what you were put on this earth to do, baby," she said.

Love. And be loved.

That was her motto. Nothing else mattered.

But for me, I was put on this earth to act, and it reminded me again of *my* life motto, the one I'd sworn to Anthony Michaels all those years ago.

No distractions.

"I'm not a baby." I laughed.

"You're always my baby boy."

When Lizzie came back, she brought something she thought would fit our mother, and Mom's jaw dropped to the ground. Sensing I might get roped into dress-up if I stuck around, I let the girls have their fun and found my way to the blue room.

LATER THAT NIGHT, I listened to the sounds of the ocean outside my balcony window. The waves crashing against the shore held such a peaceful rhythm, and in the lulling stillness of its melody, I almost forgot everything was such a mess.

I thought of Ivy again, her bright smile and her shiny red hair. I thought of the way she laughed and how she'd moan *please* in my ear with her breathy sigh. I wondered what they were doing. Were they happy together? Were they miserable? Had they found in each other a comfort that Miri and I were desperate to find for ourselves?

I traced my thumb over her name in my phone, the last text we sent to each other still on my screen.

Ivy: *Carter, I love you. But my mother doesn't want me in contact with you anymore. If my phone gets hacked, if we get found out—I'm finished. We said we wouldn't hold each other back. I need that now. Please don't reach out to me again.*

That was three days ago. This was the longest we'd ever gone without speaking to each other. I wanted to reach out to her in the worst way, maybe plead with her to take me back, maybe promise her the world if she'd let me say filthy shit to turn her cheeks red.

Maybe I'd get her to finger herself while I watched and urged her on.

Maybe Lex would walk in...

Maybe they would...

I stopped myself.

Ivy broke up with you.

Ivy is marrying someone else.

Ivy is marrying your best friend.

Pictures of them walking together on the street haunted my social media feed, Lex's arm over her shoulders, her fingers in his, that puppy dog gaze in her eyes. It was the way she used to look at me.

It's all for show, I reminded myself.

Other memories flickered through my mind—the way Lex had kissed her at the pub in Ireland, the way he'd pulled her into the woods at Midsummer, how he'd fucked her when the lust took hold of us again in our dorm room. He hadn't fought the arrangement because he loved her, truly loved her, even if he couldn't admit it.

And there was the proof—right there on the internet for all the world to see.

I knew this would happen. I knew this was coming. But tears still burned my eyes, and rage boiled in my heart.

I wanted to call them both and cuss them out. I wanted to make them fuck on screen so I could watch it and see for myself how real it was. I shook with fury for both of them, all of them, all of us, all together again.

The only thing that kept me sane, the only thing that kept my jealous rage in check, was the ring on her right ring finger—the opal I'd given her before I left.

Representation.

In every picture I saw of her, it was there. Sort of like her signal to me that despite her text, she still loved me and she always would.

And poor pitiful me, I still had nothing to offer.

Not yet.

I clicked my phone off, put it on my nightstand, and fucked my fist as I remembered our last time together. When I came, silently moaning into my pillow, I thought of steel-gray eyes and a tattooed forearm holding me down.

5

MIRI

I had always hated Los Angeles. It wasn't the beautiful, glamorous place most people thought it was. It's little more than a trash heap. Admittedly, some of the surrounding areas were nice, even if everything was so…brown and they had to ship water in from somewhere else to make the plants grow. I tried to garden in containers, and I did what I could with a planter in the backyard, but being this close to the salt water and the drought in California meant I couldn't get much going.

I longed for the summers in Scotland. I missed the trees.

The trees know, one of my nannies used to say.

Know what? I'd asked her.

The trees know all.

Hell, I'd take Virginia humidity over this bloody barren wasteland. The dry air reached inside me and sucked the moisture out of my soul, making me feel as empty and lifeless as everything around me.

I knew better than to let that show. Especially after Sandra, the PR rep for the royal family, used my vacation as an avenue for press events. That was how we found ourselves at this charade.

The formal charity on the sign said, "Children with Cancer," but it was obviously an opportunity for the host to boost his ego. He'd hung giant portraits of himself and his family all over the mansion, and the only people in attendance were other A-listers. I narrowed my eyes at this year's *People's Sexiest Man* and smirked.

He wasn't even that hot, not compared to Lex, and definitely not compared to Carter, who was currently laughing at a story some other famous actor told him.

Strange how well he fit in here like he'd been born for the notoriety, his personality that perfect blend of charisma and relaxed confidence. I'd done the best I could in the few weeks since we moved. His mother and Lizzie were delightful, and they reminded me what a normal family was supposed to be like—teasing and loving and touching.

Most people came out to LA and struggled for years, but the trick was networking, right? My family had afforded me knowledge of everyone, or at least, it had afforded everyone knowledge of *me*. I walked into spaces and doors opened for Carter on their own.

That was what I did for the people I loved. I gave them all of me to make them whole. That was what got the princess locked up in her ivory tower in the first place, wasn't it? Some stupid curse that required her sacrifice to rescue her idiot family members from the horrible villain.

Everyone got what they wanted, but what about the princess?

What did I want?

Carter's eyes met mine from across the party and he pulled one side of his mouth into a dimpled grin. I bit a cigarette between my teeth and lit it, taking a deep inhale that made me think of Lex. This was his brand—his smell, his taste.

"What are you doing over here alone?" Carter said, shoving his hands in his pockets as he sauntered toward me.

"Thinking." I held the pack out to him.

He sighed and took it, pinching one in his fingers so he could bring it to his lips. "Should I even ask?"

"Change. Nothing ever stays the same for long."

Carter blew out a breath. "Fuck, that's heavy."

Too heavy. My heart matched. Changing the subject, I said, "You fit in here."

He smiled and inhaled on his cigarette. "Can I tell you a secret?"

"I suppose. We are married, after all."

"I'm an actor." He winked. "I fit in everywhere."

I chuckled and raked my gaze over him. "That's the key, isn't it? Fake it until you make it."

"Roll with the punches. Whatever cliché you can think of."

Sadness echoed behind his eyes before he hid it away, and I ran a hand through my hair, taking another drag on my smoke as I brushed my curly strands back.

"What do you think they would say if they were here?" Carter gestured to the party behind us, the rich people in their fancy clothes sipping champagne and nibbling caviar.

"Lex would roll his eyes and call everyone a sycophant," I said.

"And Ivy would dazzle the crowd while counting down the seconds until we could leave."

I grinned, noticing how Carter's eyes shimmered in the dying summer sunset. He truly was beautiful, but not in the same jagged way that made Lex appealing or in soft, lively curves like Ivy. Carter had a *boy-next-door-hit-puberty-like-a-lumberjack* thing about him. He'd grown into someone who would tie you up and throat-fuck you while coddling you and whispering sweet nothings to make you feel precious.

"Why are you looking at me like that, Juliet?" He stabbed his cigarette out in the ashtray between us.

"Just regarding you," I said. "Can't I appreciate a pretty sight?"

He cleared his throat and stared down at me from under hooded lids. A few quiet moments passed between us until he finally stepped closer and murmured, "You ever think about that night in Ireland... that night Lex went to get Ivy from the library."

I licked my lips and smiled as memories flicked through my

mind. "You mean the night you made me ride you while reciting Shakespeare?"

He laughed and the muscles in his throat constricted. My tongue suddenly ached to trace over them. I blinked back the urge, unsure of where exactly that was coming from.

"That one. Yes," he said.

"What about it?" I stabbed out my cigarette and immediately lit up another one.

Carter took another step closer and pushed my brown hair back behind my ear, cupping my cheek. The scars from our vow brushed against my jaw, and the sensuous touch sizzled all the way down my spine to my toes and back up again.

I chalked it up to a human female response to a gorgeous man being this close, especially since the last time I'd been touched intimately, he'd been involved. Carter and I were friends. That was it. That was all. We were married to the same people, which made us metamours at best, and romantic rivals at worst. Sure, we'd slept together, but only as it related to whatever had happened to *all* of us. Never on our own. Never like this.

"I miss them," he said. "And some part of me always will, but I'm happy you're here, Juliet." He kissed my temple. "We're a team. All we have is us."

"I'm happy I'm here, too," I said, pulling back enough to look up at him. Carter's blue eyes were mere inches away, his lips so close I could taste the whiskey on his breath. He smelled enticing, like deodorant and cologne and *man*. I shouldn't want him. I knew I shouldn't. Despite what we'd all agreed, Ivy wouldn't like it and neither would Lex. But I *yearned* for him with a sick desperation. It seemed like he wanted me, too.

I pushed up on my toes to close the distance between us, but someone called to him from inside the house.

"Hey, Carter. Come check this out!"

"Yeah," Carter said. "Be right there." He looked down at me and kissed the tip of my nose. "Hold that thought, okay?"

I nodded and smiled while he disappeared inside.

After we'd drank and schmoozed our way into oblivion, my driver took us back to the house and I quickly disappeared to my bedroom. Carter likely expected to continue whatever had started between us on the balcony, but I was too confused for that.

Did I enjoy Carter's company because I liked *him?* Or was this about Lex and Ivy? Would it always be about them? Tears threatened to spill down my cheeks and, though I tried to blink them back, they overwhelmed me once I closed my bedroom door.

Carter wasn't Lex, and I wasn't Ivy, and who were we to each other if not a link to them? Did I want Carter because I wanted Carter? Or did I want him because both Lex and Ivy did?

I needed to move on with my life—just get over this bloody nonsense already. But how could I?

What do I want?

Not this. Not crying myself to sleep every night because the chasm between my body and where I left half my heart was literally the size of America.

The door handle to my room jiggled, and he opened the damn thing like the lock was more of a suggestion than a barrier, like we had zero boundaries between us. Maybe we didn't. Not anymore.

"I beg your pardon." I balked.

"Can we not do this tonight?" He stalked into the room and gestured between us like I was supposed to know what that meant.

"Do what?" Shocked didn't begin to describe my outrage.

"That thing where we act like we don't know one another, like we don't have the same heart shattering in our chests."

I pretended like I had no clue what he was talking about. "Don't be preposterous."

He paused and sighed before he murmured, "I don't want to be alone anymore."

All the fight melted out of me. *This poor thing.* "There's nothing preventing you from finding a lover, Carter."

"You made a vow," he said, clearing his throat, blinking back tear-filled eyes. "We all...We all made a vow."

"We agreed we could sleep around," I said.

"Yeah, but—" He straightened and righted his shoulders. "I don't want to."

"I can't give you what you want." What was the point? I would end up with the Prince of Monaco or whoever my grandmother decided was worth my time. This was a distraction, one that would end up hurting in the end.

"Come on, Juliet." His eyes seemed lit from within, ignited by that infinite supply of sunshine burning at his core. He'd taken off the suit jacket and rolled the sleeves of his white button-down up to his elbows, revealing those muscular forearms I remembered so very well. His tie hung over his neck, the first few buttons of his shirt undone, his undershirt peeking through. "Can't you pretend? Just for tonight?"

It didn't have to be a big deal. Carter and I had been together before, many times. But this was different. There was no one else here, no threat of our lovers walking in on us. This would be because *we* wanted it, and I didn't know how to feel about that.

He shook his head and let out a sad chuckle, turning to face the view of the ocean through my window. "I can't bring myself to move on. They look happy, ya know? It's killing me."

"They're faking it," I said. "We both know they are."

"They've loved each other their entire lives," he said. "It's getting more difficult to remember it's a show."

I wrapped my free hand around his bicep and rested my head on his shoulder, hoping to bring as much solace as he'd given to me. He relaxed and kissed my temple before circling his arms around my shoulders to pull me into a hug. He held me so tightly, I thought he might never let go. Perhaps I never wanted him to.

"All the world's a stage, and we are merely players," I said.

He hummed in agreement. "Do you think we're a comedy or a tragedy?"

"Sort of feels like both, doesn't it, Romeo?" I chuckled, what little remained of my heart shattering into a thousand tiny pieces. "If I didn't laugh, I'd never stop crying."

He gave me one last squeeze and nodded toward the bed.

"Let me stay here tonight with you," he said. "We can keep it PG. I swear. But it feels better when we're together, doesn't it?"

I laughed quietly, remembering when I'd said that in Ireland. I still agreed with him, of course. It did feel better when we were together, and it felt the best when we were a four. But if I couldn't have what I truly wanted, then I'd have Carter.

We'd have each other and bugger anyone who judged me for it.

OF ALL THE troves of treasures at the house in Malibu, the one Carter fell in love with was the cherry red 1965 Aston Martin DB5 convertible. My uncle, the prince of Wales, had bought it in the late '90s to impress women, but he'd since gotten old and stopped coming to Malibu. He hadn't seen it in years.

The minute Carter's eyes had landed on it, he wanted to take it out.

"Just a little spin?" he asked at the time. While my uncle probably wouldn't notice, his son and my cousin, Edward, would. He came here more often than anyone, and he could be a prick if he wanted to be.

Anytime we'd go out in the garage, Carter would make a beeline for it and stand there with his hands in his pockets, admiring her soft curves and ample machinery. I didn't take him for much of a car guy, but it never failed to rope him in.

Something about *this* night in particular made me cave. Maybe it was the way the sun setting over the ocean cast bright blushes on Carter's cheeks, reminding me of Midsummer. Or maybe it was the shimmer in his eye when we heard a commercial for a gossip show that mentioned breaking news for Fairington fans…Lex and Ivy were seen *ring shopping* together. Or maybe it was because my soul was in shambles and no matter what I did, nothing could repair it.

Ivy's words replayed in my head over and over again, crushing my heart.

"Please accept my boundary. I can't deal with this right now."

Boundary.

Once upon a time, she and I had no boundaries. I knew everything about her—the taste of her sweat as she climaxed, the curve of her smile first thing in the morning, the way she smelled right out of the shower. But now, all those memories seemed worlds away.

I hated feeling like this, and the miserable puffy eyes on Carter's face told me he felt the same.

"Hey," I said, getting his attention from across the living room.

He pursed his lips and crossed his arms, clearing his throat to try to hide his emotions. "Yeah?"

"Let's go for a drive."

If he'd been a puppy, his ears would have perked up and his tail would have started wagging. Excitement swelled in his gaze, his tongue almost hanging out of his mouth. "Yeah?"

"Yeah." I nodded.

"Fuck yeah." He jumped out of his seat. "Let me go get my jacket."

I narrowed my eyes. *Jacket?*

Whatever. I grabbed a silk scarf to wrap around my head so my hair didn't get tangled in the wind, and I headed to the key box in the garage, searching for the right one among the rows of options. I found it just as he came in, and I had to take a moment to steel myself against his appearance.

He wore the white shirt and jeans he'd been wearing earlier, but now he'd added aviators and a brown bomber jacket, giving him a James Dean vibe. My lower stomach clenched, and my heart almost skipped a beat, a sizzle of lust sparking between my legs. I ignored it. Carter being gorgeous was hardly a new concept.

I tossed the keys out to him. "You're driving."

"Wait...what?" He looked so damn adorable when he was confused.

I put my hands on my hips. "Well, you certainly don't expect me to chauffeur myself around, do you?"

His mouth fell open. "Miri...if I break it..."

I rolled my eyes and yanked open the passenger door, shoving my body inside it. "Get in. If you break it, I'll buy it."

Still, he stood there, swallowing and looking at the car like touching her might cause her to explode into a thousand pieces.

"Carter Scott," I finally snapped, getting his attention. "I demand you drive me around in this ridiculously expensive relic. Will you deny me?"

He twisted his lips into the biggest grin I'd ever seen, and his eyes shined like they used to, back when we were home, back when we were with them. He practically skipped around to the driver's seat and got inside, giving me a huge kiss on the cheek once he did.

"Don't call her ridiculous." He ran his hands seductively down the steering wheel. "She's a masterpiece."

I laughed while he started the ignition.

"Tonight, we wallow," he said. "Tonight, we do the sunset walk on the beach, eat pints of Ben & Jerry's, and watch the sappy rom-coms. Tomorrow, we move on, yeah?"

I sighed. "What if I can't?"

He grabbed my hand and squeezed before driving us outside. "Pretend."

Pretend.

Yeah. So easy. Never mind my breaking heart. Never mind my lost soul. I wished I had Carter's drive for *anything*. But I didn't. Whenever I thought about my future, I'd always envisioned doing my part for my family — being the dutiful princess, attending the events, and rebranding the royal name. But that didn't spark the same excitement in me that performing did in Carter.

Being in my garden did. Being around my spouses did. I couldn't turn that into a royal charity.

I traced my thumb over our vows while Carter drove, the setting sun on the ocean even more beautiful because I had him next to me. Vibrant tangerines faded into blush rosy pinks, and I thanked my lucky stars again that we were together, that I wasn't going through this public grief alone.

Patsy Cline played on the radio, the cool ocean wind mixing with the warmth of the dying light on my cheeks, the whole thing making me nostalgic. Like this, we could have gone back in time to the golden age of Hollywood and he really was a James Dean heartthrob and I was his Grace Kelly princess. Together, we were the perfect power couple that no one could tear apart.

Eventually, Carter parked the car on an overlook, perfectly situated for us to enjoy the rumbling sounds of the waves below us. He grabbed my hand and flashed me one of those classic Carter smiles.

"In case I forget to say it, thank you for this."

I shrugged and waved him off. "It's nothing."

"It's not nothing," Carter said. "Nothing you've ever done for anyone has been nothing."

That got my attention, and I whipped my focus back to him, clearing my throat to swallow a sob. I'd spent my whole life shoving my emotions down, not letting them show, pretending to put on a big smile. These last few weeks, they'd felt so close to the surface, like I was only one spilled cup of milk away from having an utter mental breakdown.

I hated my family and my entire life and this separation and their engagement. Everything. I hated it all, and it made me so tired because being hateful was exhausting. It was much easier to be apathetic. But I cared too much, especially about them.

"You think no one notices," Carter said. "But I do."

My heart pounded. "Notices what?"

"How selfless you are," he said. "How you bring out the best in everyone you love."

I rolled my eyes. "That's you, Romeo." I tickled his ribs, making him squirm away and giggle and try to tickle me in return. It turned into a slapfight, right there in the front seat. Me hitting at his hands, him trying to grab my wrists to stop me.

I laughed and laughed while we playfully smacked at each other, the song shifting to "She's Got You" in the background. It was the lightest I'd felt in weeks, and when Carter grabbed a hold of my wrists, he yanked me until our faces were inches apart.

The mood shifted instantly.

His exhales coasted across my cheeks, and I shivered from the heat radiating off his body. His dark indigo eyes bounced between mine, perhaps looking for permission for what he wanted to do next. I wanted to let him. Even though guilt snaked around my poor pathetic heart like a python, I wanted to tug him closer and pull him down on top of me and demand he take me in my uncle's status symbol.

I loved Lex and I loved Ivy, but there was something about Carter...something about his love for them and their love for him that had me tearing off a chunk of my soul to trust in his safe-keeping.

Tires pulled up next to us, and I broke away from him.

"Miriam! Miriam!" someone shouted. Bright lights flashed in my face and bodies swarmed the car on either side.

"Get us out of here," I said. "Go, go, go!"

More cameras flashed. More questions. More paparazzi.

Carter shoved the car in reverse and backed up, pulling out onto the 101 to take us home.

"Fucking vultures!" he shouted, shifting the car into third.

The scenery whooshed by us, my scarf long since yanked down to my shoulders. My wild curls whipped around my face, the rush of going fast rising in me. But it wasn't a good rush, not like a roller coaster. No. This was worse. Ever since the accident, I'd dreaded driving, even more so when the driver couldn't keep it under the speed limit. I didn't like chases, and I *definitely* didn't like the paparazzi tailing us so closely.

It brought back flashbacks of that day—the sickening crunch, my mother's screams, the terrifying nothingness, blinking awake in the patch of grass far away from my dead family.

"Carter," I managed to say, my breathing coming in heavy pants, my vision narrowing. "Carter." I tried again, but my mouth wouldn't work. I grabbed his arm, the one he used to shift gears, and my nails clamped into his skin. "Slow down. Please." I barely whispered the words. I couldn't breathe. I couldn't think.

Slow down.

Slow down.

Carter stopped the car, and when he yanked on the parking brake, I sighed in relief because we were back in my garage. Behind the closing doors. Away from prying eyes. He wrapped his strong arms around me, pulling my torso to him, unclicking my seat belt so he could tug me into his lap. My knees went to either side of his hips, and even though it was a tiny space, he squeezed me to him so tight, so secure, that nothing would ever hurt me again.

Tears streamed down my face, deep heavy sobs coming from a bottomless abyss in my chest. I let it all out, everything I'd been holding on to since the wreck, since the breakup, since we'd come here. He held me through it, rubbing my back, saying sweet soothing words to me.

"It's okay, Juliet," he said. "You've still got me."

I pulled back and stared down at him through tear-blurred vision. I must have looked like a mess—wild hair, red eyes, snotty nose. He rubbed his thumbs over my cheeks and smiled, leaning up to press a chaste kiss to my lips.

I'd kissed Carter dozens of times before, but this was different. It was sweet and told me he had my back, no matter what. At that moment, I swore I'd have his until I died.

All we have is us.

The kiss turned more passionate, and Carter twisted his fingers in my hair, tugging me closer, and I dug my nails into his shoulders, holding him firm underneath me.

My pelvis rocked against his, my clit suddenly pulsing as it rubbed over the thickening length in his pants.

We shouldn't do this, some part of me thought. *This isn't right.* But God, it felt right, like the only thing I needed in the world. Ivy had broken up with him, broken up with both of us. So had Lex. Were we free to now have each other?

The thought made me break away with a gasp, touching my lips as I stared down at Carter.

"We shouldn't do this," I murmured.

"I know," he said. But he didn't move.

And neither did I.

6

CARTER

Of all things I'd ever done, fucking Princess Miriam in the Prince of Wales's fancy car might have been the stupidest. I knew that going into it. Not only would our spouses disapprove, but probably most of the royal family, too. Maybe most of England.

But staring up into those big brown eyes with my breaking heart and my pounding cock, nothing in the world could have stopped me.

"We shouldn't do this," she said again.

"I know," I repeated.

"Are..." She stopped. Swallowed. My gaze zeroed in on the way her throat moved. "Are we?"

I didn't know what to say.

Yes?

No?

Maybe just the tip? Just to see if we like it?

God, my head was so messed up.

I loved Ivy. I loved Lex. I loved them so goddamn much that I couldn't see past it.

Now they were gone. Was I filling the hole they left with the only person who could commiserate? Or was there something truly there for Miri? Did I really love her or only think I did because it made missing them easier to bear?

"Hey." She put her hands on my jaw, cupping my face, and lifted my gaze to hers. "It's okay. I'm conflicted, too. I love them, and I don't know what to think about you."

I laughed a sad noise, pretending not to feel like a cheap date.

"But I know that I cannot do this without you," she continued, "and you cannot do this without me. Is that not love?"

Is that not love?

A different kind, maybe. Different from the one that burned in my chest for Ivy and Lex. But no less powerful or significant.

I kissed her again, and this time, we twisted so her body was laid out across the seats. Somewhere deep down inside, I envisioned Lex doing this to Ivy behind my back. I envisioned his lips on her neck, his teeth digging into the blushed X he loved to hate, and I burned with shame and guilt and envy.

Because they should be here, and they weren't.

Because I should be there, and I wasn't.

I needed something besides that hollow ache in my gut. I needed this connection more than I'd ever needed anything else. *Take a lover*, Miri had said. *Find someone else.* But I didn't want anyone else.

I just wanted us.

I just wanted *them*, and if we couldn't have them, then we'd have each other.

I opened the door so I could move my long legs to the ground and kiss my way down her body. Shoving my jacket off, I tossed it in the back seat and kneeled on the cement floor. My knees would hate me for it later, but I didn't care.

Her panties came off. Then her skirt. When she was naked from the waist down, I wrapped my hands around her thighs and yanked her closer, sliding her so she sat close to the edge. I hadn't eaten pussy since that last night together, and Miri was about to reap the benefits of my withdrawal. I ached to taste her. I yearned to lick those most secret places.

I met her honey-colored gaze and searched for any objection to this. We'd both been heartbroken about what we'd lost. I kissed up the inside of her legs while she spread herself and, when my mouth touched that familiar skin, she curled into the contact, her hands in my hair, urging me on.

Fuck. Yeah.

I licked her, sucking at her clit and flicking my tongue over her the way I thought she liked. Taking my cues from her reactions, I worked her into a frenzy, right there in her uncle's expensive car.

It made me think of Midsummer, of being in the woods with her and *them,* the sticky sweet scent of sex on my tongue, the moans of other people's ecstasy surrounding me, the dizzying thrum of a buzz behind my eyes. My cock throbbed, and I adjusted it through my pants while I lapped at Miri, relishing in her groans.

I sucked her clit, twirling it around between my lips before pushing a finger inside her. She liked it slow like this, soft and delicate. When I played with Ivy, she wanted it rough nearly as often as she wanted it sweet, but Miri wasn't like that. She used sex to be intimate, which surprised me since she'd been with Lex for so long. He didn't strike me as the soft and sweet type of guy.

One finger became two, and I delighted in her moans, her desperate pleas for me to go faster, harder, deeper.

"Please," she moaned. "Please, Romeo. Please."

I could tell she was close, so I kept at it, increasing pressure when her cries became more desperate. When she came, she dug her nails into my scalp and nearly crushed my head with her thighs. I held them open as best I could with my shoulders, but she squirmed away from me, gasping for air.

I grinned at her, licking my lips to swallow down her taste. She gave me a lazy sigh and ran the back of her fingers over the side of my cheek. Sadness flicked behind her gaze, indicating the *want* of them and how *almost* perfect this felt.

"I wish they were here," she murmured.

I pushed up to kiss her, confirming I felt the same. My heart raced and my cock throbbed, but the hole they once filled sat like a heavy weight between us. We needed this to remind us of how great it used to be, how much we were missing.

It started slow and sweet, a caress, but she soon grew hungry and shoved her tongue in my mouth, greedily devouring the taste of her sex on my lips. Then she tugged me into the car by the back of the neck, laying down so I had to climb on top of her.

I sank one hand into the cushion next to her ribs, grabbing the door over her head with the other, my palm folding over the crease of the rolled-down window. She twisted her fingers in my jeans button, yanking the zipper down so she could get my cock out.

Miri gave it a few quick pumps, but I was already rock solid for her. She positioned me at her entrance and looked up, big eyes pleading, *begging,* me to take her, to make it stop hurting.

"Promise me one thing," she said, her warmth such a tempting embrace only millimeters away.

"Anything, Juliet," I said, kissing the tip of her nose. Her forehead. Her temple. Her hair. "Anything."

"You and me, we're a team. Always." She stared up at me, wild vulnerability lacing her big doe eyes. "Whatever it is. Whatever comes for us. They have each other. All we have is us."

I nodded, wincing against the pain at the thought of Ivy. Once upon a time, all I had was her. Now I didn't even know when I'd see her again. I ignored that, and it was my turn to shake as I slid all the way home.

God, she was so warm and tight. Like Ivy, but so different in so many ways. Not better, not worse, just different.

"This isn't going to last forever. You know that," she said, drawing my attention back to her. "This is just until we're not broken anymore, all right? Until it doesn't hurt."

"I know," I murmured. "I know."

With one hand behind my neck and her forehead on mine, I

pulled out only to surge back home again, sighing into her mouth, swallowing down her moans. God, it felt so good, too good. I could have stayed in that garage with her forever, if only so I'd never have to know pain again.

"Look at me, Romeo," she said, her hands coming to my cheeks. She tilted my face to hers, and the tension in my body softened. We might not have been the ones we would have chosen, but we were all each other had left. My heart had been broken, and Miri was the only one willing to sit in the wreckage with me.

In each other, we had found some semblance of peace. I wanted to wrap myself in the vitality of what we created and never let it go, which made it worse. This wasn't supposed to feel good. None of it. I was supposed to be with Ivy; she was supposed to be with Lex. We were supposed to be a four; I had the scars on my hand to prove it.

The more I thought about it, the more I noticed it. While the physical euphoria was enough to distract me, to have me pumping into Miri like my life depended on it, the incomplete emotional connection hummed just under my skin. I loved my Juliet, I did, and she loved me. But something was missing...two somethings.

She came with her eyes locked on me, and when I emptied myself inside her, I was surprised by how close to ecstasy I'd actually risen. I never thought I'd feel that again. I never thought I could have it with anyone but *them*.

EVERYTHING after that was a blur of fucking Miri and working my ass off.

My agent had gotten me a gig at LA Fashion Week, which was almost unheard of for a newbie. But it launched my career. From there, I had shoots every other day. Whenever I wasn't working, Miri and I were fucking. It was like sipping from a chalice where the alcohol content was *just* below my tolerance level. We sated each other. We got each other by.

It seemed like she felt it, too. It was in her gaze, in her soft expression during the comedown. After we'd both climaxed and we lay next to each other with our hearts pounding in time, inhaling each other's pants, her eyes softened and a glaze shuddered over them like she'd blocked out any thought of our spouses because of how much it pained her to think about it.

We made each other feel good. We took care of one another. But she longed for them, the same as me, and neither of us could be what the other had lost.

Despite this, I fell in love with her easily and more deeply than I had before. She was fun and spontaneous. She had a twisted sense of humor that made me damn near piss myself laughing. I understood why Lex and Ivy had cared so deeply for her, why Ivy had spent four years pining for her. Up until now, she'd been my friend, my cast mate, my ideal stage partner. She'd turned into a soul mate, someone in whom I placed delicate care of a piece of my heart. We understood each other's pain in a way no one else ever could, and that brought us closer together.

Miri was like that first spring day after winter when the air still had a crispness that hung in every breath but the sun shined warmly on your skin. Which was appropriate because she thought I was the opposite—cool autumn air and dying summer light, campfires and the smell of falling leaves. Her energy made you want to burst with life; my energy made you want to toast s'mores and cuddle.

We explored Southern California together. She showed me the places she'd been before, and we fucked in some places she hadn't. After a few weeks into our vacation, I couldn't imagine my life without her. We talked, *really* talked, about everything. About things we'd never discussed between us before. About our childhoods and what we wanted for the future. Some of those conversations I hadn't even had with Ivy. Before long, Miri knew more about me than anyone had before.

"You want kids?" I asked one night. It was late, or really early, depending on the point of view. Naked in our bed, her legs twisted in mine, my arm around her shoulders, I ran my fingers through her hair strewn across my chest.

"Yes," she said with a smile, glancing up at me. "A lot of them. Do you?"

I hugged her tighter, my heart nearly bursting with how much I wanted the same thing. "Yeah."

"Did you think you'd have them with Ivy?"

That brought me back to earth. I sighed and cleared my throat, hoping my voice didn't crack when I spoke again. "We always knew we'd probably break up at the end of college. But I'm a hopeless romantic. I saw little ginger-haired Washington-Scotts running around."

She softly laughed, squeezing my torso tighter. "Lex and I wanted them, too. We'd adopt a few. We'd have a few. I wanted a house overrun with family."

My heart yanked because it was a pipe dream, wasn't it? Lex and Ivy would have their own family, and I'd probably end up alone, wishing I could be a part of something bigger.

"You come home to me," Lex had once made me promise, *"and you come home to Ivy and Miri. And in the end, it's us."*

When I'd agreed to that promise, I'd meant it. He promised to take care of Ivy, and I'd come home as soon as I could. We'd given each other forever. How pitiful those words seemed now that we were scattered.

"If we don't have any by the time we're forty, let's you and I have them. How about that, Romeo?" she asked.

"Sounds nice," I agreed, though it was only a half-hearted jest. Lord knew, Miri and I would never...*could never*...have children together. The royal family would certainly have something to say about their darling princess having little majestic babies with some nobody actor from Chicago. Despite how close the two of us were, our romance would not be tolerated by the Crown.

"Have you spoken to your dad since you've been out here?"

"Talk about family disappointments." I ignored the slice of agony in my chest at the mention of my father. No, I hadn't talked to him, and if I never did again, even that might be too soon.

"Still haven't seen your little brother?"

I shook my head, wincing against the damnable tension in my gut. That one cut deeper.

"Do you want to?" She wasn't asking to be mean or bring up old wounds. Miri seemed genuinely curious.

I considered this. He was a baby now, but would my dad even tell him about me when he got older? About my sisters? Or had he completely reinvented himself? Knowing that conniving asshole, he'd likely go on pretending none of us existed. It was like he left my mom and all thoughts of his four children fell out of his idiotic head. Either way, it wasn't the kid's fault our father was a prick. Why should either of us suffer for it?

"Maybe," I answered. "One day. If he wants to see me."

She smiled and leaned in to give me another kiss, soft and tender, putting the weight of her adoration into it. "That's one of the things she always loved about you." Miri's grin pulled to one side. "Your big heart."

"You're one to talk." I squeezed her tighter to tease her with my response.

She rolled her eyes, apparently refusing to believe me. "Please."

"I'm serious," I continued. "To keep Lex as enamored as you have all these years? You must have a heart the size of the Grand Canyon and ovaries as tough as steel."

"Yeah, well." She sat up and readjusted herself so she could lie back against the headboard, the sounds of the ocean roaring in the distance. "It wasn't enough." Miri fiddled with a piece of thread between us. "It doesn't matter. Gran is setting up my engagement to the Prince of Monaco, anyway. In a few short years, I'll be the queen consort of Monaco with all the titles and endowments that entails." Forcing a tight grin, she let out a sarcastic laugh. "Lucky me."

"The prince of Monaco?" I scrunched my nose as I recalled a guy in his late forties with a bald head, expanding waistline, and jowls that reminded me of a bulldog. "Isn't he like a hundred and ten?"

"Doesn't matter." She laughed. "It's not about love or age. It's about royal babies. That's all it's ever been about."

I paused, debating what I knew about middle-aged men with how old that stuffy bastard probably was. "Can he even get it up?"

"I suppose I'll find out."

I ignored the burning stab of jealousy that flared in my gut.

One of her eyebrows lifted up her forehead, a mischievous look in her eye. "Unless..."

I didn't like the tone she used. It usually precipitated some silly idea that would likely get us in trouble.

"What if you and I got married in Vegas next week?"

"What?" I laughed, rolling toward her so I could grab her waist and give her a soft kiss on the forehead. "That's ridiculous. Your grandmother would kill us."

Miri mulled it over before replying, "She'd have to find us first."

I narrowed my eyes, shifting them between hers when she didn't start laughing with me. Was she serious? There was no way her family would let that happen. And when Ivy or Lex found out? Good lord.

Of course, what leg did they have to stand on?

Miri blew me off when I didn't immediately respond with a yes. "It's only a thought."

"Miri"—I didn't know what to say—"anyone would be lucky to have you. Lex knows that. Ivy knows that."

Tears formed at the corners of her eyes, but she blinked them back and wiped her grief away. "Not lucky enough to announce it to the world, though."

I would if I could. I would if it meant anything. But it didn't. What good would it do? Her grandmother would make her come home and deny it. The paparazzi would swarm us more than they already did. I was a nobody and a nothing and not good enough to so much as kiss the ground she walked on, let alone marry her in some dramatic elopement to Vegas.

I could just imagine the headlines on *The Puck:* "Beautiful Titled English Princess weds relative peasant from nowhere...Hey, wait, wasn't he dating Ivy Washington?"

"I love you, Miri," I told her, leaning in to give her a tender kiss. "I may not have always shown it. But I do love you."

"I love you, too." She kissed me back, cradling my face like it was precious to her. The thought warmed the piece of my heart that had started to beat for her and her alone. "Thank you for being here for me. I couldn't have done this without you."

I sighed and leaned up to kiss her again. "No, thank you, Juliet. We have each other, yeah?"

"Yeah, Romeo. We have each other."

I rolled between her legs again and slotted myself inside her warm, soft body. Up until now, we'd taken our emotions out on each other. Fucking and clawing and bleeding our pity in the space between us. But now, it was different. Now, I made love to her the way I'd done to Ivy thousands of times. Miri and I filled a space in each other that we'd never made room for before.

When she left, when this was truly over, it would hurt.

But I'd be better for having it.

7

MIRI

Carter wasn't in bed when I woke up. He'd left a note that said, "Went for a run. Be back soon," but I heard the shower in the bathroom suite, so I assumed he had already returned.

I stood and stretched, walking to the balcony to open the doors on the beautiful beach below, squinting into the afternoon air. A dying plant on the table next to me caught my attention, and I touched a finger to its leaf, giving it a momentary prayer.

"Hang on, darling," I thought before going into the room for a glass of water. I hadn't had much luck before now, but maybe I could perk her up at least a little. When I returned to the balcony, I startled and dropped the glass of water where it shattered on the ground.

The plant, which I swear had been wilted only seconds ago, now stood upright, perfectly in bloom. It had grown at least an inch and flowered two new sprouts.

"What the bloody hell?" I murmured.

I hadn't imagined that...had I?

Blinking, I walked closer, touching the small purple bud. The second my finger made contact, the flower opened and grew another few centimeters. I jerked my hand back and froze.

I did that.

I definitely did that.

"Bleeding Christ." My heart raced, but I tried to keep my wits about me.

Certainly, I was hallucinating. Maybe the result of what happened to us in Ireland? There could be no other explanation for why I suddenly had the greenest thumb on the planet.

I thought about Ivy, about what she believed happened. *The Fairies.* I had survived a car crash that killed everyone else in my family. If anyone had reason to believe in the miraculous, it should have been me. Yet, there I stood, staring at my own fingers, wondering what was wrong with me.

I went for my phone, every instinct I had telling me to call Ivy and let her know. I hesitated because I didn't have her new contact information, and she didn't want to hear from me anyway. Besides, this was too unbelievable. What exactly did I plan to tell her? That I could *grow* flowers with my bare hands?

If it got out, my gran would lock me away. They'd lobotomize me, and no one would ever see me again. No, this had to stay with me until the grave. Not even Carter could know.

My phone buzzed in my hand, startling me back into reality.

Gran.

Like I'd summoned her, and if she'd taken the time to call me personally outside of our regularly scheduled one-on-ones, then that meant I was in deep royal shit. *Fuck.* I answered and tried to keep my voice level, like I wasn't having a complete internal freak-out. "Hello, Gran."

"Hello, Miriam, darling," came her saccharine high-pitched voice. "How are you?"

"Oh, you know..." *Discovering I have mutant powers. Nothing completely out of the ordinary.* "Gardening."

"You and your flowers," Gran said with a small chuckle. "Such a lovely talent. You should foster that. Turn it into a humanitarian effort.”

I needed to get her off the phone so I could figure out *how the hell I could grow plants with my hands!*

“What can I do for you? This wasn’t in my schedule—”

“Have you seen *The Puck* today?” Gran interrupted. “You know how I feel about public displays of affection. You and this boy from Chicago walking on the beach together. This after that fiasco with your uncle’s car. Miriam, he’s *still* furious.”

“Gran,” I tried to say.

“No, enough.” Her tense tone indicated *exactly* how far I’d stepped out of line. “I’ve tolerated this summer holiday for longer than I’d wanted. The time has come to return home.” My heart sank. Carter was in the background, rummaging through the drawers, looking for clothes that had long since mixed with mine.

All I could focus on was how terribly this was going to crush both of us. We’d only just started to feel better, started to heal. In each other, we found a solace we never knew existed. It couldn’t last. I knew that going into it, but it still hurt like hell that it had to end so soon.

“Sharon has lined up a few more events,” she continued. “Make yourself useful and show up on time. I’ve sent someone to bring you home.”

Bloody Christ, who the hell could that be?

“When it’s time to go,” Gran continued, “it’s time to go.” The slurping sounds of her sipping her tea radiated through the other side of the phone, the universal sign that the conversation was over and my input was no longer needed. “I’ll see you when you return. Love you, dear.” She disconnected the call.

My stomach filled with concrete and my eyes stung. I wanted to stay with Carter. Everything in me, every molecule, every fiber of my soul, needed to be close to him. The thought of leaving tightened my chest and made my blood run cold.

My arm brushed against the irises I'd grown, and I refocused on the most important thing that had happened.

How had I done it?

I didn't have a good answer. I needed to test it with other plants and figure out how to get rid of its errant energy buzzing under my skin. Like the rush of blood in my veins, the iris's energy hummed through me, both foreign and familiar.

This meant something.

Carter wrapped his arms around my waist and rested his chin on my shoulder. He smelled like soap and man, and *hell,* I loved him so much.

"You know," he said, pointing to a spot in the backyard. "We ought to build you a greenhouse right out there."

He was trying to be sweet, but I couldn't focus. Too many thoughts raced through my mind, too many complications, too many things happening all at once. It irritated me—the paparazzi and the media and the public obsession with my life. They couldn't leave me alone. They couldn't leave Ivy or Lex alone. And the more famous Carter got, the worse it would be for him. He thought he was nobody now, but that wouldn't last for long. Roxy had big plans for him, and based on what he'd accomplished thus far, so too did the universe.

Fuck the paparazzi. Fuck my family. Fuck the whole bloody lot of them.

I sank to my knees, right there on the balcony, and sucked Carter's cock until he exploded down my throat, his fingers gripped in my hair, the back of my head banging against the concrete balcony wall. Then he lifted me up and set me on the edge, wrapping my legs around his head so he could return the favor.

I came loud and hard and hoped they could hear me in England.

Fuck all of you, you bastards!

For the next week, I tested the limits of my newfound ability. I walked barefoot on grass, astonished when it grew inches behind me. I held flowers, purposely asking them to flourish or not based on my whim, and they listened.

They listened!

The spirit of every plant I touched surged in my veins like manifestations of the great beyond. It tingled through my body with little vibrations. My connection to the earth had never been as great as standing in the wild with the thrill of nature's energy coursing over my skin and down my throat to my lungs. I'd never felt more alive, more human.

Lying in bed next to Carter without telling him took work. In the two months we'd been here, he'd become my best friend, my confidant. I'd told him things I hadn't even mentioned to Ivy or Lex. In many ways, Carter had become my best friend. With a heart full of sorrow, I pondered whether he might be my *only* friend.

He had a screenplay open on his lap, and I pretended to read a smutty novel one of my cousins had sent me. But I couldn't focus. I chewed my bottom lip, thoughts racing through my mind.

"You know," Carter said, "of the four of us, you always were the loudest thinker."

I sighed in exasperation. "That's not true. Your precious Weeds thinks a lot louder than me."

He tilted his head in my direction. "What's bothering you, Juliet?"

"Have you"—I shook my head, trying to keep it cool—"noticed anything strange recently?"

He chuckled and closed the script, setting it on the nightstand before rolling on his side to face me and putting his head in his palm, balanced on his elbow. "Strange things happen to me all the time. What's going on?"

I sighed, rubbing my tired eyes. "It's just—I have this feeling in my gut. I think Ivy might have been right about the fairies."

"Fairies?" He narrowed his eyes. "What do you mean?"

I swallowed and put my book down, sinking farther into the mattress so I could lay on my side and face him, mirroring his pose. I grabbed his hand, linking our thumbs, brushing our vows up against each other, palm to palm. "I have this intuition. Something's changed." I stared at him, looking for any sign he was lying, that he *had* experienced something like growing flowers with his bare hands. But his furrowed brow and the confused expression in his puppy dog eyes told me he had no idea what I meant. "Gran is sending someone for me."

Carter frowned, a defeated look haunting his gaze, and he kissed my knuckles. "We knew that would happen eventually. How long do we have?"

"Days. Weeks. I have no idea." I hated how much my life had never been my own.

He hummed and rolled on top of me, positioning his hips between my thighs, his half-erect cock poised right at my opening. Tingles shot through my body when he kissed my neck, followed by little nibbles that went down my collarbone.

"Guess we ought to make the most of it, huh?"

He disappeared under the covers and yanked my panties down to my ankles. Then I forgot all about fairies and focused on other magical fingers.

A FEW DAYS LATER, we went to an event in Las Vegas that Sharon had arranged—a charity dinner with a bunch of aristocrats I'd never met before. Carter had agreed to come, so I didn't have to go alone. Per my grandmother's instructions, we kept the PDA at a minimum and when journalists asked who he was, I said he was a good friend from college. When they asked why we'd been caught hugging on the overlook, Carter smiled and chimed in with, "Don't you hug your friends?"

"We've been through a lot together," I added.

"Are you referring to Lex Fairfax and Ivy Washington?" one of them asked. "Didn't you two used to date?" came another question from someone else. "How do you feel about them coming out as a couple? Did they cheat on you?"

Questions flew at us faster than we could answer, and I plastered that fake veneer smile on my face, pretending like they didn't hurt.

Did they cheat on you?

Yes. And resoundingly...no.

"What a personal thing to ask," I said. "Such bad manners." I waved a finger at them and chidingly tsked before heading inside to the banquet. Despite having Carter with me, the whole thing was long and tedious, and I couldn't wait for it to be over. The minutes churned agonizingly by. The only upside was the money we raised for the Danae Foundation, a nonprofit aimed at curbing climate change and building sustainability.

Sometime after dinner, I stood at the bar, sipping a glass of wine and waiting for Carter to return from the bathroom when a familiar deep voice said from behind me, "Red wine? You know how that makes you an insufferable twat."

"Bleeding Christ." I jumped and nearly spilled my drink on my new dress. When I set my glare on the intruder, my heart sank into my stomach. I understood then what Gran had meant by sending someone to fetch me.

My cousin, Edward, the second son to the heir to the throne, stood next to the bar with a smug grin. Like me, he'd been a royal fuckup in his youth, but he was male and a few years older, so he'd gone through the worst of it in the days before smartphones. He hadn't taken the brunt of the social media scrutiny the way I had.

Still, it pleased me to see family, and I liked Edward when he wasn't being a righteous shit. I gave him a hug and a kiss on each cheek. "She sent in the artillery, huh?"

"Please." He rolled his emerald eyes. "I was overjoyed to get away from that cesspool for a few days." He picked at my plate of hors d'oeuvres, selecting choice bits of cheese and charcuterie to eat. Then he set his stare on me and smiled like a cat that had cornered a mouse, now deliberating the most entertaining way to torture it. "I heard a rumor about you."

"Oh, yeah?" I took another sip of wine. "What's that, love?"

"You're sleeping with some American knob," he said. "The staff talk from here to Kensington and back again."

"It's nothing serious," I lied. It was everything serious. It was my last link to the greatest love of my life. "Nothing for you to worry about."

He raised an eyebrow. "Gran thinks it is. You know how protective she is of her princess."

"You're here to drag me home by my slutty little pigtails, is that it?"

He barked out a laugh and straightened, snatching the glass of wine out of my hand before gulping down the last sips of it. "Eventually." He put the chalice down and gestured to the bartender to bring me another one.

I pursed my lips and scrutinized him like a proverbial little sister. "I figured you'd be elbow-deep in blondes by now."

"Who says I wasn't?" He flashed that charming grin, the one that made the ladies swoon. "But a party is a party, darling." He trailed his eyes over a cute brunette that passed and put his hands in his pockets, the hunter officially on the prowl. "And you know I live for free booze."

I took a moment to admire his features. He'd inherited the same genes as his father and our grandfather, the same slope to his nose and the same set to his dark eyes. His elder brother, Arthur, had always looked more like their mother, something everyone in the family had seen as a blight after she'd released a tell-all documentary about our deepest, darkest secrets once the divorce had been finalized. Arthur may have looked the most like his mother, but Edward acted the most like her. He threw a big finger in the face of our traditions and dared anyone to do anything about it. I'd always admired him for that.

I caught Carter across the room, laughing as he charmed a group of strangers he'd probably just met.

"So that's him, is it?" Edward's gaze followed mine, and he leaned back on the bar. "Is he wearing my suit?"

"Oh, please," I said. "That suit's been at the beach house for so long, you forgot you owned it."

"He sleeps in my room," Edward teased. "He wears my clothes."

I rolled my eyes. "Don't start."

He shrugged. "It looks better on him, anyway."

"He's trying to break into the film industry. I'm helping him." I straightened and grabbed my new glass of wine when the bartender set it down. "Roxy's taken him on as a client."

"Roxy's involved?" Edward shook his ginger-colored head at the mention of our estranged cousin, a fellow black sheep. "Are you trying to see what it'll take to make her put you on lockdown?" He meant our grandmother. "She sent me to bring you back; now I understand why."

"What's that supposed to mean?"

"My little cousin moves in with some American nobody, and you're surprised I came to sort you out? And here I thought you were the smart one." He wrapped those giant arms around me and pulled me into a bear hug the way he used to do when we were kids, lifting me off the ground while I struggled.

"No." I tried to squirm away. "No, no, no!" It got tighter and tighter and tighter.

"Say mercy," he said. "Say mercy!"

"Let. Go. Of. Me!" I elbowed him in the ribs, and he dropped me.

"God love ya, little coz." He gave me a pretend punch to the chin and winked. "Okay, now say your goodbyes to your Hollywood heartthrob. I'm going to find someone to suck my cock, yes? And then we'll head home."

"What? Right now?"

I couldn't leave now. It was too soon. I hadn't gotten my greenhouse started. I hadn't had my fill of Carter. I hadn't—

"Yes, right now," he mocked. "Gran's got that debutante dinner thing tomorrow night. She insists you attend."

"Ugh." Despair coiled through me, lining my stomach with dread. "I'd rather cut off my right foot."

"When it's time to go, it's time to go." He repeated Gran's favorite phrase before winking and disappearing into the crowd.

I took a deep breath and set my focus on Carter. This would hurt almost as bad as it had when I'd had to say goodbye to our other two halves. I grabbed Carter's shoulder, interrupting a story that must have been hilarious considering how hard everyone was guffawing.

"Excuse me, Carter," I said. "Can I steal a dance?"

"Of course. I'll see you guys."

I led him out onto the floor, and Carter grabbed one hand, putting the other around my waist to pull me in. We left room between us for Jesus and Gran's rules, but the live band played a version of "I'll Be Seeing You" by Billie Holiday that forced us to get close anyway. We swayed back and forth to the slow, sultry rhythm, and I tried not to let the weight of what I had to tell him pull me under.

I wished we'd met at a different time, a different place, when it could just be the two of us. Not that I would forgo what I had with Lex and Ivy, but Carter and I could have made sense in another life.

"You look so beautiful tonight," he said. "You look beautiful all the time, but especially tonight."

I smiled, relishing the warmth that oozed from my heart into my legs and up my spine. "Such a charmer, Romeo. Are you trying to get into my pants?"

He leaned and pressed his lips to my ear. "Is it working?"

I chuckled, committing everything about this moment to memory. I didn't want it to end. I didn't want the song to finish and force me to leave this night or the beautiful thing the two of us had found in our grief.

"I need to tell you something," I said, the words tasting like garbage as I uttered them. "It's not a good something."

His expression softened as he met my gaze, but he must have seen it there because he nodded and frowned like understanding had finally hit him.

"It's time, isn't it?" he said. "The clock's struck twelve, and you're about to turn into a pumpkin?"

I nodded, blinking back tears. "My cousin's here to collect me."

He pulled his lips into a thin line and looked down to the ground between us, holding me tighter, squeezing my hand harder.

"Listen to me," I said, tilting his chin up. "You can stay at the house in Malibu as long as you need. No one will bother you. You have my word. I love you." I nodded toward the rest of the room. "They love you. The whole world's going to love you, Romeo."

I wanted to kiss him and hold him and tell him Ivy and Lex would always have each other, but all we had was us—Malibu and the Aston and the stage. I wished I could abscond with him. I wished I was like my cousin, able to sneak off into a private coatroom to do what I pleased.

But if he and I disappeared together? It would be all over *The Puck* by morning.

"I love you," I told him again. "I love you."

"I love you," he repeated back, his voice cracking as he blinked back tears.

"Until the end," I said.

He took a deep breath and blew it out slowly in a desperate attempt to keep his composure. "Until the end."

I enjoyed the rest of the song, forcing myself to stay in the present with him. Eventually, my cousin found me, and I let him take me back to our ivory tower. That was when I knew the dream was finally...truly...completely and totally...over.

8

CARTER

When Miri left the party in Vegas, she took with her the last piece of my heart capable of loving someone else. Not the superficial beam of sunshine that I forced on strangers. Not the facade of the professional I gave to my agent and the other models. No, Miri knew the *real* me. We had years and years of history.

Alone in the city of sin and broken dreams, I wandered the Boulevard for hours. Thinking. Reminiscing. Trying to decide what to do next. I was melancholic enough to pack up my shit and go home. Maybe a few months in Chicago would do me some good. I could be with family again, maybe find that thing inside me that used to want this career.

Eventually, I sat at a roulette table, drinking whiskey and putting random chips on random numbers. I'd never been a betting man. I made money to save or buy necessities. But when in Rome.

Besides, I was depressed and feeling sorry for myself, and what better way to make that worse than to get shit-faced and blow a bunch of money I didn't have?

"Hey there, cutie," a drunk blonde said from the seat next to me. "Put a bet down for me."

"Sure thing, sugar." Why not? It wasn't my money. I grabbed some of her chips and put them on twenty-three red. I, likewise, did the same to mine.

"No more bets," the dealer said, and we watched the ball spin around the wheel and land on twenty-three red. "Winner!" He pushed our earnings toward us.

The woman shouted and threw her arms up in the air, wrapping them around my neck and giving me a big kiss on the cheek.

"I got lucky. I got lucky," I said.

"Do it again!"

This time, I put it down on sixteen black. The dealer spun the ball in the wheel, and it landed on the same number and color.

"Winner!" he called again.

"Jesus, cutie pie," the woman said. "Do you have a horseshoe in your pocket?"

Apprehension slithered around my spine, and I shivered. From what, I didn't know. The analogy rocketed through me, not because I actually had a horseshoe, but because there was something about me being lucky. It wiggled around in my chest like a fucked-up monster from an '80s movie, preparing to bust out of my rib cage and kill us all.

"Okay, one last time." She handed me a big stack of chips.

"That's too much," I protested and tried to push them back.

"Don't tell me how to spend my own money." She slurred and tumbled on her heels, but I caught her and pushed her back upright.

"All right," I conceded, and I placed another bet.

We won again, but this time, we won big. Really big. To the tune of half a million dollars. It drew the attention of the dealer and the security staff, who came over to "monitor" the game. It was enough to scare me off, especially because I didn't know what was happening. Could it have been a coincidence? Sure. Nothing was impossible, only highly improbable. But I'd made myself and a stranger a lot of money in a very short amount of time.

The house always wins, right?

Not tonight.

"What's your name?" The blonde slung an arm over my shoulder, leaning on me as we walked out of the casino. She smelled like cigarettes and gin and regret. "I'm Candy."

"Carter," I said.

Once we were on the sidewalk, she put a cigarette between her lips and eyed me up and down.

"Candy and Carter," she repeated. "A match made in heaven."

I snorted a laugh and ran a hand over the back of my head. I could have her, if I wanted. I could take her back up to my room and fuck her brains out and forget all about Miri and Lex and Ivy. But my cock shriveled at the idea, revolting at the images coursing through my brain.

"I should go," I said. "It was nice meeting you."

"Yeah." She flashed me a grin. "Likewise. Take care of yourself. Thanks for the luck."

That uneasy feeling choked my windpipe again, the one that had me wincing and trembling with anticipation.

Luck.

I'd never been superstitious. I didn't believe in ghosts or things that went bump in the night. Something strange had happened to us in Ireland, sure. There were things about that experience that I would never be able to explain, but there *was* a logical explanation for it, whatever it was: someone had drugged us, someone had burned marks into our hands, someone had fucked with Ivy.

I needed a way to test this, a way to be one hundred percent sure.

A stupid idea rattled around in my idiot brain, but once it was there, I couldn't find a good reason not to do it.

I went to another casino a few blocks down, one where I'd be able to get in and get out before their facial recognition system picked me up again.

One game. Just walk up to the first table. Put it all down. See what happens.

I found a blackjack table and sat down to bet it all on the first hand. Half a million dollars. *Bam!* Right on the green.

"Sir," the dealer said. "Are you sure you want to do that?"

"Yep." I looked ridiculous, like I didn't know what I was doing, but I'd come here penniless, and if I left that way, I'd call it square.

I had a point to prove. I needed to know I wasn't cursed, that I'd just had a good night in Vegas and the odds were *still* stacked against me just like any other—

"Blackjack," the dealer said, and the lights above the table went off, drawing the attention of everyone in the vicinity. The guards. The other patrons. The girls dancing in the cages nearby. "Winner! Winner!"

I'd just won...$750,000...totaling $1.2 million...in one night.

This drew *loads* of attention, and after a tense conversation where I managed to convince them I'd *just gotten lucky,* the hotel personnel kindly escorted me to the airport. They even stuck around to make sure I got on the flight.

What a couple of gentlemen.

But I could no longer deny the truth. Something was definitely wrong with me.

"She said she gave me a gift," Ivy had told us. *"You don't think fairies are real...do you?"*

"I have this feeling in my gut," Miri said the other night. *"I think Ivy might have been right about the fairies."*

I'd heard about them in stories and read about them in plays from the Renaissance. There wasn't a part of me that believed they could exist. But...what if they did? What if Ivy was right? What if Siobhan really had fucked with us?

I should tell her. I should tell someone. But what proof did I have? A gut feeling and a good night of gambling? Who would believe me? I barely believed myself...until I got back to LAX.

That short flight had never felt more lonely. I raged against

Evelyn Washington and Kellan Fairfax and the whole royal family. At the stupid media and the paparazzi and a public hungry to eat it up. I hated Lex and Ivy and Miri, all three of them. If I'd never met them, I wouldn't be so heartbroken. If I'd never fallen for them, never followed them into those stupid fucking woods, I wouldn't be wondering if I was having a quarterlife crisis.

Was there such a thing as being *too* lucky?

I suddenly regretted not having paid more attention when Ivy did all that research. Why had she blocked me? Why wouldn't she just talk to me?

To make matters worse, the plane was an hour late getting in due to someone on the flight before us having a medical emergency. We sat on the tarmac for another two hours while we waited for a gate to open up.

Going to California was the stupidest thing I'd ever done, and for what? I had an agent, but no real career prospects. I'd lost my best friend, my girlfriend, and my star-crossed lover. My father thought I was a joke. Maybe he was right. Maybe this was a pipe dream. Maybe I should've thrown in the towel and gone back to Chicago. I had enough money to set myself up now. I could buy a nice house, find a partner, and settle down with two-point-five kids and a golden retriever.

My bitterness burned my eyes, tasting sour on my tongue.

Getting off that plane, I hated my life. I hated LA. I thought I'd made the worst decision anybody could make, all for the sake of ambition. I wanted Hollywood with a fury, and I'd do anything to get it. But my mind had never been more filled with doubt than it was trying to catch a taxi back to Miri's Malibu dream pad. I had to pack up my shit and find a place more my speed. I had to figure out if I was delusional or actually possessed by some rotten form of a fairy "gift."

I went for the handle on the yellow car door at the exact same moment as someone else, and I jerked my hand back, looking up to meet the eyes of the person I'd have to fight for the ride home.

My jaw nearly hit the ground.

Anthony Michaels, my director from the Royal Theater Company, stood in front of me with an astonished look on his face. He hadn't aged a day in five years.

"Anthony?" I said.

"Holy shit!" He threw his arms out to give me a hug. "Carter! Look at you! You've filled out."

I laughed. "It's good to see you."

"Where ya headed?" His grin nearly blinded me.

"Malibu."

Anthony's eyes twinkled as he shook his head. "Not anymore. Get in the cab."

I furrowed my eyebrows but did as he said, if only so I could have the time to catch up with him. I mean, c'mon, this chance encounter on this random Tuesday at one of the busiest airports in the country? One in a million.

"What are you doing in LA?" he asked once we were on the road.

"Going for the big time." I told him about my agent and how I'd spent the last few weeks auditioning and modeling.

"You've only been out here a few weeks?"

"Since the end of June," I said.

Anthony shook his head and sighed. "You're the luckiest little shit in the world right now."

Yeah, no kidding.

I snorted and raised an eyebrow, ignoring the rising staccato in my chest. "What's that supposed to mean?"

"I'm here because *Fractured Crowns*, the screenplay I was writing back when I met you, has been picked up by a major network. I'm not at liberty to say which one yet, but there's a B and an O in the name."

My excitement rattled through my torso like a dose of some high-quality club drug. "Really? That's great, Anthony. Congratulations."

"No, you don't understand," he said. "Carter, I was writing that when I first met you. Remember? I said you had natural talent and you'd be good for one of the parts."

"I asked if you were offering me a job."

"Yeah," he said, giving me a big Cheshire grin. "You did."

I paused for a moment so the meaning of his innuendo could finally dawn on me. "Are you offering me one now?"

"Yeah," he said, nodding. "I am."

What the fuck? What the actual fuck?

"Carter, I wrote this part with you in mind," he said. "You still have to audition with the studio execs, but I'm directing most of the first season." He turned in the seat and gestured to the phone in my lap. "Call your agent. Get her on the first plane out here. I'm one hundred percent serious when I say you have the part as long as I can get the studio on board. I'm almost certain that I can."

Hands shaking and sure this was a dream, I called my agent to tell her the news, but she was conveniently still in LA. When we got to the studio, I did my song and dance with the producers, putting on the charming act even though I was exhausted and smelled like Vegas and regret. They didn't seem to mind, and two days later, I'd been cast as the lead in the next mega show to blow up on premium television.

ACT II

You draw me, you hard-hearted adamant.
But yet you draw not iron, for my heart
Is true as steel.
-Helena, Act II, Scene I

9

MIRI
TWO YEARS LATER

Time slipped through my fingers quicker than ash. When I left Carter at the party, I told myself it wouldn't be long before we saw each other again. I told myself I would visit as often as I could and call whenever the opportunity struck. Like my promises to Lex and Ivy, that too floated away on the wind.

We sent the occasional text and called at important milestones, but Carter's filming schedule had ramped up after his premiere on *Fractured Crowns* and now? Who knew where he was? Australia one day, Czech Republic the next.

It hurt to think about them, to talk about them. I didn't have much to say these days anyway.

Ivy and Lex crowded the headlines. The paparazzi loved their relationship, and when they announced their inevitable engagement, my heart turned to stone and died. I hadn't talked to either since I left Virginia, but every part of me remembered every part of them. I brushed my thumb over the scars on my other hand, vows we had made to each other all those years ago. Vows they also carried. Vows they'd broken the minute we were separated.

Part of me wanted to be angry at them. Part of me wondered if they'd done us a favor. Perhaps it was better to rip off the bandage, quick and clean.

"Miriam?" my grandmother's voice brought me back to the present, where I sat at tea with the Prince of Monaco, a man twenty years my senior who had been barking up my skirts since I turned fourteen. (Gross, I know.) "Reginald asked if you had any plans to turn your skills into something more substantial. An exhibit garden, perhaps?"

I forced a smile and took a sip of my Earl Grey, but it tasted rancid despite the cream and sugar. "Yes. Well, my nonprofit aids in building sustainable infrastructure for regenerative horticulture."

When I'd come home from LA, I'd been obliged to join the royal family and take up my noble cause to give back to the society that sustained me. My grandparents had wanted to turn my image around, make me more palatable to the general public. In an effort to take up the mantle as my father's daughter, I'd dedicated myself to something I loved, and saving the environment became my number one priority. I'd joined forces with Danae Enterprises and accepted a position as their royal ambassador. Together, we hoped to push political agendas in a more environmentally favorable direction, which was where I stepped in.

I'd been schmoozing rich wankers like the Prince of Monaco out of their assets since I could talk. But I did love to garden, and given my particular ability, I made lots of things grow where they never had before.

"But after I save the planet?" I gave a nonchalant shrug in an attempt to be charming. "Maybe a garden or two would suffice."

Reginald laughed in a dark chuckle. He seemed like a nice man, someone who would allow me to sleep around provided he could do the same. We'd have to have children, of course. That would be required. But I could close my eyes and think of England a few times a year. Hundreds of my grandmothers had done it before.

I took another leisurely sip of tea and wished there was whiskey in it. Or arsenic. Anything would be better than this.

"Well, you should see the rose gardens in Monaco. They are beautiful in late spring," he said.

"The prince has dedicated several to members of the family," my grandmother added, like I was supposed to be impressed. All this talk about plants and gardens only reminded me of the sowing I had to do at Aberdeen. I hadn't been in a few weeks, and though I paid people to tend to it in my absence, I preferred to work the earth myself, to feel the dirt between my fingers. It brought me so much solace in this chaotic world.

As if putting a cherry on top of that thought, Reginald said, "Shall we talk bride-price?"

I nearly spit out my tea through my nose.

Later, after I'd promised a trip to Monaco in exchange for a *generous* contribution to Danae's cause, I wandered the halls at Kensington, reminiscing about the first time I met Lex. I'd led him through this very corridor to the secret stairway, taking him outside so we could get stoned and gossip about the high holy patriarchs and their high holy plans.

Ages had passed between now and then.

I loved him the same.

I still loved all of them the same.

I'd become a ghost here, haunting this ancient castle as relics of my foremothers hung on the walls to remind me I was the latest in a long line of women who'd been auctioned off to the highest bidder. I had hoped the world would have changed after all these years, and maybe it had for every other person. But for me, someone burdened with thousands of years of history on my crown, it was more of the same.

I couldn't have who I wanted. I never could. So why did it matter who I married in the end? Be it the prince of Monaco or some other old man with a fortune. I was nothing more to my family than a face and a name to be traded.

I'd tried to take lovers in the time since I'd left Carter, but I couldn't get *into* it with anyone else. I revolted at the touch of someone else's kiss. My lover would trail their fingers down my stomach, and I'd grab the hand to stop it. Nothing about any encounter made me *want* the way I'd wanted with them. It was like tasting the best chocolate in the world and then being forced to live with cheap petrol-station sweets for the rest of your life.

Fine. I'd marry the prince of Monaco. I'd spit out his children because they'd be my children, too. At the end of the day, family was all I really wanted—someone to call my own.

My vows came back to me from Midsummer, as they often did when I gave way to despondency and broodiness.

"I'll love you, all of you. I'll honor you and respect you. I'll never betray you. I'll never hold you back from your dreams or each other. I'll be honest with all of you. From today. Until the end."

When I'd made that promise, I didn't realize how far away the end would feel when I was slogging through the middle.

Working for Danae was more than appearances. Yes, it had started because I needed a grand cause to support, but going in to see the staff a few days a week gave me purpose, something to look forward to. It was the only time Gran let me out of the castle unsupervised and unscheduled.

It wasn't much, and if it were up to me, I'd work full-time. But being HRH Princess Miriam Stuart, duchess of Aberdeen, didn't afford me the luxury of being normal. Between my grandmother loaning me out to her royal friends and the agenda Sandra thrust on me the minute I returned home, I barely had time to breathe, let alone hold down a full-time job *outside* of public service.

But if I could...If I'd been born any other person in any other household...I'd rule Danae Enterprises with an iron fist. I wouldn't stop until I squashed the bleeders destroying this planet. I wouldn't stop until I'd healed every last piece.

The scars on my hand itched, and I absently rubbed at them with the thumb on my opposite hand. Just when I'd decided to take the stairs toward my apartment, a wave of lust hit me in the gut so hard, I nearly toppled over. I held on to the metal railing to keep myself upright and gripped at my lower abdomen, clenching my thighs around a cunt that throbbed and demanded attention. It had come out of nowhere, like I'd swallowed a handful of arousal pills with no chaser. My blood thrummed through my veins, making me run hot and sticky.

It felt like...It felt like...

No. It's not possible.

It had been two years since Midsummer, and I'd been trapped in this palatial prison for weeks now. The only person who prepared my food also did so for the king and queen of England.

This can't be happening. This...can not...be happening.

Yet, another round of arousal assaulted me, forcing me to clench my eyes closed and squeeze my legs together, exactly like it had that day in Ireland when we were out in the woods or three days later when it took us in the dorm room. Now, it slammed me behind the legs and I fell to my knees on the staircase.

I couldn't stop myself.

I had my hands down my pants and my fingers rubbing my clit in seconds. I prayed that no one walked in on me like that. How could I explain it? Me in agony. My vulva so puffy and swollen, I might squirt from a gust of wind, unable to stop myself from seeking release.

They used to commit royal women who had mental breakdowns as recently as the '70s.

What would they do with me?

I couldn't focus on that. I could only work myself over as waves of euphoria pumped through my blood, making me sweat and convulse with each agonizing pulse.

Somewhere in my molecules, a release came...but it wasn't from me. My soul responded to another's climax...the cold waves of an icy deluge shooting down my spine.

Lex.

Sparks of fire came next, amping up my own impending explosion. *Ivy.*

A few minutes later, the warm burst of dying autumn echoed in my veins, tasting like Carter's delicate skin. It was him, his orgasm, his culmination.

Anticipation of my orgasm amplified the ethereal experience of three people on the opposite side of the world being so intimately connected to me. If they were in person, I'd think they were waiting on me to complete the orgasm cluster. The exquisite magic of being tethered to them again, of *knowing* their energy inside me the way I knew my dear plants, it broke me. I came hard, in loud panting gasps that ricocheted up the narrow stairwell, my nerves fried, my muscles tensing so tightly, I feared they'd rip apart. I clung to the railing, one arm slung over it, my knees protesting the hard metal steps. I saw stars behind my eyes.

Thankfully finding myself still alone when I was done, I struggled to my feet, smoothed my hands over my hair, and continued to my rooms on the top floor. The last time this had happened, the sensation had gone away once we all climaxed together. We'd given it what it wanted; now it would cease. But once I was there, safely behind a locking barrier, it hit me again—the rush, the passion, the wave of uncontrollable whatever it was.

Damn it all to hell.

I went for my Hitachi this time, but when I climaxed again and the rush only escalated, I knew I was screwed—royally and utterly screwed.

There was only one way to end this, and that meant I had to get out of this prison and on a plane to DC as quickly as possible.

ESCAPING PROVED to be more challenging than I'd initially anticipated. I didn't know where they lived, nor did I have their phone numbers. Even if I did, I'd been blocked for years. They didn't want to speak with me, but given the circumstances, they had to relent. I couldn't see how they wouldn't.

One of my cousins had been a computer genius their whole life. I didn't relish the thought of stalking my former lovers, but at this point, I was out of options.

"Why didn't you come to me first?" my cousin said.

"Because I didn't want it getting back to Grandmother."

He balked and laughed. "Look, I can't get you much, but I have an address. Evelyn Washington bought a three-story row home for them a few weeks ago. They're in Georgetown."

"Thank you," I said, hanging up.

I tried Carter again, but he still didn't answer. His odd filming hours had made it damn near impossible to reach him. When I'd talked to him a month ago, he'd been in the Czech Republic. He could be anywhere by now.

A wave of lust hit me hard between the legs, and I nearly toppled over, texting him Ivy and Lex's address before packing the rest of my things into my suitcase.

Now began the tedious task of getting out of the castle. Gran had paid off all the guards to keep me here, and if any of them saw me attempting to leave, they were on strict orders to detain me.

Still, I'd been sneaking out of this place since I was a teenager, and all I had to do was wait for the change in shift by the door. My most loyal guard and driver had already brought the car around. By the time I'd made it down the hallway and stairwell to the first floor, Sandra had caught up to me.

"Where are you going?" Her voice boomed over the click-clack of her kitten heels.

"Damn it." I kept going, hoping I'd get to the car before she caught up.

"Your Highness!"

"I'm leaving, Sandra," I called. "It's non-negotiable."

"You have engagements." She chased after me. "You can't leave."

"Cancel them," I said, lugging one of my suitcases over to where

Frederick grabbed it from me and hauled it into the trunk. "This is an emergency."

"What emergency?" Sandra's wide eyes hinted at her panic.

"It's a friend." I grimaced against the rush that went through me. "They're sick. Real sick." I was sick, too, but she didn't need to know that.

"Miriam," she said. My gaze snapped to hers at the use of my formal name. She corrected herself. "Your Highness, please."

"My grandmother's going to be upset," I said. "And I apologize for that. But this is really an emer—"

"Emergency, yes, you've said that. But if it's not a direct family member, I can't authorize—"

"Authorize?" This time, I cut her off. "I'm twenty-four years old. I don't need you to authorize anything."

Which was technically true, but the rules of the general populace did not apply to those with HRH in front of their name. I barely gotten in the limo and slammed the door in her bird face before the wave became too overbearing to stand. I put up the partition, cranked the music, and worked myself to another agonizing climax.

At this point, my pussy hurt to touch and my wrist ached from bringing myself there time and time again. What choice did I have? This wouldn't be over until we were together, and like it or not, I had to get to them.

Everything in me urged my compliance. It was a compulsion like none other I'd ever known, like magnets seeking out their counterparts, pulled together despite gravity and the space between. The flight nearly killed me, and when my driver got stuck in traffic on I-495, I clenched my legs together and took deep inhales, focusing on anything but the pain and agony of lust.

The scars on my hand burned like they'd been made yesterday.

Every jolting stop...start...stop...start...sent my blood pressure higher.

Be calm. Almost there.

When the limo finally pulled up in front of the townhouse, it only then occurred to me that I had no idea if they were home or if they'd want to see me. They had a bodyguard posting sentry out in front of their house, and a few people with cameras hung out on either side, already focused on my limo, waiting to see who would get out of it.

"Drive around back," I told my escort, and he circled the block while I debated what to do. It had been years since I'd talked to either of them, so long that this seemed idiotic. My heart beat wildly in my chest and my hands shook, sweat beading on my forehead.

I should have had no reason to be nervous. It was *them*, after all. Ivy and Lex. The two people I'd loved the longest in my life. I should have figured out a way to contact them before now. But no, I'd blindly flown over here assuming they'd see me.

They couldn't refuse me...right? *Oh, God.* What if I came all this way for nothing? What if I was the only one experiencing this? What if I was all alone in my misery and had been all this time?

My driver stopped in front of the garage behind their townhome, and I got out, quickly darting through the backyard to the door. A bodyguard held up his hands to stop me.

"Whoa, whoa," he said. "That's close enough."

"It's okay," came the sultry voice from the back door. "She's an old friend."

I met Lex's hazel gaze and every feeling I'd ever had for him rushed to the center of my chest like a shock wave, like the first time again.

My prince of darkness.

His hair had gotten longer and his body had filled out with muscle, but his eyes were as piercing and intimidating as I remembered. The cheekbones were more defined, accenting the angles in his face. He looked at me like I was fresh air, and he'd been suffocating for decades. None of it had dulled since I'd last seen him. He wore gray sweatpants and nothing else, his tattooed body red and flushed from the last twelve hours of what we'd been through.

I did my best to slowly ascend the stairs to their back door, minding my manners, while he said, "We're expecting another person, Carter Scott. If he happens to show up, no need to stop him. Let him through."

I took two steps inside, Lex shut the door behind me, and I jumped into his arms.

I didn't care about the two years between us. I didn't care that he'd gotten engaged to my former best friend weeks ago or that he'd broken up with me via text.

I needed to have his body pressed against mine. I needed his depravity and perverse gentleness, just like he'd used to give it to me. I just needed *him*.

Our lips collided, and I tasted sex and cigarettes and weed, a familiar cocktail for my deviant prince. The magic inside me, whatever it was that tortured us with this madness, vibrated at the slide of his skin against mine again.

His tongue explored my mouth and his hands, strong and familiar, went to my backside, squeezing me tighter to him, rubbing my cunt up against his cock, which had been hard since he saw me.

Footsteps to my right brought me back to my senses, and I dropped my legs as I broke the kiss to look in that direction. I *felt* her before I saw her, hot and vibrant in my molecules, like summer had been personified in real life.

Ivy.

"Miri?" Her breathless whisper coated my skin in adoration, and I ran to her, throwing myself in her arms the same way I had with Lex. My skirt flew up to my hips and my heels clinked together at her back as she caught me. Together, we laughed and we cried and we kissed.

God, we kissed.

Tears streaming down my cheeks, I held her face in my hands and devoured her soft, delectable mouth in front of her fiancé. It must have pained him to watch, just as it pained me to taste him on her lips. Of course, they had taken advantage of each other while they waited. I would have done the same, but a sharp stab of jealousy zigzagged down to my gut anyway. I wanted to be here with them. I wanted to be in the middle of whatever they'd taken out on each other.

I stepped back to admire her as I had with Lex. Her long ginger hair hung in a messy plait down the side of her body, and she wore one of Lex's old *Nirvana* shirts with nothing on underneath it. Bite marks glowed on the insides of her thighs, matching a few hickeys on her neck, and that envious inferno ramped up another notch in my gut.

"You look amazing, darling," I said, running the tip of my finger over a bite mark on the spot where her X appeared.

"I missed you." Ivy grabbed my hands to stop me, twisting our fingers together, the touch soothing and invigorating.

"I missed you, too." I gave her another kiss because in all the years I'd known her, I'd always wanted to put my greedy mouth on her. I'd had about a week of free rein before life tossed us in opposite directions. Now, it hurt *not* to touch her.

"You guys feel it, right?" I asked. "Please tell me you feel it."

"We feel it," Ivy said, nodding. "It started last night."

"For me, too," I said. "It won't go away. I've given myself carpal tunnel on the flight over here."

Ivy laughed as Lex lit a cigarette, and it felt almost perfect.

Almost.

If this were different circumstances or perhaps we were different people, there would have been the awkwardness of the breakup and subsequent time span between us. Maybe once this rush was over, that tension might seep back into whatever tatters of a relationship we still had. But under the influence of this clawing, needy thing, it was like we'd pressed play on a song we paused long ago, a song we all knew the words to. We picked it back up without missing a beat.

Ivy pulled me into the living room, Lex went to the kitchen to get us some water, and I knew two things immediately.

We were in for a sweaty, confusing night.

And I was finally home.

IO

MIRI

I wasn't sure what to expect, showing up at their front door the way I had. In retrospect, that was risky. I had no idea what the relationship between them was *really* like, despite the fact that I believed they faked their public one, and I didn't know how they'd feel about me, given the manner in which they'd ended things.

We didn't talk about any of it, not at first. Perhaps we were waiting until Carter arrived to sort it out. Perhaps there was nothing to be said while the lust had us.

I lay on their guest bed in the third-story loft, perched up on my elbows, stripped down to my lingerie, spread open and vulnerable for them.

"What do you think we should do with her, X?" Lex asked, with his arm slung around Ivy's shoulders. He raised an eyebrow, his lips twisting into a cruel grin.

"I don't know, Lucifer." Ivy crossed her arms, pushing her breasts higher on her body. She looked like a bombshell, and every queer impulse I'd ever had inside sat up at attention.

They both were wrecked; we all were, but there could be no stopping what was about to happen.

"She stole our boyfriend and ran off to Malibu," Ivy said, the gleam in her steel eyes just as incinerating as Lex's. Together, they looked like twin gods, come to earth to torture a mere mortal such as myself. The lust surged inside me again, twisting my cunt until it throbbed, and I gasped in an effort to contain my anticipation.

Lex made a small groan, and Ivy took a deep breath, the wave evidently rising in them as well.

"She did," Lex said, returning to the game. He ran a fingertip over my knee and down the front of my calf, making me shiver. "She turned him into a TV star."

"Should we punish her?" Ivy tilted her chin up and looked down her nose at me like an inscrutable queen. Like maybe I was the princess of a foreign territory that had been captured on their soil and now I had to answer to them about my trespassing. To be fair, that wasn't entirely far from the truth.

"We should," Lex said, stroking his cock through his boxers, which was only erect because of the surge between us, not because he had anything else in him. "But I honestly don't know if I can fuck anyone else."

The small break in character made us both laugh, and Ivy elbowed him in the ribs, quickly getting back into it.

"I have an idea." Ivy went to a dresser drawer, and I trembled while I waited for her to rummage through it. When she eventually returned, she'd wrapped a black leather holster around her waist, a huge rainbow-colored dildo hanging off the front. "I think the princess should tend to your aches and pains while I take what I want out of this sweet pussy."

Ivy trailed her finger along the inside of my leg, and I spread my knees wider.

"What do you say?" Lex looked at me, awaiting my permission.

They had it. *They always had it.*

I rushed to get on all fours, my pulse thundering against my ribs and echoing down to my cunt. Lex walked around the side of the bed to slide in front of me, relaxing against the headboard like a king in repose.

His queen took the spot behind me, coasting her warm hands over my hips and down my spine, easing me into a better pose with my ass up in the air. The bed dipped where her knees bent between mine, and I heard the lube cap open while I pressed my lips to Lex's mouth.

I loved Ivy, I truly did, and I loved her well before I loved Lex. But he and I had seen the best and the worst of each other. He completed me. So many times I had been in this position, bowed before him, his dick in my hand, his intimidating stare trained on me, beckoning me to do all the dirty things I knew he liked.

After pressing my lips to the tip of his cock, I licked at the spot that drove him wild—soft and sweet, knowing he was sensitive from all we'd done up until now. He twisted his hand in my hair and hissed in a breath like it hurt and felt amazing.

I knew it did. I sensed his bliss under my skin. When I circled my lips around the head, flicking my tongue over his slit, he groaned and tilted his head back on the headboard. There were many things I loved doing to Lex, but sucking his cock had to be in my top five. He was so responsive, so greedy, and it made me feel truly alive to be wanted that desperately by such a powerful man.

Ivy positioned the dildo at my entrance and inched inside of me. My skin stretched, accommodating her entry. For as tender as she'd always been with me, she wasn't nice about this. As soon as she positioned it, she shoved forward, sending me off balance and shoving Lex's cock down the back of my throat.

I gagged and Lex gasped, jumping under me and kicking his legs out. Ivy let out an evil laugh, followed by, "There's a good girl."

"Fucking hell, X." Lex tightened his hands in my hair, soothing the ache of having choked on his big dick.

I loved the familiar taste of him, and when Ivy found that spot inside of me that made me moan around him, we all learned Lex had lied earlier. He *could* fuck something else as long as it was my face.

They descended on me like monsters. Ivy spanked my ass and pulled my hair, forcing my mouth open wider so Lex could get farther inside. My eyes burned, and my throat constricted around the girth of him, but I wouldn't have stopped it for anything.

Having their joint attention on me blew my entire world apart. The last time we were together, they had barely discovered the strange new friendship between them. Now, it seemed, they had learned the same thing Carter and I had—what it took to be a team.

The undercurrent of their rivalry still burned between them, but instead of turning it on each other like they would have done in the past, they turned it on the world, and in this case, on *me*.

Lex fucked my mouth harder and, when I choked and drooled, he gave me little reprieve.

"Aww, my poor princess." Lex fake pouted and pulled out of me to wipe the spit from my chin, smearing it over my face. "Is my cock bigger than you remember?"

"No, I've just gotten used to your best friend's," I teased. "He likes to have his balls licked."

It may have been the wrong thing to say when Carter wasn't there to defend himself, and I'd only said it to goad Lex, to be his brat-princess once again. But Ivy tightened her hands around my waist, digging her short nails into my skin, and Lex's eyes widened at the taunt before flicking to Ivy over my head.

I'd confirmed what they must have suspected but hadn't yet asked—that the two of us had fucked outside of our square. That after they'd broken our hearts, we'd taken out our grief on each other.

I waited for the other shoe to drop, for Ivy to pull away and look at me with an unyielding jealous heat. My heart pounded. My skin flushed. Just when I was about to apologize, to say I hadn't meant it, Lex grabbed my head and forced my mouth lower.

"Well, then," he said, "get to it."

I did, licking and lapping at him like a good princess. A few minutes later, I came with Ivy pounding into me like a savage. She and I had never used a strap-on before, but she had skill. I wondered if it was Carter or Lex who enjoyed being pegged and decided it might be both.

"Fuck yeah," Lex said, pumping down my throat again. "Your mouth is so fucking perfect." I swallowed him, groaning as Lex's climax rushed through me. Ivy came last, using the vibrating portion of the holster to rub against her clit until it echoed through the three of us in an incriminating display of euphoria. I rolled to the side, panting down my hormone-laced ecstasy, and Ivy collapsed next to me, the strap tossed somewhere to our left.

Then we waited to feel Carter.

Our orgasms were like a siren beacon to him, reverberating through our souls and whatever joined us together. It reminded us of our obligation. We had promised *until the end.*

We needed him now, and he needed us. But he didn't come, figuratively or literally. It ached like an itch on a limb that had been amputated, like I couldn't reach it no matter how hard I tried.

Lex sighed and rolled to the nightstand, grabbing a pack of cigarettes and handing one to each of us. I took it and inhaled when he brought the lighter toward me, wondering where my Romeo had gone, wondering when he'd come for his Juliet.

The lulls between episodes were longer, seemingly quelled by the three of us being together, but they hadn't gone away entirely. He had to be on his way. I'd texted him the address. He wouldn't just leave this to go unanswered. The lust had to be sated, and if it wasn't, we might suffer the terrible consequences to no end. I reached for my phone and called him, but it went to voicemail again, as it had every time I'd tried.

"Where is he?" Ivy asked, a scowl forming between her eyebrows.

"Fucking off wherever he is." Lex took a deep inhale and ran his free hand through his head of thick, dark hair.

"He'll be here, darling." I coasted my fingers down the side of Ivy's face while she bit her bottom lip, her gray eyes unsure despite how badly she must have wanted to believe me.

The loft was a wide open area that ran the length of the house with a spare bed they kept up here for overflow guests. Aside from that, it was stacked to the brim with boxes from their parents' places that contained old clothes, trophies from their childhoods, and costumes from Halloweens gone by. We'd come up here to find their stuff from TW, maybe even something from Ireland that would help us figure out what was going on. The lust hit us again just as we started, and we didn't have a choice. Deciding I wanted to get some nonsexual movement in before it came back, I got up and walked to a box in the far corner.

"Old dresses, huh?" I asked, flipping open the lid.

"I have to go through them." Ivy followed me while Lex stayed in bed, one leg bent, the sheets twisted around his hips, eyes set on us. Still the same brat he'd always been, my prince of darkness had not changed in all these years.

"Look at these." Ivy went to the next plastic tub. "I should donate them."

"I have an idea." I held up a sapphire piece that flared into a mermaid skirt at the bottom. "Let's play dress-up."

"And I'm out." Lex rolled out of the bed.

"Oh, come on." I grabbed his hands. "Let me put you in Vera. She has a thing for long legs."

"I think you should wear the Vera." Ivy gathered a blush-colored poof of fabric that threatened to swallow me whole the minute I put it on. It was beautiful, and I remembered seeing Ivy in it at some gala a year or two ago. "I'll wear the Tom Ford and..." She leaned in so she could whisper something in my ear. "...we'll put Lucifer in the Anthony Wang."

I gasped, and we both set our sights on Lex, who looked between us like a rabbit that already knew it had been trapped but was still trying to find a way out.

II

CARTER

I was on set when the lust hit me like a sledgehammer behind the knees. My head went woozy, and blood rushed to my cock. I mumbled something about feeling nauseous before racing back to my trailer and pumping myself twice so I came.

The weird part was…the rest of them vibrated inside me, at the back of my mind like a splinter in my brain. I knew the instant Lex climaxed, a burst of coldness behind my eyes. Ivy came shortly after him, complementing that rush of ice with her special brand of fire. Something broke inside me when Miri finished us out, fresh dew and springtime energy.

Good fucking Lord.

I collapsed on the ground in front of my couch and panted, my face in my elbow, my other hand still down my pants, but my traitor fucking cock only got hard again. And again. And again. Nothing would stop it. The lust had taken me the same way it had in Ireland.

What the hell is happening?

Miri texted me the address, but I hadn't had a chance to respond.

Miri: *Come to DC. We're waiting for you.*

I opened the screen to do it, but another wave of lust hit me so hard, I grimaced against it, banging my fist on the floor.

I'm so screwed.

I still had two days of filming left. How the hell was I going to get through this?

By the grace of God and a helluva prayer.

I told everyone I had food poisoning, and that gave me the freedom to hit my trailer every hour or so, but those two days passed at a glacial pace. I jacked off so much, my skin burned. By the time I was free, I hadn't eaten in forty-eight hours. My throat ached, my hands were raw, and I was so damn dehydrated, I could barely stand.

I was sure I'd lost at least fifteen pounds by the time I made it to their DC townhouse. The closer I got, the less it hurt.

The tight ball of anxiety in my chest loosened when I lugged my backpack and suitcase up the steps to their front door. If the paparazzi were watching, I didn't care. I had to get inside. I needed them like I needed air.

"Carter Scott?" one of their bodyguards said.

"Yeah?"

He opened the door and nodded. "They've been expecting you."

"I fucking bet," I murmured as I entered, my shoulders relaxing, my cock stiffening. Every molecule in my body trembled with the anticipation of seeing them again. The whole house reeked with the tang of sex and the spicy aroma of weed. They had dimmed the lights in the main corridor, which I was thankful for because my eyes burned and ached for sleep. Footsteps raced somewhere on the other side of the wall to my left, followed by a girlish giggle.

Miri.

Another set of footsteps ran after her, this laugh louder and more commanding.

Ivy.

When I turned the corner, I froze.

What a sight.

Miri sprinted through the far side of the house wearing mountains of peach-colored fabric, looking like a Renaissance painting come to life. Ivy chased after her, wearing a pair of trousers, black suspenders, and a fedora.

Lex sat on the couch facing me, his naked feet outstretched in front of him, legs parted in an inviting V that begged for me to drop down between them. He, too, wore trousers and suspenders, but where Ivy ran around bare-breasted, Lex had on a white tank top covering his amazing tattooed chest. One of his arms stretched along the back of the couch and the other bent at the elbow to bring a lit blunt to those perfect pink lips. His head tilted to the side, making the top hat on his crown lilt off balance.

"Welcome home," he said, inhaling deep, the orange cherry illuminating his chiseled features. Smoke curled around him in tendrils, warping reality as dozens of misty arms stretched out to me, grabbing me, luring me in. He was the king of the circus, and I'd just become his new favorite act.

God, it was so good to see him.

I took a deep breath and clenched my fists at my sides. Desperation poured off me in thick, suffocating waves. I could smell it. Could he?

They'd had each other for the last seventy-two hours. And I... well, strung out didn't begin to cover it. I hadn't slept. I hadn't eaten. I stank to fucking high holy heaven. I could barely stand. The last time I looked in the mirror, my bloodshot eyes had big, dark circles under them and my skin had turned pale and clammy.

Lex looked totaled, but not as bad as me.

I expected him to rip me a new asshole for taking so long to get here. Lex never had any problem being accurately cruel. But he took mercy on me instead.

He held up a finger and waved me closer.

Like the action had complete control over me, I dropped my bags in the middle of the entryway and took a step, shoving my hands in my pockets so I could pretend to be nonchalant about the whole thing. Inside, I was cracking at the fucking seams.

"Where are the girls?" My voice sounded gravelly and raw, and my cock throbbed, but I ached to see Ivy. I didn't know where I stood with Lex, especially given what I'd done with Miri in Malibu, so I reached for the one person I knew would want me no matter what, the one who still wore the sign of my devotion on her finger.

"Around." Lex gestured vaguely toward the dining room off to the left and lifted the blunt to me.

I took it, my hands shaking as I brought it to my lips and relished the buzz. This thing, this lust, whatever it was, had made me jittery and frustrated and hell, I needed to come.

"Look at you. You're trembling." He reached up to grip the back of my neck. "My poor Chicago. Come here."

I tensed at his touch, at once so familiar and foreign, but I bent when he pulled me down so he could kiss me.

I melted. Immediately. I buckled at the knees and dropped to that vacant space between his legs. His body felt exactly the same. His muscles were firmer, his jaw wider, but his mouth hadn't lost that mystical quality that drew me to it in the first place. I dropped my palms to his thighs, blowing smoke into his mouth, unable to hold it in anymore. He inhaled it like he could inhale me with him. Maybe he could. Maybe he did.

Lord help me, I still wanted him, after all these years.

I took what I needed, and when I trailed my free hand down his chest, quivering with the weight of being away from them during the grips of this terrible thing, he groaned and tugged me closer. Scrambling for the waistband of his trousers, I tried to undo the button, but he broke the kiss and shook his head.

"No, no, no." He took the blunt so he could inhale another puff and put it in the ashtray. "I can't stick my dick in anything else."

I laughed and hung my head. "Things I never thought I'd hear you say."

He cupped my jaw and tilted my face back up to him, resting his forehead against mine. "What do you need?"

"Please get me off," I whispered. "Please. For the love of God. Make this end."

Lex pushed me flat on the living room floor and straddled my legs, tugging at my jeans so he could get my dick out.

I swear I saw the heavens part when he closed his lips around the tip and sucked me all the way back. I dragged my hands through his soft, thick hair, the way I had all those years ago, and I groaned loud and slow and satisfying. He chuckled but took his part seriously, like he needed this as much as I did.

Had he pined for me the way I had for him? Did seeing me impact him just as much?

I panted and hissed in a breath as the pain mixed with pleasure, bursting up my spine and down my legs to my toes.

It didn't take long. A few good minutes had me clenching my fingers into fists and coming in the back of his throat, a moan barreling out of the depths of mine. He let me use him however I needed and, once I was a writhing mess, Lex sat back on his haunches and sighed as the spell lifted. The ache in my gut subsided, the fog in my head cleared, and this heavy anvil in my chest finally let go.

Whatever it was, whatever it needed from us, it had finally been satisfied by my arrival.

"Welcome home," Lex said with a pleased smile, patting my chest.

"What the fuck was I supposed to do?" I rubbed my knuckles over my eyes as I sat in their enormous bathtub, Lex on my left, Ivy directly across from me with Miri in her lap. "I had to stay to finish filming. I'd breach my contract if I didn't."

"You filmed like that?" Miri rested her head on Ivy's shoulder, grinning mischievously at me.

"The last four or five scenes, yeah." The thought made me laugh. "I told them I had food poisoning. Thank God for black pants, right?"

"I was in the UK." Miri sighed, shaking her head. "I ran away. I'm sure my grandmother will send the royal army to retrieve me any moment."

"We were in bed," Ivy said.

"Woke me up out of a dead sleep," Lex added.

My focus drifted to Miri, who wore the same expression of curiosity-laced jealousy that throbbed in my heart. *They* were in bed? Doing what? I wanted to know, I needed to know, but would I be able to bear the brunt of the truth once I did? What if they were fucking? Would that hurt? Would I be excited?

"You two seem good," Miri said for me, pointing between Lex and Ivy.

"Surprisingly well adjusted," I added.

"It's all a show," Ivy said, rolling her steel eyes. "Don't be fooled. Lex and I hate each other even more these days."

"I don't believe you ever hated each other," I said, because what the hell? We might as well be honest with each other. We had too many years of bullshit between us to start lying now.

"Maybe Ivy hated Lex," Miri added. "But Lex has always had it bad for our Weeds." She tickled Ivy, who squirmed and sloshed around in the water. Ivy grabbed her hands and trapped them between their bodies, and Miri bit her bottom lip, eyes going from playful to sinful in a heartbeat. Ivy, bless her, reciprocated. Part of me wanted to egg them on, the same part that wanted to devour both of them until we couldn't stand. But after the last three days, I needed to sleep for at least ten.

"We're not together," Lex said, lighting a cigarette and inhaling deep before pinching it between his index and middle fingers. "Not the way the media thinks."

"All of this"—Ivy gestured to the bite marks on her neck and arms—"it's because of the lust. It only happened a few times after..." She cleared her throat. "Well, just after."

After the breakup.

After they ended this amazing thing over text.

After they told us never to contact them again.

I looked at Miri because she and I could not say the same. We had fucked each other into oblivion in Malibu.

Until it doesn't hurt. All we have is us.

That was what we'd promised.

"What about you two?" Lex nodded to me and Miri. "Summer getaways and Malibu Dream Houses?"

"That was two years ago," Miri said.

"But you were together, right?" Lex raised his eyebrows, expecting a response.

I sighed and ran my hand over the back of my head, trying to find the best way to break this news. "It's complicated."

"We were," Miri said.

"And now?" Ivy's voice cracked, and she blinked back a telltale redness that threatened to spill tears down her cheeks.

"And now"—Miri stole the cigarettes from Lex so she could light her own—"I'm the duchess of Aberdeen and Carter is the noble knight of Denwater." She took a deep inhale. "And we speak every month or so." Miri tapped ash in the crystal ashtray before looking at me. "It was because you broke our hearts over text message, which is so bloody rotten, I can't even stand it."

Lex lifted his gaze to Miri before shooting right over to Ivy, who furrowed her brows and gaped.

"No," she said, looking at me. "Carter sent a group text. It said you two needed space and not to contact either of you again."

"You called her Weeds," Lex added. "You called me DC."

Ivy held out her phone, showing a message I'd never sent from my old number.

"What the fuck? This wasn't me," I said, dread filling my stomach. "No way would I have ever done that. I tried for weeks to get in touch with you both."

"It said the number had been disconnected," Miri said. "You blocked both of us online."

"*You* blocked *us*," Ivy said.

Utter silence followed as the gravity of this massive misunderstanding settled between us. We'd spent two years pining for each other, all because someone *somewhere* had purposely driven us apart.

"No," Ivy said, but it came out like a whisper, like she was just putting the pieces together. She looked to Lex. "You asked your father."

"I did," he said. "He didn't know anything about it."

Her features dropped. "We never asked my mother."

"Asked her what?" I cut in.

"After we got the text, and you went radio silent, I suspected our parents might have done this to fuck with us. To keep us from contacting you and risking the marriage." Lex shook his head, inhaling deeper on the cigarette. "I believed what he told me. There's a lot more to the story, but I'm too tired to talk about it tonight."

"If he didn't, then there's another obvious choice." Ivy pursed her lips. "I told you we should have asked her, too."

"Then why didn't you just use your little telepathic mind trick?"

"Because yours is less obvious, Lucifer," Ivy snapped.

"My father still thinks I drugged him." Lex pinched the bridge of his nose, his agitation rising to the surface. "I'm not doing that shit to anyone else in our family. I told you that already."

"Okay," I cut in. "Calm down." I didn't even know what they were talking about. Telepathic mind trick? What did that mean? "Look, the point is, we're back together again. We can spend the rest of our lives figuring out the rest."

Ivy looked between me and Miri, but I knew what those sad eyes meant. Nothing had changed. She and Lex still needed to get married. I still had a tight filming schedule. Miri had the royal family. And yet...everything *had* changed, hadn't it? We couldn't be apart without this weird wanton compulsion eating away at us.

"How do we stop this from happening again?" I asked. "Because I sure as shit can't go through that a fourth time."

"You looked terrible when you got here." Lex's attention drifted to me.

"We need to get the band back together," Miri said. "That's obvious, isn't it?"

Ivy snorted and dug her fingers into Miri's waist, making her twist away so she floated over toward me.

"What about you, Romeo?" Miri raised an eyebrow and leaned in to kiss me, soft and tender. "What do you *want* to happen next?"

"Getting back together sounds nice." I would love to know I had these three people to myself for the rest of my life. *Until the end* and all that.

"It's not that easy," Ivy protested. "We can't go public with this."

"Ivy's running for Congress in two years," Lex explained.

"I'll be the youngest in history," she said. "Younger than my mother. I have a good shot at winning."

"We can be discreet, darling." Miri drifted over to Lex and put her hands on his knees to kiss him, slower and deeper than she had with me, but just as affectionate and thereby making her point. We belonged together—the four of us.

"Can you?" Lex pursed his lips at our princess. "The press follows you the most, and you've never been one for monogamy."

"I can pretend." Miri gave him a teasing little smile. "Ask your boyfriend. We pretended a lot in Malibu."

He narrowed his eyes and stabbed out his cigarette, grabbing hers to stab out next. Lex whispered to Miri and grabbed her by the back of her neck, bringing her closer so he could devour her mouth. But I shifted my attention to Ivy, my cheeks heating, my stomach dropping somewhere around my knees.

Miri likely meant the comment to be harmless, and if we'd handled this thing like actual adults instead of burying our heads in the sand, it might have rolled off our backs.

But I saw it in Ivy's expression—the momentary lapse where her guard was down and all of the emotions from the last two years bled through those steel-gray eyes—the jealousy over Miri and me, the equally intense feelings about her and Lex, the lust and the want and the *yearning.*

Shit, I'm right here.

"Weeds," I said in that tone that used to get her to drop to her knees.

Now, it brought her gaze to me, and her shields snapped right back into place. She curled her lips into a fake smile, a version of her mother's politician grin, and stood, water dripping down the front of her body like Aphrodite in the seas of Olympus. All she need do was beckon, and I'd worship every inch of her.

"I'm exhausted," she said. "I'm going to bed. You guys hang out a while, okay?"

"X?" Lex grabbed her wrist to stop her, and the intimacy in that tiny connection set me off. The way he said her nickname used to be a taunt, but now it sounded like a term of endearment. Ivy said they weren't together, not in the way the media made it sound. *Only a few times.* But I zeroed in on his thumb tracing circles around her pulse point while she talked. That meant more than sex.

"I'm fine, Lucifer," she said, taking a step away. "Just exhausted. I'll see you in the morning. Love you guys."

Their hands slid palm to palm as he let her go. It was a small caress, but it said so much. Years ago, he wouldn't have dreamed of touching her like that. If he did, she'd yank away from him and snarl something about minding his own business. Now there was tenderness. My own words came back to me from that day in Ireland, when I'd pinned Lex under me and made him helpless to do anything except heed my demands.

Because you love her, I'd told him. *And you love me, and you love Miri, and what we have is special, even when you want to destroy it.*

I'd made him swear to take care of her, to put her back together again when every instinct in him wanted to tear her apart. In that one touch, that one moment of gentleness, I saw two years of his efforts.

She smiled and kissed Miri's temple before heading toward her bedroom with barely a passing glance at me.

"We have a lot to talk about tomorrow. Have a good night." She slid the door shut behind her. Miri and Lex both looked at me, and I glanced between them while I struggled with the urge not to strangle Lex. I'd asked him to take care of her, and he had.

Only a few times.

The visual of him fucking her in Ireland assaulted me, but I quickly brushed it away. I'd fucked Miri, and I'd fucked Lex, and the boundaries between us were blurred from the start.

I should go after Weeds.

But how long after she left would I have to wait before it wasn't awkward?

"That was an invitation for you to follow if I ever saw one." Miri nodded toward the door.

I looked at Lex. Was I asking permission? Or was I staking my territory? Fuck, I didn't know, but did it even matter?

"I told you, Chicago," he said. "I tried, and I failed. She still wants you."

Well, that wasn't entirely true. There was friendship there now, real friendship, like what I had with Miri.

I ran a hand over the back of my head, considering this. Was that why she'd ignored me the whole night? Was that why she'd barely looked at me? Barely touched me?

I got up and swung my legs over the side of the tub.

"Give us a few," I said. "We'll talk tomorrow."

"Agreed," Lex said.

"Good night, Romeo," Miri called.

"Good night, Romeo," Lex mockingly echoed.

Then I went after my girl.

12

CARTER

"Weeds," I called after her. She wrapped a robe over her shoulders and walked down the hallway to another room at the far end. Her room, I realized, when I recognized her enormous bed and her fresh white furniture. I followed Ivy into the walk-in closet, my knees shaking and butterflies rolling through my stomach. She startled and turned to face me when I closed the door behind me, her wet hair in the beginnings of a braid down the side of her chest.

"Carter." She gave me a small smile and went back to riffling through her drawer. "What are you doing?"

"Miss Washington," I said, attempting to revive the game we used to play, the gentleman slut and his lady whore. I took a step closer, straightening my shoulders so my broad chest seemed even more imposing. She used to like it when I was fresh out of the shower. Proving my point, Ivy licked her lips and moved away.

Some things never change.

"You and I should talk." I stepped closer, my hands linked together at the base of my spine.

She hummed and pretended like it had no effect on her. "About?"

"About the two years we spent thinking we didn't want each other." I danced my fingers over a lace panty set that caught my eye.

"Oh." Her expression turned cross, eyebrows arching, stare eviscerating me where I stood. "What about the two years you spent fucking my best friend?"

And there it is. The reason she'd ignored me. The reason she'd rebuilt her barriers. The reason we couldn't be who we were, not until we sorted this out.

"It wasn't two years," I said. "And don't pretend like you didn't do the same."

"Lex and I—" she started.

"You and Lex have been in love with each other since you were kids," I said. "Everyone on the planet can see it except for you."

She didn't say anything, just clenched her jaw and continued flinging stuff around.

"It still hurts," she mumbled. "I'll get over it. Just...give me a minute."

"Get over it?" Another step toward her brought me close enough to feel the heat radiating off her tight body. "You think I don't like that you're jealous? That the thought of me with anyone else makes you run red hot?"

She bit the corner of her lip, her eyes searching mine for signs of trickery.

Oh, I knew my Weeds so well. She was waiting for me to pull the rug out from under her, to tell her this was all a big fat lie and I *did* love Miri more than her and perhaps I always would.

No, Weeds, I wanted to say. *It's you. It's always you.*

"'Cause the thought of you with Lex is making me want to choke the life out of *my* best friend," I said. "Or fuck him. Or maybe both. It's all very confusing."

She giggled softly, and the sound was like a church bell calling me to kneel at her altar and beg her for redemption.

"Miri and I..." I shook my head and looked down between us. "It was to make it not hurt so much. I won't say it meant nothing, because it didn't. Miri means a lot to me. I love her."

Ivy swallowed and nodded, her attention going back to the dresser.

"That doesn't mean"—I softened my tone, slowly reaching out to cup her cheek and turn her face toward me—"that I don't love you, Weeds."

Bloodshot gray eyes met mine, tears trailing down her cheeks, and I wiped my thumbs across her skin so I could capture her pain and clear it away.

"I missed you so fucking much," she said on a sob, clutching my wrists.

"Shhh." I wrapped her in my arms, tucking her head under my chin the way I used to do. She smelled the same, vanilla and sugar and girl, and when I pressed my mouth into that velvet ginger hair, I almost came apart. The first girl I'd ever loved and lost, right here in my arms again. "I missed you, too, Weeds."

"I'm sorry," she said, pulling away, speaking in hushed whispers that came from some deep well inside her. Almost like she'd been holding on to this for eons and being trapped in this closet with me had forced the dam to break. "I'm sorry I didn't go with you, that I didn't fight harder. I shouldn't have believed that stupid text. You'd never do that to me." She was frantic now, shaking her head, tears streaming down her cheeks. "I shouldn't have stopped fighting for you. I know better than that. I do—"

I collided my mouth with hers, and even though her lips were wet from crying, the kiss vibrated through every cell in my body. We'd spent the last few hours getting to know each other mentally again, but this physical connection? This was inevitable.

Our bodies gravitated to each other from the start. I wanted her the moment I set eyes on her and every day since then. Her skin on mine brought out a side of me I thought was lost forever.

After the last few days, I was exhausted. My dick hurt, and my balls felt like they'd run a marathon. But when Ivy tucked her fingers under the edge of my towel and yanked, my cock sprang free. Instantly hard. Instantly ready for her.

We needed this intimacy in the worst way.

I tugged at the waistband of her robe and ghosted my palms over her waist to her shoulders, dancing my fingertips underneath the satin to slide it down her arms.

Standing naked together, I let myself look at her. *Really* look at her. My beautiful Weeds.

She had bite marks on her neck and thighs, nail scrapes going up and down her arms and torso, palm prints on her ass and hickeys on the mounds of her breasts. None of that was put there by me. It only added fuel to this infernal need to consume her, to take her again, to be so deep inside her that I could wipe out Lex and Miri and anyone else who'd come between the last time and this.

"You're still my favorite girl," I murmured.

Ivy let out a breath that sounded like it weighed a ton, and she sprang into my arms.

Fuck yeah.

She crossed her ankles at the small of my back and tunneled her fingers through my hair, nails dragging over my scalp in a way that urged me on. I lowered us to the ground so I was on top of her, my elbow pressed into the fluffy carpet near her ribs. I would spend ages going down on Ivy if I could, but we were beyond foreplay at this point.

I positioned myself at her entrance with my free hand and thrust home, all the way to the root.

"Fuck. Me." It came out as a groan, my nose buried in her neck. I'd wanted this for so long, ages and ages, and now that I had it, I shook in her arms. My shoulders could barely support my weight, and I felt like I was in that treehouse again with Stephanie Hoppenheimer or the tiny dorm room with Ivy for the first time. I'd never trembled so hard in my life.

If I hadn't spent the last seventy-two hours acting like I'd just discovered the world's first cock, I wouldn't have lasted thirty seconds. Good Lord, she felt like heaven here on earth, so familiar and welcoming, and a shiver went down my back even though I tried to hide it.

"You're so tight, feels so good." I pulled out a little and surged back in, and she moaned, her forehead pressed to mine.

"I can't believe you're here." She coasted her hands over my shoulders to my chin, cupping my face like I was precious, like I was made of porcelain. "Really here with me."

"I'm here, Weeds." I kissed her. "And I'm not going anywhere again. I swear."

I'd swear and swear and swear. I couldn't leave her, not after losing her once and getting her back. I had a desperate clawing desire for Lex, yes, and I definitely had deep abiding affection for Miri. But Ivy was it for me. She was my sun and my moon and all the stars in my sky. I loved her like I'd loved no one before or since. To make sure she knew that, I intertwined my fingers in hers and brought her knuckles to my lips, carefully kissing each one while I rocked inside her.

Then I brought her hand to my heart and kept it there while I broke her to pieces. We took our time in that walk-in closet. We explored each other the way we used to when we were younger. We made each other moan and cry out for release, but instead of the heated frenzy of the lust, this was special.

This was a reunion of souls.

When I brushed the hair out of her face in the aftermath of our lovemaking, I saw the girl I used to know—guard down, boundaries blown to shit, just me and her and the years of trust between us.

"There she is," I said, smiling and kissing on the tip of her nose.

"I love you, Mister Scott," she murmured, trembling in my arms.

I brushed the tip of my nose over hers and grinned. "I love you, Miss Washington, and I always will."

13

MIRI

After Carter left me with my prince of darkness, most of the tension inside eased. Not that I didn't love Ivy and Carter, but Lex was my most favorite person in the world. He and I matched in so many depraved ways, and I'd never found anyone else who reveled in the grittier side of life like I did.

Lex's mouth still curled the same and his hands were just as rough as they used to be when he glided them across my soft, wet skin.

"What does my princess want, huh?" He nibbled at my throat, his fingers working between my legs, teasing at flesh that ached.

After these last three days together, I shouldn't yearn for him the way I did. I shouldn't want anyone this desperately. Hadn't I had my fill? But I couldn't stop myself. I had to get more.

"Tell me you missed me." I kissed him and wrapped my hands around his neck, positioning his cock at my entrance.

"I missed you more than you can ever know."

"Do you still love me?" I knew he did, of course he did, but I wanted to hear him say it.

"I'll always love you." He grabbed my wrists and twisted them behind my back, holding them at the base of my spine, pinning me to him. I sank lower, sheathing Lex's big cock inside me, arching into the agony and the nirvana mixing together. He took my nipple between his teeth, biting and pulling as he worked himself in and out, sending a tremble up my spine and down my legs.

"Tell me you love me, too." He gave the other nipple the same attention before grabbing me by the back of the neck and pulling me upright, his hand in the back of my hair. "Tell me I didn't lose you to the Hollywood heartthrob."

I laughed and rocked against him, smiling as tingles of electricity shot through our connection. I was sore, but in the soothing warm water, I'd do anything for him. I craved his body as much as it appeared he craved mine.

"I love you. I love you. I love you."

We took each other the way we always did, with nails and teeth and filthy words. When my climax claimed me, wrenching from my body in a combustible mix of pain and ecstasy, I moaned into the space between his neck and his shoulder, delighting in the kick of his cock inside me.

"Fucking hell, Miri." He kissed me, groaning and gasping, making me feel so damn lucky to have him.

"My prince," I murmured between gasps. "My love."

In the aftermath, he helped me out of the bath and dried me off, wrapping the towel around my shoulders with a wink before grabbing his own.

"Are you happy, darling?" I asked. "With all this?"

"Happy?" Shaking his head, he snorted and pushed the lever for the drain on the bath, gesturing me to go in the opposite direction of where Ivy had left, into his room. "No, none of us is happy."

The walls were painted a gunmetal gray and decorated with black-and-white photographs. I got closer and realized they were places from his life—our college, our old dorm, the Naval Observatory where he lived as a child, and finally a stunning one of Ivy.

It took my breath away.

She sat naked on a chair, facing the floor-to-ceiling window in a former apartment, the Washington Monument and the Capitol in the distance. One long leg crossed over the other and a high heel dangling from her toes, she had her elbow on her knee and a cigarette hanging between two fingers. She'd been crying, but the way she absently stared out at the DC skyline indicated the scenery wasn't the cause of her tears.

It was beautiful, and it said so much about Ivy as a person—facing the physical manifestation of her legacy, crying because, at the end of the day, she was human like the rest of us.

"Who took this?" I asked, desperate for a copy of my own.

"I did." Lex walked up behind me and wrapped his arms around my waist. "When you don't fuck everything that moves, you have a lot of spare time on your hands."

I turned in his hold.

"You're not slagging around?" This surprised me. Of course, I had stopped all my extracurricular activities as well. But when we met, we were equally as disreputable.

"No," he said. "After Ireland, it didn't feel right." He walked to his dresser, digging through his clothes to find something suitable to wear. "I tried with Ivy for a while."

"Oh?" I pretended that didn't hurt. It did and it didn't. I couldn't act like I hadn't done the same thing with Carter. We'd needed each other in a way only we understood. Lex and Ivy had to have felt the same way. To distract myself, I went to my luggage so I could find my own sleepwear. "How did that go?"

Another sardonic laugh. "About as well as you'd imagine."

"That great, huh?" I smiled, remembering how they used to fight.

He sighed as he bent his arms through a shirt to pull it over his head. "She's convinced whatever's between us is just because of some fairy curse." He shoved his long legs into gym shorts. "And I don't have a good enough reason to argue with her."

"Fairy curse." I thought of my gift, of how I could grow flowers. In two years, I hadn't told a soul. Maybe I should have said something to Lex right then and there, but I imagined what he'd think of me and held my tongue, and it wasn't him I needed to tell first. If anyone deserved that honor, it was Ivy.

"Yeah," he said. "Siobhan and the ring and the nightmares."

That got my attention. I pulled my leggings up to my waist and yanked an old T-shirt over my head before turning to face him. "Nightmares?"

He nodded, putting his phone and a pack of smokes into his pockets. "Sometimes. They were bad right after we got home from Ireland. it's been quiet for a while. Until...well...until this."

I raised an eyebrow. "Right."

"I don't know what to make of it." Lex sighed, staring out the window to the DC skyline beyond it. "There's no reason we should still feel like this. There's no reason for this to happen. Unless—"

"Unless she was right," I said.

"Yeah." It came out like a sigh, and I let the topic drop because I was exhausted. Tomorrow, we'd talk. Tomorrow, we'd ask the hard questions and spill all our secrets. But tonight, I wanted to disappear into the abyss of being with them again, of being complete. Because certainly, I'd never known wholeness like I did standing in that room with him, knowing Ivy and Carter were on the other side of the house. We were together again, perfect in a way we hadn't been in two years.

I traced a finger over a black binder on his desk, touching a photo that stuck out at an odd angle. I flipped it open and turned it so I could see another picture of Ivy. This time, she was looking at the camera with that haunting mix of vulnerability and malice. She had a lit cigarette hanging out of her mouth, holding up a hand to give the camera...*Lex*...the middle finger.

"Wow," I said, flipping to the next page. This one was a boudoir shot on her giant bed. Naked, she arched her back and bent her knees, the curves of her body dark against the white sheet behind her. My lower stomach clenched, and a shiver of arousal went straight down my center at how amazing she looked.

"Ohhh, no, no, no." Lex rushed over and flipped the binder closed, scooting his body in between me and the desk. "Uh-uh. You're not supposed to see those."

"What?" I balked, half amused, half surprised. "Why?"

"Because I promised," he said. "I pinky swore no one else would ever see them except for the two of us."

The cut stung. "Certainly, I don't count. I've seen both of you naked a million times."

Lex pulled his lips into a *devil-may-care* grin and put his hands on my neck, pulling me in for a kiss to distract me. "I promised, Princess." Another kiss. "You know I always keep my promises. Even to stuck-up gingers like X."

I rolled my eyes and huffed, going for them again.

"Don't be a spoiled brat," he teased, biting my lower lip as he circled his fingers around my wrist to stop me. "You don't own everything."

"Why can't I see, darling?" I asked. "She's my best friend."

"She's my best friend, too," Lex said. "I needed help with a project, and she offered. But this was just for us. For her."

I narrowed my eyes at him and relented, pleased by his respect for her and surprised that he had called her his best friend. Until two years ago, that title had been reserved for Carter. It had taken all their lives, but Lex finally saw what I had in our American sweetheart. I wrapped my arms around his neck and pressed my body against his, all the way from our chests to our knees.

"You know I think it's sexy when you tell me no," I murmured.

"I remember." He slid his palms along my biceps and down my torso to my waist, sending chills over my skin. "And if I wasn't so fucking wrung out, I'd deny you. All." A kiss. "Fucking." Another. "Night."

How I'd missed him.

"You think they're sufficiently reacquainted?" He nodded toward Ivy's room.

"The moaning stopped a few minutes ago, so I'd say we're in the clear."

He chuckled and guided me into the hallway. As I took one last look at that solemn picture of Ivy on the wall, I told myself I'd get my paws on one of those prints somehow, no matter what favors I had to promise in return.

He didn't knock on Ivy's door, just twisted the handle and went inside, where we found Carter and Ivy huddled together in her massive Alaskan king-size bed. It dwarfed them, swallowed them whole in a poof of blankets and pillows.

"Are we all caught up?" Lex crawled onto the mattress and sat back on his haunches, while I walked on my knees across the bedding so I could slip under the covers next to my wife.

"We're good." Carter hauled Ivy in closer to him. I smiled and kissed her before I went to Carter and kissed him, too. They both tasted like sex and each other, but that didn't bother me. It felt right. All of this just felt so right.

I grabbed Ivy's hands and cuddled closer to her while Lex scooted in behind me. We teased and prodded each other for a few minutes, but peace eventually fell on our achy bodies. We drifted off to an easy slumber, once again in the safety of each other's embrace.

14

MIRI

I slept better than I had in years. I didn't know if it was because of how tired I was or the warmth and coziness of sharing a bed with my three spouses. I peeled my eyes open when a streak of bright sunlight snuck in through the blinds, hitting me in the face. Ivy still slept behind me, but Lex was gone. When I sat up, I saw Carter was gone as well.

Just me and my wife.

Just me and my girl.

I ran a finger down the side of her face, tracing the way her cheekbone dipped and became her jaw. She cracked open her gray eyes and focused on me before curling into herself and stretching, reminding me of a grumpy cat that had been unceremoniously awakened.

"Good morning, darling," I said, giving her a sweet kiss.

She reciprocated with a smile. "Good morning."

"How do you feel?"

"Sore," she said, her voice gravelly from sleep. "And tired. But good."

"Me too," I said. "I didn't mean to make you upset last night. With Carter."

She shook her head. "This whole thing is hard. I spent so long thinking neither of you wanted me. I was jealous of you. And of him. Of everyone."

"I never wanted you to feel like that." I kissed her again. "We're in this together. No matter what."

"Until the end." She grabbed my hand with hers, rubbing our vows against each other.

"Make me a promise, darling."

"Anything," she said, eyeing me with sincerity.

"Don't let me disappear on you again," I said. "If you think I don't love you, show up and ask me. I'll do the same for you."

She sighed and blinked back tears, kissing my knuckles while she said, "I promise."

"Good." I gave her a quick peck on the forehead before pushing the covers aside to climb out of bed. "I know it's first thing in the morning, but I need to show you something."

She narrowed her eyes, now more serious, and sat up. "Okay."

I cleared my throat and walked to the wilted plant in the window. It looked healthy enough; it just needed some water. When I touched it, the energy surged through me, zipping right into the orchid. It perked up and grew a few inches before I pulled my hand away.

Ivy gasped and shot to her feet, closing the distance between us. "Holy hell, Miri."

"Shhh." I grabbed her arms. "Lex and Carter don't know. No one knows."

She took a deep breath and pursed her lips, meeting my eyes. But it wasn't surprise behind her expression. It was resolution, as if showing her my deep, dark secret had cemented something in her mind.

"Don't freak out, okay?"

I prepared to ask what she meant, but she grabbed my wrists and tugged me close. Her eyes went white before something tightened in my mind, like someone had taken a battering ram to the mental room that held my secrets.

Memories from California whirled around us. When I first found out I could do this. When I shoved Carter up against the balcony and sucked him off for all the world to see. When I said goodbye to him at the gala and my shattered heart broke in half again. I couldn't stop the images from flicking like a movie montage, and with them came the emotional turmoil of those months apart, like Ivy could rip the agony right out of my body if she wanted.

What is happening? What is she doing?

Everything stopped the minute she let go, and I gasped, covering my mouth with my palms. "What the bloody hell was that?"

She sighed and rubbed her fingers over her eyes. "C'mon. We have a lot to talk about."

We found Carter and Lex at the breakfast nook in the kitchen. Lex had a cigarette between his fingers, a coffee in the other hand, a huge grin on his face. Carter fried eggs on the stove, the smell of bacon permeating from the oven while he entertained Lex with a story about filming the notorious threesome scene in the first season. The king had just learned James was in love with his queen, and instead of reprimanding him for it, he instead invited him into their bed.

I'd had to rewind it four times during my first watch through. (For purely educational purposes, of course.)

"Lorne got so fucking hard," Carter said, "he had to sit there for a few minutes after Anthony called cut."

"Was it you or Alexandra?" Lex asked.

Carter winked, and Lex threw his head back to guffaw.

I loved seeing him laugh. I got the sense he so rarely did when we weren't here. I had loved the old version of Lex, the college fuckboy with a chip on his shoulder and an axe to grind with the whole fucking world. But this Lex? The man who'd grown to capture the world through his own lens? I *adored* him.

"Good morning," Ivy said, kissing Carter before grabbing the carafe of coffee and pouring two mugs.

"How did you sleep?" Lex asked.

"Amazing," I said.

"Same," Carter agreed. "Haven't slept that well in years."

"Since Ireland," Ivy added.

The room fell silent, and my attention went to Ivy. She handed me a mug, and I took a sip. Hmm...she still knew how to make it the way I liked, the perfect mix of sugar and cream. Then she looked to Lex.

"Go on, X," he said. "Tell them."

She licked her lips and straightened, and Carter furrowed his brows, glancing between us. "Tell us what?"

"Remember the woman, Siobhan, and the ring she gave me?" Ivy blew on her coffee before taking a drink.

"Yeah," I said. "You lost it in the woods, didn't you?"

"I did. Or, at least, I thought I did." She sighed before taking a deep breath to continue. "About six months after we got home, I had a dream where I found the ruins again. Siobhan waited for me there. She told me I looked terrible, and that I wasn't taking care of her gift. When I told her I lost the ring, she said, 'Did you think that was the gift?' Then she disappeared." Ivy brushed a stray piece of hair behind her ear. "I haven't seen her since. When I woke up, the ring was in the bed with me."

"In the bed with you...how?" Carter asked.

"It was just there," Ivy explained.

"That's not all," Lex said, straightening. "I told you last night I asked my father if he had anything to do with you two ditching us, and he said he didn't. I believed him because..." Lex cleared his throat and took a deep pull on his cigarette. "He confessed to wishing it had been me that died instead of my brother. He told me things he never would have said had I not *made* him."

"Made him?" I asked, my eyes going to Ivy. She nodded, confirming Lex had the same special gift we did.

Oh...

OH...

"Are you saying you can make people tell the truth?" Carter said.

"I could make you tell us every filthy thought you've ever had about everyone in this room," Lex said.

"Well." Carter playfully rolled his eyes. "I'd never lie about that."

I chuckled, and Ivy smiled before sobering and setting her focus on me.

"Miri," Ivy said. "Show them what you can do."

I cleared my throat and went to one of their houseplants, touching the leaf to make it preen and grow.

"Fuck." Lex ran his hands back through his hair with one hand and stabbed his cigarette out with the other.

"How long have you known you could do that?" Carter asked.

"I found out in Malibu," I admitted.

"The irises," he said, as if it was all coming together in his mind.

I nodded, a tinge of guilt burning my cheeks. I probably should have told him, and maybe it revealed something sinister about us that I hadn't. Lex and Ivy had obviously shared their secrets. Were they closer because they lived together? Or did Carter and I share a bond only because we were bonded to them?

Carter sighed and ran his hand over the back of his hair. "Okay, my turn. You got a deck of cards?"

"Sure." Ivy pulled a small white box out of a junk drawer next to the stove.

"Shuffle them," Carter said. "Shuffle them really good."

Ivy did as he asked, then held the deck out to him.

"Jack of spades," he said. "Flip over the first card."

She did, and it was a jack of spades.

"Two of diamonds."

Correct.

Then she went rapid-fire.

"Four of hearts, queen of diamonds, ace of spades, seven of clubs, six of diamonds."

Bam. Bam. Bam.

He guessed them all.

"Lucky guess," Lex said.

"Exactly." Carter returned his attention back to the eggs still cooking on the stove. "I'm banned from two hotels in Vegas. I won over a million dollars in under three hours."

"Jesus Christ," Ivy said.

"Yeah." Carter thinned his lips, looking equally embarrassed and proud of his status.

I shifted my attention back to Ivy. "And you can read minds."

"Telepathic mind trick," she said, holding up a hand to wave in front of us. "Your droids are not here."

Carter snorted a laugh at her misquote and shook his head. "Close enough, Weeds."

"Look, for a long time, I didn't want to believe it," Lex said. "I thought someone was fucking with us. But this? It's something I can do to anyone. I can't stop it."

"None of us can," I added.

"What the hell is going on?" Carter asked as he put the finishing touches on breakfast.

Silence.

"I have an idea," Ivy said, just as Carter put plates in front of us. "After Ireland, we said we would move on and forget it...but I couldn't. I was obsessed." She bit into a piece of toast, and starving, I dove into my eggs. "I'm still kind of obsessed. I came across a story about two couples that went into the woods on Beltane. They claimed they'd only been gone a few hours, but the townspeople said they'd been lost for a week. They said they lived with the fairies and married each other. *For none could stray from the others without knowing terrible ecstasy.*"

"Terrible ecstasy?" Carter whistled incredulously. "That sounds about right."

"I think it means we can't be apart," she said. "We have to stay together until we can figure out how to break the curse."

"Why would we want to break it?" Lex asked, scrutinizing Ivy with his piercing stare. "None of this sounds bad to me."

"You don't think having to get together to fuck or risk going rabid is a bad thing?" Ivy raised her eyebrows at her fiancé.

"You do?" Lex mirrored her expression, half facetious, half serious.

She rolled her eyes and shoved at his shoulder. "Shut up."

"What if we can't?" I asked. "What if we have to live with it for the rest of our lives?"

"Would that be the worst thing?" Carter shrugged and reached across the kitchen island to grab my hand. "That the four of us share a future. A family. I mean"—he pointed to Lex and Ivy—"half of us have been together since birth."

Ivy flushed, and Lex curled his perfect lips into a smile.

"I've wanted that since the day we got hitched in the woods," Lex said. "The cottage and the kids. The four of us old and gray and creaky together."

"All four of us?" Ivy raised an eyebrow at him.

"Yeah, X." He ran the back of his fingers down her cheek. "All of us. Who's going to give me shit every day if you're not there?"

She laughed, returning her attention to Carter and me. "I'm not giving up hope we can end this. If Siobhan did this to us, then she can undo it. I've had Kit looking for her since we got home from Ireland."

"Kit knows about this?" Lex said. Suddenly, his sincerity and affection were replaced by that telltale challenge in his eyes, like he was coiled in the grass and waiting to strike.

"Not all of it," Ivy said, trying to calm him. "She knows I need to talk to Siobhan, and she's got access to all that facial recognition bullshit."

Lex took a deep breath and rubbed his fingers in his eyes. "You said you wouldn't tell anyone."

"Kit doesn't count," Ivy said. "And she doesn't know *everything.*"

"You can't keep things from me, X," he said. "We're partners."

"Oh, I'm sorry, Lucifer. Do you need a play-by-play of every minute of my life?" She said it, but not in the harsh or cruel way she once might have done. Now, amusement hung in every bantering word. "Carter fucked me in the closet last night. You want to know how that was, too?"

"I'm sure it was fantastic, X," he retorted with a chilling bite in his tone, widening his eyes for debate. "If you feel so inclined, I'll gladly take a reenactment."

She pursed her lips and her eyes twinkled with wild amusement as she muttered, "Maybe later."

"All right, kids," Carter cut in with a laugh. "Can we eat breakfast in peace?"

I giggled at how so much had changed between them, evident in the way they co-existed peacefully, not to mention the pictures of Ivy in Lex's room. But in a lot of ways, so much had stayed the same. They still got under each other's skin like no one else could.

"How close is Kit to finding Siobhan?" I asked.

"I don't know. I have to go to family brunch in a few days, so I'll ask then." Ivy rubbed at her neck and took another sip of coffee. "That's not all. The lore talks about a fairy king and queen, these powerful beings capable of terrible things. Sometimes, they're benevolent. Sometimes, they trick humans and enthrall them."

"Do you think they're real?" Carter asked.

"If fairies are real, they must be, too." She brushed hair back behind her ear, steel eyes meeting each of us before she continued. "All I'm saying is we need to be careful. If even half those stories are true, this won't end well for any of us."

Carter reached across the table and grabbed her hand. "I'm with you, Weeds. Until the end." He paused before adding, "For real this time."

Ivy cleared her throat. "How long are you staying?"

"A week or two, at least," I said. "Until my grandmother loses her patience and sends someone to fetch me."

"I have a month before I'm supposed to visit my sisters," Carter said. "I think I can hold my agent off that long."

I warmed at the thought of Lizzie and Renee. "How are they?"

"Great. Lizzie asks about you a lot."

"I miss her," I said. "I should call her."

The conversation drifted to stories about our time in Malibu, and they told us about law school. We laughed, really laughed, and my heart became so light and free.

I could stay here forever. I glanced around that breakfast table with the loves of my life. *I could stay with all of them forever, and I'd never regret a thing.*

15

CARTER

It was like we picked up right where we left off. Except now, we were two years older, and we knew the agony of being separated. I took every opportunity to put my hands on Ivy. In the shower, her face pressed up against the tile. On the couch, buried under throw pillows and blankets. When I caught her alone in her office, bent over her desk with her paperwork crunching under our bodies. Reconnecting with her had made me the happiest and horniest I'd been in a long time.

It wasn't just her.

Like me, Lex was an early riser. Or perhaps a light sleeper. He usually got up when I did. I liked to work out first thing in the morning, so I hit their gym and put in at least five miles on the treadmill before he made his way down to find me.

I had my headphones in while I was doing pull-ups, pushing my body to stay in shape for the next season. My eyes were closed when the hairs on the back of my neck stood up like someone was watching me. When I opened them, I focused on the mirror in front of me where my gaze connected with the reflection of Lex Fairfax leaning against the doorjamb. Shirtless. Smoking a cigarette. All those tattoos on glorious display. The way he looked at me screamed filthy things...perverse things...things I'd been dreaming about for two long years.

I froze and slowly lowered my feet to the ground.

My heart pounded, and not because of the way I'd pushed myself in the workout. Sweat dripped down my torso and the side of my face, and I wiped it off on a towel before I turned to face him. Grabbing a water bottle, I squirted a mouthful and swallowed, yanking my headphones out of my ears.

"Morning, DC," I said.

"Good morning, Chicago." He tilted his head to the other side, eyes running over the length of me. "Or is it good night? The sun's not up yet either way."

I'd long ago drenched my shirt. It lay in a crumpled ball on the ground. So I stood there, naked chest heaving, my gym shorts hanging low on my hips, the waistband of my Calvin Kleins peeking out.

"What's up?" I asked.

He frowned and shook his head, shrugging. "Can't a guy hang out in his own house?"

"The way you've been smoking, I know you're not down here for cardio."

He let out a low chuckle and pushed off the wall, stabbing the cigarette out in the crystal ashtray he'd brought with him before setting it on the water cooler next to the door. Such a contrast, Lex and this gym. They'd built it for Ivy. She liked to exercise to keep her mental health in check. But I scoffed to look at this hedonist in such a place—covered in tattoos, reeking of cigarettes and last night's sex and eternal damnation.

I shifted my shoulders and ignored the strain in my cock.

"Do you remember the last time it was just me and you, Chicago?" he said. "That time in Ireland when you made me swear to take care of your Weeds as long as you promised to come home to us."

I cleared my throat and took another gulp of water, nodding. "I remember."

"How would you say I've held up my end of the bargain?" He took a slow, lazy step forward.

I understood the heady look in his hazel eyes and the predator's gate in his step. Lex wanted to play.

"She seems like she's in one piece," I said.

He hummed, circling me, his hands linked behind his back. "Pretty damn good, if I say so myself. I take care of her. She takes care of me."

"I noticed." I thought of his hand on her wrist in a soothing gesture that meant so much.

He came to stand in front of me. We'd always been almost equal in stature, Lex only an inch taller. He was long and lithe, and I was bigger through the chest, but together, we were formidable.

"And what about you?" he asked.

This was a game. Lex wanted to bat me around for a bit like a toy mouse, and I, ever the slut for him, could never resist playing along.

"What about me?" I asked, sinking into temptation. "I'm here, aren't I?"

Ohhh, what a thing to say. I'd only come because of the lust and the sickness. If that hadn't happened, I'd be sipping scotch in Eastern Europe somewhere, daydreaming about what my three spouses were doing on the other side of the world.

He shook his head, tsked, and moved so our broad chests touched all the way down to our pelvises. His cock pressed next to mine, half erect, begging for someone to pay it attention.

"You're here." Disapproval dripped from every word. "Is that supposed to satisfy me? Two years, Chicago. Two years. You don't call. You don't write."

I cleared my throat. "We've already established that I tried—"

"Yes, but *you're* the one that promised *me.* You should have tried harder." He leaned in so his bright teeth snarled inches from my face.

"You left me hanging for a long, *long* time. Instead, I have to watch you dry hump some B-rate actress on premium cable."

I twisted my lips into a smirk.

"Don't you dare laugh at me." Heat radiated off him in thick, suffocating waves.

Good Lord. It reminded me of the first time, when he'd looked up at me from between my legs before stuffing my cock down his throat. Or that time in the woods, when I told him I could have him any time I wanted, and he'd fucked me to prove my point.

"How was it?" he snarled. "When you fucked my princess like you had any right?"

I snapped my gaze to his.

Maybe this is getting too personal?

But if he wanted to play rough, fine. I could swing it.

"Fucking fantastic," I said. "She sucks amazing cock. You show her that, or did she learn it on her own?"

He licked his lips, trying not to break character. "And what about my fiancée? You enjoy her last night?"

"No." I steeled my gaze and gritted my teeth. "You don't get to claim Ivy. You didn't want her until I had her, and even then, you treated each other like shit. She's mine, and she always will be."

He squared his jaw, now so close, I was breathing his exhales.

"And what about me, Chicago?" he murmured. "Am I yours? Will I always be yours?"

"You were mine first, DC," I said. "Nothing can change that."

We didn't kiss so much as crash like two meteors that had been swinging around each other since the dawn of time. His lips were demanding, and he forced his tongue inside my mouth, claiming me, seeking all the attention I'd denied him for nearly two years.

God, how I wanted him. How I'd always want him. This eagerness. This urgency. Like we couldn't contain it if we tried.

Done with pretense, I dropped to my knees in front of him and clawed at his shorts, freeing his cock and sucking the tip into my mouth. His velvet skin was exactly as I remembered and tasted even better for the absence. I worked him the way I knew how, swallowing him down and moaning when he dug his nails into my head, twisting my hair, guiding me to his own pleasure.

Lex and I could be harsh with each other in a way we couldn't with the girls, so when he yanked my head back by my hair, it nearly brought tears to my eyes. I hissed in a breath and grimaced, but looked up at him to await his next demand.

"That's right, Chicago." He leaned down so he could claim my mouth again. "And you're mine."

I'd just pushed my body to the limit with an hour and a half workout. My legs trembled, my arms shook, and I needed something to eat before I crashed. But when he brought me to the ground so he could flip me over and yank down my shorts, I did nothing to protest. The waistband dug into the middle of my thighs while I held myself on all fours, my shoulders screaming, my quads burning.

The cap of the lube popped open before the cool liquid hit my ass and slid down to my balls, making me snicker.

"What are you laughing at?" He slapped my ass with one hand and played with my entrance.

"You have random bottles of lube lying around?"

"No, Chicago." One finger probed inside, testing me, and I groaned before almost falling over. "I came down here to fuck you." He pulled out and eased two fingers in this time. The fronts of his thighs hit the back of mine, and I ducked my head down between my arms, the fulfilling sensation too fucking much. He wrapped his other hand around me to grab my cock, stroking me as precum leaked out of the tip. "I brought lube because I'm a fucking gentleman."

I laughed at the audacity that he assumed he'd get to fuck me again. To be fair, I'd wilted with barely any argument.

I hadn't been screwed since the last time with Lex, and now that I was prone and exposed to him, I thought I might blow my load in seconds. I suspected, even if I did, Lex would keep pumping into me until he'd had his fun.

He leaned over my back, bringing his teeth to my ear so he could nip at the curve. A shiver erupted down that side of my body, making my skin prickle, and I couldn't hide my shaking then.

"So can I?" he said, seemingly asking for permission to take what he already owned. "Can I fuck you?"

"Hell," I hissed. "I might die if you don't."

He nudged the tip of his cock against me, and I pushed back on him, bearing down so he could easily slip inside. He took it slowly, letting me enjoy the contact, letting me enjoy the burn of his branding.

And once he was in, he twisted his hips and immediately found that spot that made my arms go weak. I sagged under my own weight and euphoria, pressing my face down on the cool rubber floor and stretching my arms over my head, unable to support myself.

"That's fucking it." He laughed a sick, dark sound and put one palm on the side of my face, the other on the back of my shoulder blades, holding me in place while he took what he wanted. He pulled out only to surge back in. Deeper. Harder. Rocking my whole world and my body with it.

"You like that, don't you, Chicago?" he said. "You're so fucking good at your job because you already live that life. You know what it is to give your soul to someone else. To several someones."

"Fuck," I groaned, the sound coming from a deep, secret place inside of me. My cock wept with the fury of his taking. All I could do was lie there and receive it.

"This ass," he said, squeezing my fleshy muscle so hard I'd have nail imprints for hours. "This cock." He wrapped his fist around my dick, pumping me, squeezing the tip in just the right way to make me gasp. He made me feel so good, taking me like I belonged to him. "This mouth."

He grabbed my chin so he could twist my head toward him,

claiming my lips again with his own, biting and devouring me. I played along because I knew, deep down, that as much as Lex said I was his, he was equally mine. We had belonged to each other since that night in London, despite the years and heartache in between. Nothing about that would ever change.

"All fucking mine, right?" He growled, clawing at whatever skin he could find, fucking my ass like he could permanently imprint himself inside me. It ached and it throbbed and I loved every filthy thing about it.

"Yours, DC," I said.

"You're coming home to us, right?" He slowed his pace, more gentle now, as if to coax me into agreeing.

"I will," I said, jolts of ecstasy ricocheting through my body, curling my toes against the floor. "I promise. I will when I can."

I didn't know if that pleased him or incensed him more because he snarled, gripped my hips, and fucked me deeper, maybe to remind me of the sincerity in my vows to him.

A few pumps later, I came like a firehose—hard and fast, spurting over the place and embarrassing myself. Lex laughed, the sound of his degradation making my cheeks burn, but that only spurred him on.

"Oh, such a quick trigger. Glad some things haven't changed." He kept going, picking up his pace, sinking his nails into my skin to hold me down, to mark me as his the way he'd marked Ivy and Miri.

Perhaps that made the most sense. We all belonged to Lex and he was our king. No matter what we did or where we went, our loyalty to him was written in our hands, as was his to us.

With a loud grunt and a hard shove, Lex came inside me. His groans of euphoria sent a fresh shock of arousal down to my half-hearted erection, and if he willed it, I would have lain there to force that moan out of him for the rest of the day. Instead, he eased himself out and smacked my ass hard enough to sting.

"Woo! And you thought I didn't come down here for cardio." Another slap on the other side. "Let's see if we can go another round in the shower before the girls wake up, huh?" He leaned down to plant a rough, demanding kiss on my lips before trailing his lips to bite my earlobe. "I love you, Chicago."

Then he was gone—up and out of the gym, heading for the shower while I tried to pry myself off the goddamn floor, blissed out and wrecked and put back together.

16
CARTER

My version of heaven would be eerily similar to that week we spent in Lex and Ivy's townhouse after the lust finished with us. Nowhere to go. Nowhere to be. Ivy and Lex took time off school, Miri had convinced her grandmother to give her some space, and I'd already planned this vacation.

I spent my mornings fucking my husband and making breakfast for my wives. After that, we talked and researched fairy history, speculating about what could be wrong with us. In the time since Ireland, all of us had seen doctors and had bloodwork done. Nothing seemed out of the ordinary with us physically or mentally, which meant this was some other kind of problem.

Dare I say *magical?*

I wasn't ready to admit that out loud yet, even if it made the most sense. Siobhan hadn't come to Ivy since we'd been together, so short of her brief encounter two years ago, we didn't have much to go on.

"We have to assume all the lore is true," Ivy said, rubbing her forehead.

"If we do that, then there are things that contradict each

other." Lex lit a cigarette and leaned back on the couch. We'd been in their study for hours, going through Ivy's massive book collection. She'd accumulated enough for a doctorate. "For example, H. R. Murphy says there's a portal in the woods. O'Kelley says the fairies abduct you from your bed. There are mentions of sacrifices—"

"Sacrifices?" Miri asked with wide panicked eyes.

"Only life can pay for life," Ivy explained. "In some cases, one person agrees to stay with the fairies in exchange for another person to be set free."

"That's cruel." Miri furrowed her eyebrows and scowled.

"Siobhan led us out into the woods," I said. "Does anyone remember crossing through a portal into a different world?"

"That Midsummer festival was off from the beginning." Miri flipped another page in her book. "But the wine was what did me in."

"All the lore says to stay away from the food of the fae," Ivy added.

"Noted." Three pairs of eyes shot to me. "For next time."

"Next time?" Lex narrowed his gaze and furrowed his brows, letting out an exhale of smoke.

No one said anything, and I shrugged. "They always go back."

"What do you mean?" Miri cut in.

Ivy cleared her throat and touched her neck, hiding the X that currently snaked up her windpipe.

"In the lore," I explained, pointing down to the book in front of me, "any human that escapes Faerie usually goes back."

"Why the fuck would they do that?" Lex inhaled his cigarette before stabbing it out in the ashtray on the coffee table.

I shrugged. "The realm has a hold on them forever."

Lex looked from me to Miri and eventually up to Ivy. "You think that's what's happening here?"

Ivy pursed her lips. "I don't know, but it makes sense."

"In the end, you have to go back to the beginning," Miri said, pulling one side of her mouth into a grimace. "I really don't want to see those woods again."

"I don't know if we'll have another choice." Ivy sat back in her seat, her features softening as the weight of the situation landed on all of us.

"I hope we do," Miri added.

Yeah, me too.

Nothing in me wanted to return to Killwater, especially now that we suspected the fairies had done something terrible to us. What if they made this worse? What if we went back and we could never leave again? There were stories about that shit, too. I'd just read one about some entitled fairy falling in love with a human, only to keep them as a consort until everyone that human knew had died. I didn't want to end up like that poor dude.

When our brains turned to mush, we moved to the kitchen where we made dinner together like a family. Lex and Ivy debated politics while Miri antagonized both of them and I tried to play peacemaker. We cuddled on their oversized couch and watched movies until we couldn't keep our eyes open. Then we dragged ourselves back to Ivy's massive bed where we'd take our fill of each other. We'd pass out in a heap of hormones only to wake up and do it all over again the next day.

It was perfect. But like all perfect things, it couldn't last. About a week and a half into our staycation, Ivy came home with news.

"Kit found Siobhan," she said.

Miri and I sat on the couch, watching a popular show about meth dealers in Albuquerque, when Ivy and Lex came through the front door following brunch with their parents.

"Where is she?" Miri said, pushing to her feet.

"She's back in Ireland," Lex said.

"She showed up three days after the lust took us." Ivy looked between us. "She bounced around Dublin until yesterday, when she stopped two kilometers outside Killwater." She showed us a grainy black-and-white photo of someone I sort of recognized at a cash register.

"Are you sure it's her?" Miri asked.

"Kit is," Ivy said. "Her computers are smarter than everyone in this room."

"Computers are still programmed by humans," Lex said.

Fair point.

"It's obvious she's heading to Killwater," Ivy said. "Back to the woods."

We fell into a brief silence where the suggestion hung between us, unsaid but undeniable. We all knew it.

"No," Lex said. "Absolutely not. We talked about this."

"Why not?" Ivy said.

"The last time we went into those woods, we lost a whole day of our lives," Lex said. "Who's to say it's not a month or a year this time?"

"This is the only way we'll know for sure," Ivy said. "We have to get answers from her. We have to demand she tell us the truth."

"Ivy," Lex said. "Think about this for a second. You can't drop everything to fly to Ireland on a whim."

"This isn't a whim. This is proof that Siobhan is there."

"This is a grainy image of a brunette at a gas station." Lex furrowed his brows, looking at her like she'd said the sky was falling.

"Kit says it's her." Ivy put her hands on her hips, a clear sign of a challenge.

"Kit has never met her," Lex argued. "Kit is still in college."

Ivy clenched her hands into fists and Lex bit into a cigarette to hold it so he could light it, competition flaming in his gaze. They lived for the thrill of the fight, especially against each other. I glanced at Miri, who pursed her lips and returned my look of reticence.

"That doesn't mean she doesn't know what she's doing," Ivy argued.

"No, it means we can't take her word for it," Lex said. "Midterm break is almost over. We have to go back to school in five days. We can't afford to get caught up in this fairy tale bullshit again."

"We're already caught up in it," she said. "This is the only way to break this curse. Don't you want to be normal again? To have ordinary relationships?"

I might have argued that none of us had ever been normal, and our relationship had *certainly* never been ordinary.

"I can't be on set constantly worried about whether the lust is going to hit me again." I rubbed a hand over my mouth. Fuck me, but I agreed with Ivy. It scared the shit out of me, but we needed to hunt Siobhan down and make her explain herself.

"That means we have to stay together," Lex said. "Which you already agreed to."

"What if it gets worse?" Miri argued.

"What if these powers come with a cost?" I remembered what Ashley told us at the orientation. "A fairy gift is never *just* a gift. There's always a cost."

Lex ran his free hand over his face and through his hair. "Fuck."

"I think we should go, darling," Miri said, grabbing his hand. "Siobhan owes us an explanation."

"Even if we can't find her, we know that's the source," I said. "It started there."

Lex took a deep breath and stared at us. "It's Samhain. You realize that, right?"

"Shit." I rubbed my hands over my face.

"This sabbat marks the time when the veil between the realms is the thinnest," Lex continued. "If Midsummer brought us this bullshit, what do you think will happen now?"

"It's a different holiday," Ivy countered, raising an eyebrow in consideration. "It's a different time of year."

He gave her a look that said he doubted that mattered. "We go into those woods"—Lex shook his head—"we don't know what's going to happen. Fairy king? Fairy queen? A whole fairy army?"

"We made it out last time," Ivy argued. "We know the risks."

"Do we?" Lex raised his eyebrows. "This is—"

"We have to try," Ivy cut in. "That's all I'm asking for. Your best effort."

He pursed his lips and raised an eyebrow. Obviously, that meant something between them.

"Please, Lex," she said. "Please do this for me."

The Lex I met in college would have scoffed and put up a front, perhaps demanding she explain what was in it for him. But this Lex softened at her plea and took a deep breath in concession. "You can never leave well enough alone, can you?"

"I wouldn't be me if I did."

"Fine." He stabbed out his cigarette and immediately lit another one. "But you're paying for first class, and I'm not staying in some violently sweltering broom closet, okay? I'm talking the best bed-and-breakfast you can find."

Ivy clapped and wrapped her arms around his neck, pulling him into a big hug.

"And," he said, "you owe me. Like, blowjob on the top of the Washington Monument owe me."

She scrunched her nose and laughed. "We'll talk about that one."

"You get us to the top of the Washington Monument," I said, "and I'll handle that one for you."

"Don't tease me with a good time, Chicago," Lex said, winking.

A few hours later, we were on a plane in first class, headed for Dublin.

ACT III

Out of this wood do not desire to go.
Thou shalt remain here whether thou wilt or no.
I am a spirit of no common rate.
The summer still doth tend upon my state,
And I do love thee. Therefore go with me.
I'll give thee fairies to attend on thee,
And they shall fetch thee jewels from the deep
And sing while thou on pressèd flowers dost sleep.
And I will purge thy mortal grossness so
That thou shalt like an airy spirit go.
-Titania, Act III, Scene I

17

MIRI
IRELAND

Killwater seemed much the same as it had the last time I'd been here. The same cobblestones lined the narrow streets. The same old townhouses sat on either side, their decaying shutters evidence of how apart from time this city really was. If I closed my eyes, I could almost be that twenty-two-year-old girl again, as if I'd never left.

Despite that, a strange vibration whistled through the air and coated my skin like electricity. As soon as I stepped out of the vehicle, the ethereal sensation forced itself down my throat like battery acid, pungent and sweet. Had it felt like this last time? Or had I been ignorant to it, naive and unaware of how dangerous this place could be?

At least the weather wasn't unbearable. We'd arrived in October instead of June.

Samhain.

Most of the town was preparing for the celebrations later in the week. I'd grown up at various boarding schools throughout England and spent a great deal of time in Scotland, so I understood some of the Gaelic legends. I didn't remember much about the fairies, but some believed ghosts walked among us on Samhain. Some believed the apparitions were fairies themselves. In either case, perhaps it was fortuitous we'd arrive at the time when it might be the *easiest* to find the land of the fairy folk, if indeed such a thing existed.

Ivy booked a room at the pub that had once been owned by Siobhan and Ashley. It was now in the possession of a retired couple named Bill and Keely.

"Have you lived in Killwater long?" Carter asked when Bill offered to bring our bags up for us.

"All my life," he said, lugging our suitcases into the top room.

"Looks like everyone's excited about Samhain," Carter said, attempting he'd see what he could get out of the guy.

"Oh, aye. It's mostly for the locals, ya know?" he said. "But you're welcome to come. There's trick-or-treating for the kids, and lots of toasting for the adults."

I walked around the space. Two queen beds sat on either side with a small window overlooking the woods on the wall opposite the door. The old furniture reminded me of Aberdeen, of how I'd taken the disregarded pieces from each castle I liked and filled my most beloved space with them.

"The bathroom's through here," he said, but my attention refocused on the trees.

They were different now, pulsing with an energy I hadn't noticed before. Taunting me. They knew we were here, that we'd returned, and they beckoned us to them like a wolf in sheep's clothing. But I knew better now. I knew that house made of candy held dark, dirty secrets, and I'd be better prepared this time.

Or at least, that was what I told myself to build the courage to see this through.

"What about the woods?" I asked Bill.

"The woods?" He raised his eyebrows as he turned to me.

"Yeah," I said. "Are there any festivities in the woods on Samhain?"

Bill's features dropped, his eyes widening, his mouth hanging open.

Fear.

The woods scared him, but in the way powerful things often did to the wary. There was terror, sure, but mixed with respect and awe. He knew the secrets that lay out in the forest, and he didn't dare tamper with them. He feared we might do the same.

"No," he said, regaining his composure. "Not that I know of. And if you were smart, you'd stay far away from there."

Lex smirked. "Why is that?"

"People your age go missing in the woods all the time." Bill cleared his throat and hiked his pants higher on his waist. "Don't come out for months if they come out at all."

"Our age?" Lex raised a curious eyebrow.

"Older folks know better," he said. "Fairies don't want them, anyway. Fairies want beauty and eternal youth."

Ivy crossed her arms. "You believe in fairies?"

"Of course," he said. "They're real, and they'll give ya a go if you aren't careful." He patted down his pockets like he was making sure he'd given us everything we'd need. "Breakfast is served between six and nine, and if you come in after twenty-two hundred, I'll ask that you use the back door so you don't wake up any other guests."

"Sure," Carter said. "Thanks, Bill."

He took one last look at us before going to the door and opening it.

"Stay outta the woods," he said. "Nothing good ever came from going in there, especially on Samhain."

None of us said anything, but when he shut the door behind him, we looked at each other.

"We should listen." Lex lit a cigarette and pinched it between his fingers, going to the window next to me so he could open it and blow the smoke out. "We know what's lurking out there. Everyone in this town does."

"That's the whole reason we came," Ivy said.

"It's a last resort, okay?" Carter said, ever the peacekeeper. "We'll check out the library. Maybe ask the townspeople."

"Let's take a moment to think before we do anything stupid," Lex added.

I returned my focus to the trees as a shiver snaked down my spine. Energy emanated from them, reverberating through my bones the same way it did with my flowers back home, but this was different. It brewed infinitely more powerful. I understood Bill's fear. I was terrified myself. The trees were strong, and they hid a closely guarded secret, one we'd only gotten a glimpse of on Midsummer.

When I was a little girl, one of my nannies had taken me on a hike in the woods behind my house in Aberdeen. I'd raced through the undergrowth all morning, and she'd struggled to keep up with me. I couldn't have been more than ten, so my eagerness to explore far outweighed my concern for her tiredness. She'd stopped to take a breath, I'd wandered off, and by the time I realized I didn't know where I was, the sun had set low in the sky.

I called out for her, but I didn't hear an answer.

As the moon rose higher, shadows played on the ground like monsters in a nightmare, their twisted limbs like long icicle fingers, waiting to wrap around my throat. I'd walked for hours until my legs went numb and my knees couldn't hold me anymore.

Eventually, I'd collapsed in a hollowed-out log, convinced that if I closed my eyes and stayed still, the monsters wouldn't get me.

The trees know all, my nanny had said. *They see all.*

Help is coming, I heard them say. *Stay calm. Stay calm.*

I listened to it until I fell asleep. The hounds found me shortly after that. Search and rescue escorted me back to my house, mostly unharmed. In the morning, I'd convinced myself I imagined the whole thing, that I'd been dehydrated and *trees didn't talk.*

But standing in the window of that bed-and-breakfast in Killwater, I thought perhaps I hadn't imagined it at all. Perhaps I'd been marked from birth, given the ability to communicate with nature in a way no one else ever could. If that was the case, then Siobhan had nothing to do with our fairy curse, and this was a fool's errand after all.

"We have two days until Samhain," Ivy said. "If we haven't found anything substantial by then, I say we take the ring and go for a camping trip."

Carter sighed and scrubbed his face, clearly as exhausted as the rest of us.

"Even if we find Siobhan, what exactly are we planning to say? Thanks for the gift, but no thanks?" I crossed my arms and turned back to the room, tugging my jumper tighter around me. "The first thing Ashley told us was not to piss off the fairies."

"We don't know she's a fairy," Lex said before quickly adding, "I can't believe that's something I seriously said."

"We don't know she's *not.*" Ivy sat on one of the beds and leaned forward so her elbows rested on her knees. "One of us should double back to the college."

"Why?" Carter asked.

"Ashley was the lore historian," Ivy said. "She and Siobhan came there every day. They were chummy with Peter Smythe, the associate professor who was friends with Stephens."

"Shit, that's right," Lex said.

I had all but forgotten about the other people who were there when this started.

"They still have the intensive every year," Ivy said. "Stephens is still the sponsor, and Smythe still works in the theater department."

"Fuck, Weeds," Carter said. "You're brilliant."

That settled, we started planning. Ivy and Carter decided to hit the local library to ask around, and maybe, with Carter's luck, they'd find someone who could be useful. Lex and I headed to campus to find Dr. Smythe. If anyone could make someone tell the truth, Lex could. How did he know Ashley and Siobhan? Was he a fairy, too? And if he was, did he know how to find our mystery woman?

When we entered the art department's lecture hall, Smythe stood at the front, giving a talk on the types of movement in theater theory. At this time of year, the students were in full study mode. We slipped in the back and took the seats closest to the door. Disguised among the sea of coeds, I relished the opportunity to assess him before we began our interrogation.

Tall and handsome with curly salt-and-pepper hair and a beard that matched, he wore wire-framed glasses that gave him an educated aesthetic. But what I hadn't noticed last time that stood out now was the tattoo on his hand: a beautiful, timeless rose with ivy vines swirling over his wrist and disappearing under the sleeve of his cardigan.

Something about him drew me to him. I didn't know if it was the streaks of gray in his hair or the way he spoke, his voice like butter and honey and molasses, sweet as decadent pie. No, there was something else there, too. Something...elemental.

No sooner had the thought skidded across my mind than his eyes settled on me. Even from the center of the hall, I sensed the danger in him. The power. The raw force of whatever made him *him*. He wasn't human, certainly. Or...he wasn't entirely human, not like everyone else in this room. Maybe he could tell I knew that about him because one side of his mouth pulled into a smile before he returned to his chalkboard and continued his speech.

"He knows we're here," I whispered to Lex.

At the end, we waited until everyone else left before we stood and made our way down the stairs. He closed his briefcase on the desk and snapped the locks in place before turning to face us with a smile, his hands folded in front of him.

"Miriam Stuart," he said. "Alexei Fairfax. I'm so pleased to see you again."

It was possible he knew our names, being children of very famous people, or maybe he remembered us from the last time we were here, although that seemed more unlikely.

"Yes, I know who you are," Smythe said. "And I know what brings you back."

"How's that?" Lex gave a small chuckle, like he was barely a blip on his radar.

"You've been marked," Smythe said, glancing at me while I narrowed my eyes at his explanation. "So have you. A group gift, if I'm not mistaken. Let me guess, there's two or three others?"

I cleared my throat, and Lex straightened his spine, his eyes widening for a moment before he locked his surprise down again.

"We need to find Siobhan," Lex said.

Smythe shrugged. "I don't know where she is."

Lex pursed his lips like he didn't believe him. "She was seen not far from here three days ago."

"Three days?" Smythe raised his eyebrows and stuffed his hands in his pockets. "She could be anywhere by now."

"It's Samhain," Lex pressed on. "If there were a reason for her to come home, wouldn't she wait until the veil between the realms is thinnest?"

Smythe kept his cool. "That depends on what you think she wants."

I looked at Lex with frustration, almost to say, *Are we done here?*

Yep, replied his stoic expression.

"Tell me the truth," he said, and I gasped at the strength in those words. They hit me like a tsunami, pulling me under his massive power, assaulting all my molecules. It affected Smythe just as intensely. He sagged into his desk, gripping at the edges to keep himself upright.

"Bleeding hell," Smythe said. "I don't know where Siobhan is. But if she did come back, she's headed for Faerie." He pronounced it like Fay-Ree, and I assumed that was the name of the fairy realm.

"How?" Lex said. "How do you get in?"

Smythe licked his lips, visibly sweating. "Please don't. They'll kill me."

"Who?"

He shook his head and whimpered, opening his mouth like he was compelled to answer, but would rather bite off his tongue than do it.

"You know who," he said. "You don't have to ask. You know."

"Ashley," Lex said. "Siobhan."

"All of them," Smythe confessed. "I'm half fae. They kicked me out a few years ago, but I've been trying to get back in. Ashley and Siobhan, they were helping me. We were helping each other."

"What happened?" I asked.

Smythe rubbed his cheeks, wiping away tears. He obviously didn't want to tell us, and part of me felt conflicted about forcing it out of him.

"Maybe we should stop," I cut in. "This feels wrong."

Lex only took another step closer to Smythe. "Tell me how to get there."

"In the woods," he blubbered, spit flying out of his mouth. He cracked open like an egg, tears now streaming out of his eyes, sobs ripping from his chest. "Full fae like Ashley can come and go as they please. The same with Siobhan before she was banished. Me and you? We need a key. An invitation."

Lex looked at me as the puzzle pieces clicked together in my mind.

"The ring," Lex said. That was how we got there the first time. Siobhan had slipped the ring into Ivy's pocket, and she'd had the foresight to bring it with her when we went to find the Midsummer ritual.

"Yes, a ring. A bracelet. Something fae made. Even then, you might not be welcomed," Smythe said. "They're not the forgiving type. If the queen decides she doesn't like you, that's it. They'll kill you and not think twice about it."

Shivers went down my spine as I imagined a terrible winged beast with claws and fangs and evil red eyes, hell-bent on devouring me and my beloveds. I wouldn't let that happen, no matter what I had to do to stop it.

"Or worse yet, if she decides she does like you, you can never leave." Smythe winced, perhaps remembering something terrible. "She'll keep you and feed you ambrosia, so you stay as young as you are now."

"Siobhan's not the queen?" I asked. "Not Ashley?"

"Gods, no." Smythe shook his head. "They're pawns. Players. Ambassadors to the humans. At least, they used to be. I haven't seen Siobhan in a long time. Ashley sold the pub and her house to go home after the king left."

Lex and I exchanged hesitant looks. Ivy had mentioned a fairy king and queen, ancient beings capable of terrible power.

"Tell me about the king and queen," Lex said. "Who are they? What are they like?"

Smythe bit his bottom lip. "Please, enough. I've already said too much. If they find out it was me, if they find out I said this—"

"They won't," Lex said. "You have my word."

I ignored my impulse to gawk at him because I didn't see how he could promise that. We couldn't even guarantee our own safety. There was a good chance this wild goose chase was going to lead us right into those woods, and once it did, I feared Smythe might be right. We may never come out again.

Smythe curled into himself as the weight of his confession brewed on his tongue, seemingly defeated by our arguments and show of force. "The queen looks favorably on the humans that live in Faerie. The king does not. They quarreled about it before the king left. But they're dual spirits. One cannot exist without the other. The queen called her fae back to her kingdom to console her, all that weren't banished."

My heart ached for Smythe. It was quite obvious he missed his home, missed living among his fairy relatives. The fact that they had kicked him out made my stomach twist with what they might do to us, relative strangers compared to him. "Why'd they banish you?"

Tears rolled down his cheeks, and he dabbed them away, clearing his throat before saying, "I loved the wrong woman. The queen's favorite." He stole a heartbroken glance between Lex and me before dropping his gaze to the floor. "When the queen found out, she killed my beloved and cast me from the realm." He cleared his throat and swallowed back a sob. "No one can touch her ladies without her permission. She might have allowed it had we asked, but we didn't, and that is unforgivable."

"That's horrible," I said, my heart twisting for him. "I'm sorry you went through that."

He nodded and pulled himself together. "You both are marked, so I know you won't heed what I'm about to tell you. But I'd be remiss if I didn't say it anyway." He darted his tearful, bloodshot eyes back and forth between us again. "If you go into those woods on Samhain, you are looking for trouble. If the king finds you, he'll kill you. And if the queen finds you, she might keep you forever, even if you don't like it." He gave us one grim smile before sighing and turning to stuff his books in his leather messenger bag, muttering, "Whatever gift Siobhan gave you, you should learn to live with it. Leave the past in the past."

"Thank you." I nodded toward the door as if to suggest we leave, but Lex kept his suspicious gaze on Smythe.

"You know more," Lex said. "What aren't you telling us?"

"Lex." I grabbed his arm, trying to give Smythe a break. "C'mon. He's already a mess."

Tell me, Lex snarled, the power in his words almost bringing me to my knees.

Smythe balked and took a step back.

"Prepare yourself for what you might see there, Alexei," he said. "The fairies aren't happy pixies or glittery Disney princesses. These fairies will gut you and string up your insides for kabobs. They think of humans as thralls, something for entertainment. Humans and fae have a long, complicated history, and you've barely scratched the surface."

This time, I managed to drag Lex from the room, shouting, "Thank you, Dr. Smythe," over my shoulder as we went.

Smythe pressed his knuckles onto the table and hung his head between his shoulders, the weight of his regret nearly a tangible, visible thing. He shouldn't have told us, and walking out of that room, part of me prickled for making him. I didn't like it. But if it meant getting to the bottom of what was going on with us, how much of my conscience was I willing to risk?

18

CARTER

Ivy and I asked around the pub, but no one had seen Ashley since she sold the place a year ago. Some said she disappeared into the woods and never came out. Others said they saw her drive away in her truck with all her stuff piled in the back. If no one had seen Ashley, they definitely hadn't seen Siobhan.

"Three days ago, you say?" one of the locals asked, shaking his gray head. "Well, if you find her, you tell her ole Bertie's looking for her, yeah? She still owes me a pint for that Manchester bet she lost."

We went by the local library, but that was a hole in the wall compared to the one at the university. When that failed, we grabbed a coffee to help with the jet lag.

"If we don't find anything else," Ivy said, sitting at the circular table outside a cafe, "we'll go by the university library tomorrow."

I slumped into the seat next to her and sighed. For someone who'd been gifted with luck, it certainly didn't seem like the odds were in my favor that afternoon, not until the waitress came over to take our order.

"Oh my God," she said, her eyes widening. "You're Carter Scott."

My momentary shock turned to joy when I realized *I* was the one being recognized.

"You're James of Denwater. I fecking love you on *Fractured Crowns.*" Her gaze shifted to Ivy, who she didn't seem to recognize, before coming back to me. "When you had to tell King Henry you loved Princess Kalli, but not as much as you loved him—" She grabbed her chest and rolled her eyes into the back of her head with delight. "I thought my heart was going to break into a thousand pieces."

"Thank you," I said. "I'm glad you enjoy the show."

"And when you had to pull Henry off the battlefield so he didn't get hurt after his older brother was beheaded." She dabbed at her eyes like she was tearing up thinking about it. "Carter...Mr. Scott... You're one of my favorites. Can I have a picture or an autograph or something?"

"Sure," I said, agreeing to a selfie with her. I signed a napkin, "To Sunny." The name on her uniform. "All my best, Carter Scott." I ignored Ivy's pursed lips and the amusement in her gaze, that *I*, the lowly nobody from Chicago, would have fans in remote parts of the world.

"What are you doing in Killwater?" she asked.

"Looking for an old friend," I said.

"Oh?" She preened and smiled wider. "I've lived here my whole life. Who are you looking for?"

"A woman named Siobhan." It was a small town, sure, but I didn't think she'd know who we were talking about.

"Oh yeah," Sunny said. "I know her. She came through a few days ago."

Surprise flitting through my blood, I glanced at Ivy.

"She's always so nice to me." Sunny ran her hand through her bright yellow ponytail. "She stopped for a coffee and some cigarettes."

"Did she say where she was going?" Ivy asked.

She shook her head. "But she did say that if anyone asked after her to tell them, *You already know the way.*"

Ivy looked at me, raising her eyebrows up her forehead.

"Did she say anything else?" Ivy asked, seeming more excited the longer Sunny talked.

"No, sorry." Sunny shook her head. "So, what can I get for you?"

I met my wife's gaze, already knowing what she wanted to ask.

Should I do it?

It seemed like a violation to invade a person's mind without their consent, but how could we ask? And how would we explain it to her once it was over? In the end, we didn't need to.

"Two coffees," Ivy said. "Cream and sugar."

"Sure thing." Sunny touched Ivy's shoulder in a friendly gesture, but when their skin met, Ivy opened her mouth and her pupils turned completely white. Sunny froze, slamming her eyes shut like the touch hurt her. Neither moved for about thirty seconds, an entire fucking lifetime, as I waited to see what would happen. Then Sunny let go and stumbled back, righting herself on the brick wall of the building behind her.

"Okay," she said, rubbing one of her temples. "I'll be back with those coffees." She walked inside, blinking and shaking her head as if nothing had happened.

"What the fuck was that?" I whispered to Ivy, leaning over the table to get closer. "Are you okay?"

"I don't know." Ivy rubbed her eyes as a flush crept up her neck and into her cheeks. "I didn't mean for it to happen, I swear."

"I saw. *She* touched *you.*"

Ivy furrowed her brows as fear danced behind her fiery gray gaze. Not much rattled her. She had social anxiety, and she didn't like large crowds, but she'd spent her whole life preparing to argue for national policy. Ivy's skin had turned to steel.

"Carter, I think Siobhan left a message for me *in* the waitress." Ivy shook her head, clenching her eyes shut like she was trying to rationalize it to herself. "I don't know, maybe I hallucinated it."

"Tell me." I put my hand on hers, squeezing it to reassure her.

"Siobhan came here and asked for her, specifically. When Sunny came out, Siobhan took her and...I don't know...mesmerized her?"

What does that mean?

"She said she knew I'd come after her," Ivy continued, "and that she knows what I want, but she can't give it to me. Not yet. Not until we do what we're supposed to do."

That didn't make any sense. "What are we supposed to do?"

Ivy shrugged. "I don't know, but Siobhan is scared. She's running from someone. Or maybe...*to* someone."

I took a deep breath and scratched the back of my head, trying to put this new information in place with the research we'd done up until now.

"I know Lex doesn't want to go into the woods," she said, "but I don't think we have another choice. That's where Siobhan went. That's where Ashley is."

I didn't want to agree with her, but I was running out of other ideas. Maybe it wouldn't be as bad as Lex thought. Maybe my luck would protect us and make sure we returned to our realm safely.

"Siobhan told me how to get there," she said. "I already know the way. I've been dreaming about it since Midsummer."

I swallowed and sat back in my seat. Part of me wanted to go screaming for the hills. This was beyond anything I could have imagined—fairies and curses and enchanted forests—but I couldn't deny it was, in fact, happening.

Everyone in this town believed fairies existed, and the more research I did, the more convinced I became. All cultures had some variation of a fairy myth, enough to make a credible argument that there must be a source to the archetype—an original monster that scared the humans enough to make up stories and pass them down through the generations to protect the species.

We finished our coffees and paid our tab, heading back to the B&B when we got a text from Lex that they had returned with news.

"The ring is a key," Miri said. "We need it to get into Faerie."

"Smythe was scared shitless," Lex added, sucking on a cigarette.

"He kept saying they would kill him for telling us," Miri said from her spot perched by the window. "Poor bloke nearly pissed himself."

"We need to be careful." Lex drew his hand back through his hair and paced, his eyes sparkling with his trepidation. "The king and queen are real, and they're in the middle of a pissing match. If the king finds us, he'll kill us. If the queen finds us, she might not let us go."

Both of which terrified me. We were treading deep water here, and we were sorely unprepared.

"He mentioned something about ripping out our insides and turning them into kabobs," Miri added with a grimace, returning her attention to the forest outside the window.

"Great," I said as the rancid taste of dread crept up my esophagus. "Really selling me on this whole 'Into the Woods' plan."

"I'm not saying that's what we should do," Lex said. "If it were up to me, I'd lure her out onto our playing field where we know the rules and the landscape."

"Okay." Ivy held her hands out to the side, clearly exasperated by the whole conversation. "And how do you propose we do that? We have nothing she wants."

Lex sighed, conceding her point. "That doesn't mean we should go gallivanting into Faerie like a bunch of idiots."

"We can't sit here and do nothing," Ivy said.

"You've been doing research for the last two years. Tell me"—Lex took a deep inhale on the smoke and let it out in a puff—"did any of the humans in those *not* regret fucking with the fairies?"

"We don't have to fuck with them," Ivy explained, narrowing her steel eyes at our husband. "We can reason with them, tell them this was a misunderstanding."

Lex snorted a cynical laugh. "Siobhan kissed you and gave you a ring, and now you can hijack anyone's mind. What do you suppose the queen of the fairies would make of you?"

Ivy balled her hands into fists, an angry retort brewing on her lips.

"We don't have a choice," Miri cut in. "Everything's been leading up to this, hasn't it? The lust and Siobhan and the ring, it was pulling us back here."

No one said anything because how could we argue with that? It did feel like everything that happened had been designed to bring us back to where we started.

"We should get it over with." Miri sounded despondent and resigned, as if there were no other way out of this and she'd given into fate. "If we die, we die. If we end up in Faerie, we end up in Faerie. At least we'll be together."

I looked at Lex and Ivy, who both glanced at me before each other with that same furrowed worry dancing behind their eyes.

"Princess, why don't you come over here, away from that window?" Lex said. "I'll give you something prettier to look at."

Miri sighed but rose to walk over and curl up in his lap, tucking her head under his chin. But some weird thing brewed between us; we'd all been strange since arriving. Miri couldn't stop looking at the trees. Lex couldn't stop smoking. Ivy couldn't sit still. And me? Well, my skin had grown too tight for my body—like I'd used up all the good luck one person was supposed to have in their lifetime, and karma had come back around to bitch-slap me in the worst way.

Sleep didn't come easy that night, knowing the next would be spent hunting down some fairy monster in the haunted woods. Sometime around 2 a.m., I rolled over and cracked my eyes open, my focus landing on Miri. She was back at the window, smoking a cigarette and staring out at the woods with that anxious crease between her brows. I extracted myself from Ivy's limbs and slid out of bed, tiptoeing over to her. She gave me a small smile when I scooted into the alcove and took a cigarette from the pack.

"What's going on, Juliet?" I asked, cupping my lighter so I could bring it to the smoke and inhale.

She shook her head, the moonlight streaming in through the window making her seem even more precious somehow, like porcelain or ivory. Leaning in close, she whispered, "They're pulsing."

I narrowed my eyes as I studied the seriousness in hers.

"The trees," she said, holding out her hands so she could open and close her fingers. "I can feel them under my skin, the way I can with my plants."

Realization dawned on me. Miri's gift was organic. She said she could *sense* nature and give it her energy to make it grow. I'd bet those trees were like a live wire in her veins.

"Can I tell you something?" She grabbed my right hand with hers, vow to vow, our thumbs hooked around each other.

"Of course." I inhaled on my smoke and kept my gaze on her.

"I'm scared," she whispered. "This is unreal, and we're going against something we don't entirely understand."

"I know," I said. "But...with a bit of luck"—she tried to smile as I kissed her knuckles—"and some truth, and some telepathy, and some witchy plant shit, we might make it out of this alive."

That made her laugh softly, and my work there was done.

"C'mon," I said, giving her hand a reassuring squeeze. "Where's that eternal optimism?"

She shook her head, biting at her bottom lip. "Remember when I told you about my car accident?"

I nodded.

"This feels like that, deep down inside," she said, clenching her eyes shut as tears streaked down her cheeks. "Smythe said we were marked. He called it a group gift."

"We'll find out tomorrow, Juliet." I cupped her face with my free hand and rubbed my thumb over her cheek, clearing away the signs of her distress. "It'll be okay."

She stabbed out the cigarette and immediately lit up another one. "I have a bad feeling about Samhain."

"Well, you'd be silly to have a great feeling about it."

She gripped my hand tighter, and even though I had a warm bed with my Weeds a few feet away, I sat there with my princess until the sun came up. She needed what she could only get from me—a soul friend, one who had already seen her at her worst, one who could handle her vulnerability with the gentle care she needed.

19

MIRI

We waited until sunset before we headed out. The knots in my stomach were so tight, nausea rolled through me with every step I took. His warning rang loudly at the back of my mind. These weren't friendly woodland folk. The magical beings we sought were powerful and dangerous, and if they had done this to us, what else were they capable of?

Still, like a moth to a flame, I couldn't resist. The woods had been calling me since we got here, radiating with vibrance and temptation. I needed to find it.

"X, slow down," Lex shouted from in front of me.

Ivy charged ahead, the light from her torch bouncing around on the grassy path, footsteps crunching on fallen leaves.

The last time we'd walked along this trail, the sun had been low in the sky, coloring everything in a dreamy peach-colored haze. Tonight, the moon reigned supreme. Full and bright, it cast shadows of the trees on the undergrowth, like demons out of my childhood nightmares. Their long tendrils stretched in either direction, pointing to our destruction and scaring me the same as it had when I was a child. It was another reminder we were in the wild, that the trees owned this land and so did the things that lived here. In this tale, *we* were the monsters.

"It's over this way," Ivy said, pointing to her left. "I'm sure of it."

"Okay, well," Lex cut in with a scoff, "I walked these trails for hours, looking for the ruins. I'm pretty sure I know them better than you."

"I've been dreaming about them for years, Lucifer," she snapped.

"That's not the same," Lex argued, indignation in his tone. "Not at all. What you made up in your head versus what I actually walked are different things."

"Can we all agree my dreams are more than made up in my head?" Ivy looked over her shoulder and sneered. Even in the darkness, I saw the signs of her impudence directed at our husband.

"Maybe," Lex added. "That doesn't mean you know where you're going."

"Siobhan told me I did." As if that explained it all, as if we were supposed to trust some fairy that had cursed us on that Midsummer night.

"Oh, right." I could almost hear Lex rolling his eyes. "In the daydream you had when the president of Carter's fan club touched you."

"It wasn't a daydream," Carter and Ivy said at the same time.

"Her eyes turned white, dude," he added. "She read her mind."

I tuned them out and looked around as the vitality of the forest beat against me, prodding against my eardrums like a drop in cabin pressure. It recognized our strangeness and had yet to decide what to do with the intrusion. We were taught a lesson two years ago, and here we were again, as if we needed a reminder.

A chill went down my spine, and my shoulders trembled. "Maybe we ought to—"

"Over here." Ivy pointed toward a hill and charged ahead. Carter went after her, but Lex stayed back and looked at me.

"You okay?" He eyed me with that addictive mix of dominance and gentleness, like he expected the truth from me and would take it from me if I dared lie.

I cleared my throat, the static charge of the magic in the air a palpable thing, like I'd stuck my finger in an outlet. Its elephant weight crushed my chest, suffocating me, pushing all the air out of my lungs. I couldn't breathe.

"Lex, this is a bad night to be here," I said.

"Hey." He grabbed my hand and swiped his thumb over my knuckles in a caring caress. "Weren't you the one that said at least we'd die together?"

I forced a tight smile, ignoring the churning in my gut.

"C'mon." He nodded toward the trail. "I've got your back."

I went with him, each step more agonizing than the last. When we crested the hill, I recognized the valley below. Two years ago, it had burned with four epic bonfires and a sea of bodies in the middle, dancing to the rhythm of drumbeats. Now it stood barren and empty.

"We're close." Ivy stalked down the hill and through the field, likely to reorient herself with the direction she and Lex had taken off in.

"Over here." Lex headed to the left. Ivy agreed and went with him.

Hugging myself a little tighter and ignoring the rising hair on the back of my neck, I followed. Every self-preservation instinct I had told me to turn back, that this would end in tragedy and if we didn't heed the trees' warning, we would suffer the most for it.

The trees know. The trees know all.

Instead, we went deeper. We found the spot where we'd gotten into a fight and farther on, the spot at the creek where we'd made up.

"The memories from that night are still hazy." Carter gestured toward a giant rock. "But I feel like the ruins should be up that way."

"Yeah," Lex agreed.

"Miri," came a sound from behind me. At first, I thought it was a whistle on the wind, nothing but branches brushing against each other. I ignored it, clutching my jacket tighter around my torso. *"Mirrrriiii."*

I definitely heard it that time. Turning, I scanned the forest line for the person saying my name. No one else knew I was here, no one save the other three people in front of me. Who could it be? Was I hearing things? Was it the trees?

Movement off to the left caught my attention.

"Lex." My heart pounded as I reached out for him, digging my nails into the sleeve of his peacoat. "You hear that?"

"Hear what?" he said.

"Miriam, where are you?" The sound of my mother's voice raised the hairs on my arm, sending a jolt of terror down my spine and into my legs. I didn't know how I knew it was her; I hadn't heard her speak in over ten years. But it was her. Definitely.

"Miriam." My father's voice echoed next, seizing my lungs, forcing me to pay attention. I couldn't pretend they weren't there when I heard them so clearly. This wasn't the trees. It couldn't be. How could they know what my parents sounded like?

The trees know all.

"Mum?" I murmured. "Da?"

"What?" Lex scrunched his features together and grabbed my shoulder, trying to get my attention refocused on him. "Miri, what's going on?"

"My parents," I whispered, looking up into his intense hazel stare. "Do you hear them?"

"Parents?" Lex had barely uttered the word before I took off into the woods.

Objectively, it *couldn't* have been my parents. They'd died when I was a teenager. I'd personally seen their bodies lowered into graves at St. Andrews Cathedral. But the veil between the realms was supposed to have been the thinnest on Samhain. If they were haunting me, tonight might be the only night they could make contact.

I had to try to reach them. I just had to.

"Mum," I shouted, running through the woods, jumping over fallen trees. "Da!" I pumped my legs harder, cranking my arms at my sides. "Mum! Da!"

"Miriam!" The sound came from my left, and I took off in that direction.

"Miri!" someone shouted behind me, but I ignored them. My parents were here. *Here!* I had to see them. I had so much to ask them. I needed to know what they thought I should do. I needed advice from the only people who understood. I yearned for my mum to hold me in her arms and kiss my face and tell me I'd be okay, that I was smart and strong and loved. My inner child longed to hear my father call me his girl and bounce me on his knee. Sure, I knew I was twenty-four years old, but age didn't matter when the warmth of my father's affection had been withheld from me for so very long.

"Mum!" I shouted.

"Miri!" came the voice behind me again.

"Miriam! This way!" I turned right, but something big and hard collided with me, taking me down to the ground. I landed with a loud *oof,* the air pushing out of my lungs.

Lex.

"Stop it," he said, grabbing my wrists to pin them above my head when I tried to wrestle out from under him. "You can't run off by yourself."

"Lex?" came a deeper, darker voice.

Lex's features dropped. He froze, turned to ice on top of me, and lifted his head to look above us. "Marcus?"

"Miriam!" My father's voice cut through the night air again, urging me forward.

"Lex, come find me! I need to talk to you! I need to tell you something!" Marcus called, his tone worried and panicked.

Lex hopped off me, and I pushed myself upright, listening

through the gusts of wind and rattles of fallen leaves for my father again.

"Da!" I was desperate now, turning in place so I didn't miss anything. My heart raced and tears streamed down my face as I searched. *Where is he? Where is he?* I spun around, sobs pouring out of my chest as I tried to get my bearings. In the tussle with Lex, I'd lost my way.

"Da!" I called again, my voice cracking as I gasped for air.

"*Miriam!*" I took off to the right, running harder this time to stay away from Lex, the sounds of crunching twigs and fallen pine needles echoing from under my feet. I leaped over a log, my lungs heaving the crisp autumn air, the taste of metal in the back of my throat.

Almost there. Almost there.

"Mum! Da!" I stopped to listen because I didn't know where to go. I'd lost them. I heard nothing, just the humming call of the forest nightlife.

Bleeding Christ! How could I lose them? You're so stupid, Miri! So damned ridiculous.

Hands grabbed me by the shoulders, and I jumped, settling when Lex wrapped his arms around me.

"It's not real," he said, his muscles trembling as he tried to hold me still. "The fairies disguise themselves as ghosts, remember? It's not real."

"I need to talk to them. I need—"

"*Miriam...*" my mother called.

"*Alexei!*" Marcus cried. "*Save me, Alexei! Save me! I need your help.*"

"C'mon." I grabbed Lex's hand and set off toward the left. Any second, we'd duck around a tree, and there they'd be. Instead, a big structure loomed in the distance and when we got close enough, the ruins came into focus.

We'd found it!

Mum! Da!

I skidded to a halt, digging my heels into the dirt to stop myself.

Ivy and Carter had beaten us there, but that wasn't what made me freeze. A tall, brunette woman wearing a long, flowing white gown stood in front of the structure.

Ashley.

"Welcome back," she said, her voice holding a metallic tin-like quality that made her seem otherworldly. Her presence lured me in, seemingly safe and entrancing. "It's been a while. Follow me."

20

CARTER

"What's going on?" Ivy asked, trailing after Ashley. The question had been on the tip of my tongue since we rounded the bend and saw her standing in front of the same ruins where we'd once married each other.

Ashley shook her head. "This was a bad time to come asking questions, Ivy."

Two years ago, she'd given us the orientation on Killwater and the surrounding area. I remembered the tattoo of the vines going up her arms. Now, I wanted to shake her to get her to spill her secrets. I wanted to know what her sister had done to us and how to undo it.

"You chased me in my dreams," Ivy said.

"I did," Ashley agreed, apparently nonchalant about the whole thing. "I'm glad to see you again, but I do wish you had come another night."

The last time, I'd been too drunk and high to notice when we crossed over into Faerie. Now sober, I discerned the shift immediately. A strange warmth settled on my skin as my chest tightened, suddenly full of the heaviness in the air that wasn't there before. There was no door, no portal, no jilt in the atmosphere, only the acknowledgment of the magic *inside* my body balancing the magic *outside* of it.

The world had changed, and yet...stayed mostly the same.

"What do you want with us?" Ivy asked, bringing me back to the conversation.

"That ring, for starters," she said. "When you leave here, you'll hand it over and never return to look for it."

Ivy raised her eyebrow as if to suggest, *That's what you think.*

"It's a key to the portal between realms," Ashley said, scowling as she glanced over her shoulder. "My sister and I created it together. She was never meant to give it to you."

"Where *is* Siobhan?" Ivy said. "I need to talk to her."

"Hmm. Gone."

"Gone?" Lex glanced between me and Miri.

"After she cast the gift on you four, she was banished from Faerie," Ashley explained, a hint of despondent sadness in her tone. That didn't sound good. "Fae aren't supposed to meddle. Not anymore." She shrugged and frowned. "I love my sister, but she always was a sucker for a damsel in distress."

"Hey," Ivy balked. "I wasn't a damsel in distress."

Ashley raised an eyebrow and pursed her pixie lips. "She overheard your sob story and after that, she couldn't leave you alone. She said you were important."

"How?" I asked.

"No clue." Ashley turned and continued walking, leading us farther into the woods. "Siobhan has amazing instincts, and she's never wrong. But the queen had forbidden it. Siobhan knew the consequences. Now, she lives with them."

That rubbed me the wrong way, but I couldn't figure out why— something about her being banished yet turning up only a few miles away. Still, I ignored it to continue listening to Ashley's story.

"Now, *I* have to deal with the fallout from her decisions." Ashley stopped walking and turned back to us, folding her hands. "My lady queen will want to meet you. After that, she'll decide what happens."

I thought back to what Miri told me last night, about the queen killing Smythe's girl because he didn't have permission to touch her. I thought of every story I'd ever heard about faerie monarchs. None of them were great. Either she turned into an old crone, hell-bent on punishing the mortals that wronged her, or she tricked them into life everlasting here in Faerie. I didn't want either of those options, and that was to say nothing of the fairy king.

"Normally, it would be customary for me to take you right to her," Ashley explained, "but tonight is our Samhain ritual. Our queen is...indisposed."

Oh...

Ashley smiled and led us over the crest of another hill lined with fairy sentries every few feet. I admired their metal armor and heavy swords hanging from leather scabbards. The one on my left eyed me up and down, but quickly returned his attention to the forest.

I wanted to ask why they had the army on red alert, but the sight in the valley made me pause. Crawling with life and vibrancy, bodies moved around dozens of tiny fires, fairies and their consorts, preparing for whatever tonight's ritual would bring. Big white tents had been erected, dotting the landscape like a mini-city. In the far distance sat a platform with the biggest tent on top, two enormous chairs...*thrones*...were off to one side, opposite a huge table of food on the other.

"Samhain is a time of great mourning," Ashley continued, gesturing to the commotion. "But it is also a time of great hope. For there can be no happiness in life without sorrow in death."

She led us into the chaos, but instead of the jovial celebration we'd encountered two years ago, this was a much more somber affair. No one shoved condoms and lube in my face, no one forced me to drink magic-laced ambrosia wine. Groups of people huddled together around individual fires, some laughing, some playing music, some singing and slurring, already heavily intoxicated. The smell of campfires and spiced cider hung in the air, sweet and smoky.

It seemed oddly comforting, like a coming home, like we weren't supposed to leave the first time.

"In honor of life itself, our queen selects a lover to pleasure her for one complete cycle." Ashley gestured to the giant tent on the platform. "They don't stop until she is fulfilled, so we don't stop until she is fulfilled."

"I'll be plain," Miri said. "We only want the gift lifted. We didn't ask for it, and if Siobhan wasn't supposed to give it to us, perhaps it's best for everyone if it's gone."

"Right. We'll talk tomorrow." Ashley nodded before stopping outside of a white tent and holding out her hand for us to go inside. "This is my space, but I have a friend I can stay with. Make yourselves comfortable."

"Wait," Lex said. "You're leaving us?"

"Yes." Ashley seemed confused. "It's the Samhain ritual. I must attend to my duties."

"We have to get back to the real world," he argued. "We can't hang around all night."

Ashley's gentle smile turned sinister, her stare growing more intense. "You came to me, human. If you want my help, you'll wait until I can give it."

Lex glared and clenched his jaw, but didn't say anything else.

"Now," she said, her tone much lighter, "there's wine in the bladder and food on the table. Help yourself to whatever you like. You're my guests. No one will harm you, not until you've seen my lady." I didn't like the sound of that, especially knowing what I did about guests in Faerie. "I'll check on you in a bit."

Then she left us in the medieval-style tent in the middle of a different realm, all alone in a sea of magical creatures. Candlelit lanterns hung from several posts throughout the large space, and big wooden beams held the tent up. *Bloody hell,* it was made of leather, actual leather.

The bed on the other end was enormous, certainly big enough for the four of us, and covered in animal furs. When I peeled back a few layers, foamy straw stuck up from the top of the mattress. The candles burned a bright shade of rosy pink, making everything seem more dreamlike, almost like the night sky on Midsummer.

"I don't like this," Ivy said.

"Yeah, no shit." Lex anxiously ran his palms over his face before reaching into his pocket for his cigarettes.

Miri stood at the entrance to the tent, hugging her body, hesitant eyes wide as she took in the crowd.

"How you doing, Princess?" I stood next to her and wrapped an arm over her shoulders, trying to hold her close to let her know she wasn't alone in her uncertainty.

"It's not as bad as I thought." She shivered but straightened her spine anyway. "Either that, or the worst hasn't happened yet."

I wanted to be optimistic, but every part of me feared the latter. We were strangers in a strange land, and the rules we thought we knew no longer applied. My stomach growled as I eyed the roasted turkey and ears of corn at the dining table, remembering it had been hours since I'd eaten.

Lex heard it and looked at me, eyeing me up and down and raising an eyebrow. "Don't touch anything. That's what got us fucked-up last time." He handed me the pack of cigarettes.

"Shit." I didn't think I'd make it, especially not when the food smelled so amazing and looked even better. I grabbed a cigarette and lit it, letting the nicotine soothe away the hunger ache. Inhaling deeply, I tried to get my shit together but hearing ghosts in the forest earlier had messed with me. After Miri had taken off, Lex went after her, leaving Ivy and me alone by the creek.

I'd heard my grandfather first. Pop had called me, the voice so accurate, it could have come right out of my memories. I'd paused to consider the fact Pop had died ten years ago, but Ivy set off before I could stop her, calling out for Marcus. It made me despise these motherfuckers even more. What kind of monsters used people's grief to draw them into a realm on a night when they might not return?

I took another deep inhale on the cigarette.

Minutes passed like hours, hours like centuries, and the sounds from the crowd grew louder and more intense—moans mixed with laughs and cries of mourning. People wore ruby-colored robes, and a few had animal skulls over their faces like masks. At Midsummer, we had jumped over a fire and drank endless wine from leather chalices. Tonight, the revelers of Faerie chanted in tongues and sobbed in low tones among each other.

"We need to demand our answers tonight," Ivy said, clawing the nervous rash on her neck.

"We should get the fuck out of here." Lex paced back and forth, chain-smoking and pulling his hair. "This was stupid, even for us, X."

They'd been arguing about what to do for the last few hours, going in circles, arriving nowhere in the conversation.

"If we do that, we don't find out the truth," Miri cut in. "We came here for a reason."

I agreed with her. We were already here. But there was another, more desperate part of me that also agreed with Lex. I wanted to book it out of this hellhole like my ass was on fire. Everything gave me the creeps—the medieval decor and the shifty-eyed looks from everyone else around us. It wasn't like the last time, and I wondered if that was because my perspective had changed or if it was because the festival had a different meaning.

Perhaps we had been tolerated two years ago. Tonight, I felt like an intruder.

I walked to Miri, who still stood at the entrance to the tent, watching the world go by. She hadn't moved since we'd arrived.

"What're you looking at, Juliet?"

She nodded toward the stage. "I can tell which are human and which aren't."

I followed her line of sight to a blond child on the stage. She couldn't have been more than five or six, but the way her hair frizzed out around her head reminded me of Lizzie.

"She's human." Miri raised an eyebrow at me, curling her lips into disgust. "A lot of them are."

If the queen liked your company, she might keep you forever.

I watched the girl on stage hold a plate of grapes while the queen drank and laughed and picked her fill of fruit.

What was her story? How had she gotten here? What events in her life went so wrong that she'd become a servant girl for a fairy queen?

Fire swelled in my gut, and the urge to protect her had me rooting my feet in the grass to keep from launching myself at the stage. But Miri and Ivy were right. We were here to get our answers, and I needed to behave myself until then.

21

MIRI

Lex was on edge. We all were. Something heavy hung in the air, something more than the ritual or the way Ashley had ditched us. I sensed foreboding on the horizon, and I couldn't explain it. Chewing my bottom lip, I counted the number of humans while my spouses argued about whether we should leave or wait it out.

I *sensed* the fairies in attendance. Perhaps it was because of their connection to nature or because they had lived among the trees so long they were a part of the forest. Their auras shone around their bodies like halos, like I'd had my eyes open under chlorinated water too long and looking at them was like looking at white blurry lights. The queen's aura was the brightest. Did that mean she was the most powerful?

"Ashley's the closest we have to a clue," Carter said. "If she can undo the gift, we've got to try."

Lex took a deep breath and sucked on his cigarette, but stopped arguing. Maybe he accepted the lot we'd cast for ourselves and decided to wait it out.

"Okay, fuck it." Carter headed back toward the table. "I can't stand it anymore. I'm starving." He sat and pinched at the turkey to pile it on his plate.

"Carter—" Ivy moved to stand next to him. "If you consume the food of the fae, you could get stuck here."

"Yeah," Lex said. "Like Persephone and shit."

"Ashley promised not to harm us." Carter took a deep breath, raking his eyes over the spoils. "We didn't get stuck last time. How much longer are we going to wait for the queen to finish?"

No one answered him, and my own stomach growled.

"Do you want to go to your death on an empty stomach?" Carter looked at me. "If I'm not leaving here anyway, then I'd rather enjoy the time I have left."

I'd been nauseous since we left Killwater, but now that we'd been stopped, my adrenaline had subsided and left an empty hollowness in its wake. If we were here permanently, at least we'd be together. If Carter wanted to give in to temptation, I'd go with him. One of my nannies used to say there wasn't anything in this world that couldn't be fixed by a good meal.

"I've got a terrible feeling about this, but I'm with you until the end." I held out my hand to him like I had last night. He took it, hooked his thumb around mine, and gave it a shake. "You're right. This could be our last meal."

Ivy exhaled and sat opposite me, taking a piece of turkey and putting it on her plate. "Until the end, right?"

Carter and I nodded.

Lex flicked his hazel stare between us, inhaling his cigarette down to the butt before stabbing it out and walking over to the table. He resigned himself to the spot next to Ivy. "In for a penny."

Then, like a screwed-up family, we ate a Samhain dinner together surrounded by the fae. The turkey melted in my mouth, cooked to perfection and somehow still warm and juicy despite sitting out the entire time we'd been here. The wine wasn't the sweet floral decadence I remembered, but cinnamon flavored and spicy, like a warm, fluffy blanket for my veins.

As soon as it settled in my gut, the worries from my day disappeared. The taste may have been different, but the high was the same —like I floated above my body, a part of this world, but not at the same time.

"Did you guys hear voices in the woods, too?" I asked, my prior anxiety about the trees dissipating.

"My pop," Carter said, nodding. His eyes shimmered as he blinked back tears and cleared his throat.

Ivy nodded and met Lex's stare. "Marcus."

"Same." Lex gave Ivy one of his rare looks of genuine affection before nodding.

"I heard my parents," I admitted.

We fell quiet, a simple peace laced with the grief of our departed loved ones. Wasn't that what Samhain was about? Wasn't that when the veil between the realms was the thinnest? If there were an afterlife, I hoped our beloveds were watching us. I hoped they knew how much we missed them, how much we still carried them in our hearts. The thought twisted in my chest, making my eyes burn, and I clenched them shut as tears trickled over my cheeks before I could wipe them away.

"What's your favorite memory of them?" Ivy asked, reaching across the table to grab my hand.

I smiled, the visual coming from somewhere deep in the back of my brain. "My mother used to take me walking in the gardens at Windsor. We liked to pick roses." That was where my love for plants came from. "She told me the reason flowers were so magical was because no two are the same. They may look alike, and they may come from the same roots, but a closer look always revealed that each one was an individual."

Ivy smiled and looked at Carter. "What about you? Tell us about Pop."

"He took me to the Bears first home game every year—just me and Pop," Carter started, wiping at his own wet eyes while he talked. "My sisters weren't allowed to come. He's the one who always told me to stay optimistic. To keep the faith and the rest will come."

"He sounds like he was fantastic," I said. "I bet I would have liked him."

"He was." Carter grabbed my other hand. "And you would have. He would have liked all of you, too. He would have liked our strange marriage."

"Lex?" Ivy said. "What about Marcus?"

Lex blew out a breath. "Marcus was…" He couldn't finish without clearing his throat. "Marcus was so much better at this than me."

"At what?" Carter asked.

"The show. The game. Being the Fairfax." Lex shook his head and pinched the bridge of his nose, closing his eyes as waves of emotion seemed to overwhelm him.

"You don't give yourself enough credit," Ivy said.

I agreed. "I would say there are few in the game better than you."

"You guys are sweet," Lex said. "But you don't have to inflate my ego just because you're married to me."

I chuckled, and Carter patted the side of Lex's face. "I wouldn't do that. Your ego's big enough whether we're married or not."

Lex cracked up and leaned across the table to kiss Carter, grabbing him firmly by the neck to hold him in place. Perhaps I should have been jealous of the affection so freely given to my Romeo, but I loved their love. I loved to watch Lex love Carter.

"What about you, Ivy?" I asked. "What do you remember about Marcus?"

Ivy sighed and intertwined her fingers, bringing them up to her mouth while she contemplated. "He was my friend at a time when I didn't have many. He held my hand at big events, and I was braver because of it."

Lex pulled one side of his mouth into a grin, wrapping an arm around Ivy's shoulders to tug her closer so he could give her a gentle peck on the temple.

"You were brave on your own," Lex muttered, probably thinking it was too low for me and Carter to hear. But I did. "You didn't need my idiot brother."

Before I could linger too long on that tender glint in Lex's eye, I held up my glass of wine. "Cheers to the ones that came before us. May they never be far from our hearts. May the good memories see us through the bad."

Everyone held up their chalice and sipped to our departed family members.

"To last dinners," Lex added.

"Here, here," Ivy and Carter said together.

It should have sobered me and made me pause to consider how we planned to get out of this. There was no telling when Ashley would be around to check on us again, and time passed differently on this side of the veil. Twelve hours here meant twenty-four out there. Three days could be a week. We might get back to our world to discover years had gone by. But the magical side effects of the wine dulled my reasoning, and when Lex made a crack at Carter's expense, Ivy and I burst into hysterics.

The night went jovially on around us. We laughed at old stories from our college days and talked about things that had happened since then. In that tent with nothing to do, nowhere to go, and no control over what happened next, the four of us rebuilt what we had created and torn apart two years ago.

This...This was what the gift was meant to be. Stripped of titles and pretense and the weight of the world's expectations, we were free, so joyful and light.

A momentary thought passed through my mind, there and gone in a heartbeat.

What if we didn't leave? What if we stayed like this forever? Would that be the worst thing?

For the life of me, I couldn't think of a reason why it would. Yeah, I wouldn't see my family again. Perhaps I would miss my grandparents and Edward, and maybe Carter's family, too. Other than that, most humans were disappointing. I could just as easily come back to this tent with my spouses night after night. I'd cook vegetables I had harvested myself and raise our children surrounded by people who understood what it was between us, who wouldn't judge or try to keep us apart by tearing us down. Other humans lived here successfully, right? Would it be difficult for us to blend in?

"If we do make it out of this," Lex added, returning my attention to the conversation, "I want to buy a house in the country, far away from everyone."

"Agreed," Ivy said. "Somewhere that's ours. *All* of us."

"If we make it out of this, I won't go another two years without being together," Carter said, squeezing my hand tighter. "I don't care what I have to do to my filming schedule. I'll figure it out."

"We can have a big garden out back for our princess"—Lex shot me a wink—"and a gym in the basement for Weeds and Chicago."

"And a darkroom for you to develop your prints," I added, remembering those gorgeous shots of Ivy.

"Every night, we'll make dinner together," Carter said, "and then we'll fuck in our hot tub overlooking the mountains."

Ivy laughed, and the noise warmed all the parts of me that had frozen over while being in Faerie. I realized, as we sat there discussing our paradise, that I wanted it with a fury. I wanted it more than I wanted anything else in my life. If we left this place intact, if we went back to who we were, we may never get it. My life would be the royal family. Ivy and Lex would go back to their politics in DC. Carter would go on to be the next EGOT winner.

"It sure is a pretty picture," I said, a small bit of melancholy creeping into my blood.

22

CARTER

The food was amazing, even better than it smelled, and *several* bladders of wine later, we made our way to the bed. The four of us cuddled together under the furs in the order we preferred—Lex and me on the outside, the girls in the middle. Despite the fact this could be our last night alive, depending on how the queen felt when she woke up in the morning, a sense of lightness and joy hung over us. Like nothing mattered and never would again because we were alive in this moment.

"You don't think one of us should...I don't know...stand guard?" Miri asked with a small slur and a giggle.

"If they wanted to kill us," Ivy said, leaning to kiss the princess, "they wouldn't have to wait until we were asleep to do it."

"It's just—" Miri sighed. "It's strange, isn't it? It's all so strange."

I settled into the straw mattress, which was the most comfortable bed I'd ever been on. The cushioning pooled in all the right places. I had a ten-thousand-dollar Tempur-Pedic at home, and all I needed was this foamy shit. Go figure.

"Jesus, everything's better in Faerie, isn't it?" I murmured, crossing my arms under my head.

Ivy and Miri laughed, pulling back from their kissing to glance at me.

"The beds, the wine," I continued.

"The sex," Lex cut in, pulling one side of his mouth into a wolfish grin.

Ivy chuckled harder and rolled into me, draping her arm around my waist and leaning her head on my chest to bring her lips tenuously close to my neck. A moment of silence fell on us where the atmosphere shifted, like whatever was going on *out there* had finally crept its way in here. The mood grew heady and stifling, pushing the four of us closer in this bed together.

Almost like it could be centuries ago, like the story between us had been playing out for hundreds of years, and here we were, back where we'd started—in this tent, in this bed, with the gift and the love between us.

"It would be wrong to do that, right?" Lex pursed his lips and narrowed his eyes, clearly expecting a response.

"Totally wrong," I agreed. "We're here for a reason."

"It's not safe for us to be distracted," Miri said.

"But," Ivy added, connecting her lips to my skin, sending a jolt of erotic pleasure straight down my spine.

"But," I agreed, looking down at her to return the kiss.

"Tonight is about celebrating life." Miri turned to Lex and wrapped her fingers behind his neck. "We're lucky to be alive."

"Very lucky," Lex murmured, leaning down to appease the princess with a tender peck.

"They could have killed us," I said. "They still might."

"They might," Ivy agreed.

"We should enjoy it while we can," Lex said.

I needed little convincing after that. I yanked Ivy on top of me, bringing her knees to either side of my hips, slotting my quickly growing cock at her clit. I moaned when she rolled her pelvis on top of me and pinned my hands above my head, putting me in the perfect position to be claimed by her. Anticipation built inside of my chest when she kissed me, softly at first, but growing more demanding the harder she rubbed against me.

Yes. Fuck yes.

Lex hadn't been lying. The sex was infinitely better like this, drunk on fairy wine and sated with fairy food. Now, I took my spouses any damn way I chose because why the fuck not? Anyone who walked in on us wouldn't care. Hell, I'd seen *groups* of people having sex on our way here. They'd done this to us, after all, and when Ivy slid her arms down my body, landing on the waistband of my pants, I smiled and nodded, urging her on.

She kissed my stomach, casually licking places she liked the most. Lex found my mouth, coaxing my lips open with his tongue so he could steal his way inside. Hot heady arousal skyrocketed through me, and when Lex straddled my chest, I grinned and waited to see what he would do.

"Open up, Chicago," he said, and I gratefully complied. He shoved his cock in my mouth just as Ivy enveloped mine in hers.

Fuck! I nearly arched off the bed, and if it wasn't for Lex's weight holding me down, I would have. I sucked on Lex because I was made to do so, even as Ivy moaned, followed by Miri. Two sets of hands replaced her mouth, and I bucked, trying to find that warmth again.

"Focus," Lex teased, twisting his fingers in my hair while he fucked my face, his knees pinning my shoulders down. "That's a good boy."

"Lex, he's my plaything," Ivy groaned. "Be nice."

"He likes it when I'm mean to him," Lex said, winking at me.

Jesus Christ, I swear I could have died and gone to heaven. Tears pooled at the corners of my eyes, and I gagged around his dick in a delightfully sick contrast to my own pleasure, which sizzled up my spine and down my legs. I loved when they used me like this. I loved being their toy.

A warm tongue ran over my balls as another mouth rolled my tip between its lips, and hands roamed over my skin, amplifying the groans Lex made on top of me.

"Fuck yeah, Chicago." He thrust harder, pumping deeper into me. "That mouth is pure fucking sin." I tried to put my palms on his thighs to stop him, to slow him down, but his shins dug into my forearms and I couldn't move. Perhaps I liked that most of all.

I thought he might come like that, but he pulled out and slid down my body, spreading out to my side so he lay next to me. He grabbed the back of my neck and tilted my head up so I could watch our wives take each other at the end of the bed. Ivy tangled her free hand in Miri's hair while Miri rubbed her cunt in between Ivy's thighs, their mouths connected in an intimate embrace.

"Look at them," Lex said, his breath coasting down the side of my body. "Look at us. Look at our love."

After all this time, after all that happened between us, after all that would ever happen, I loved these three humans with a fury that I'd never known before. I loved the way my husband dominated my body, taking me and marking me as he pleased. I loved the way my wife licked up my torso, joining mouths with my husband while they took mine. I loved the way my other wife pleased our husband and our wife. It all sounded so fucked-up and weird and strangely...so right, I could cry.

What would that boy think, the one I was at the start of all this? Eighteen and wide-eyed, landing in London with nothing but an internship with the Royal Theater Company, my backpack on my shoulders, and a prayer in my heart? Six years later, I'd found my home, and it wasn't with some Hollywood starlet the way I'd thought it would go. It was with three other misfits I'd been lucky to meet.

The luckiest motherfucker on all of Earth, in fact.

"Hold him down, X," Lex said when Ivy coasted up my torso again. She grabbed my wrists and put them over my head while Miri positioned my cock in between Ivy's legs. I shivered when she sank on top of me, sheathing me before riding me like the world might end. Hell, tomorrow, it just might. We didn't know what would happen, but I pushed those thoughts aside.

"Get up here," Lex said, yanking Miri to the top of the bed beside me. I watched him kiss her, delighting in the soft way he always handled our princess. He could be rough and domineering with me, but with Miri, he had a sweet side. To see him so tender made my heart melt for him.

He twisted her around onto all fours and kneeled behind her, pushing into her slowly. Miri sighed and leaned down to kiss me, connecting our mouths in a delicate embrace that amplified my devotion to her. I moaned when Ivy hit a sensitive spot and shivered, my entire body quaking with her euphoria.

While she fucked me, I watched Lex take Miri from behind, digging his fingers into her hips as he slammed into her. He leaned his head back on his shoulders, his features slack with bliss, his tattooed neck exposed. I ached to sink my teeth into it, into every bit of his skin. I wanted to mark him the same way he lived to mark us.

"I love you like this," Ivy said, "I love all of you like this."

"I love you, Weeds," I said, reaching between her legs to rub her clit while she got herself off. When she crested the height of her pleasure, it set something off inside Miri, too. They came together, their deep bellows hypnotizing and intense, like they were connected on a soul-deep level. Who's to say they weren't?

When Lex had his fill of our princess, riding her through her climax, he sat back while she collapsed on the mattress at my side.

"Chicago, be a good boy and clean her come off me." He nodded down to his dick.

"I'm not done with him, Lucifer," Ivy said, slowing her thrusts but still holding me down.

Lex laughed and wrapped an arm over her shoulders, leaning in to whisper something in her ear. I caught words like "clean up our princess" and "I plan to fuck all three of you tonight."

Ivy smiled and gave him a chaste kiss before climbing off me to slot herself between Miri's legs. Lex refocused on me and raised an eyebrow, staring down his nose with expectation. I curled myself up and turned around so I bring my mouth to his cock, giving it a gentle lap from root to tip. He hissed in a breath and dived down my throat again, tasting like Miri and him and pure sin.

"That's a good little cumslut," Lex said, digging his fingers in my hair.

I wished the praise and the degradation made me hate him. But no. A perverted thrill shot down my chest, even as my throat burned and bruised with his depravity.

He didn't take my mouth for very long before flipping me around so he could squirt lube on my ass and slot himself deep inside me. I didn't know where he'd gotten it from and, once he filled me, I didn't care. One hand gripping my hip, the other holding my shoulder, he fucked me harder than he ever had before. Perhaps he, too, worried we might not leave this place. Perhaps he thought this might be the last time he could have me like this.

"You like that, Chicago?" he said through clenched teeth. "You like being my whore?"

"Not as much as you," I teased. Oh, it was the wrong thing to say. Lex slapped my ass hard enough to bruise before sinking his nails into my fleshy skin with a scalding ache.

"Weeds, be a good wife and give Carter something else to do with his mouth," Lex said. Usually, Ivy balked at his orders, but this time, she listened. Whatever he'd whispered to her must have hit all her kink buttons because she made a dark chuckle and scooted in front of me so my mouth lined up with her delicious cunt.

And what a treat she was. While Lex fucked me within an inch of my life, I devoured her, licking up the taste of myself left behind. Miri positioned herself under me and I held myself up on my elbows so she had room, but I nearly lost my balance when she wrapped her perfect lips around my cock.

Fuuuccckk.

I was putty in their hands. Miri rested her legs on top of Ivy's, and I took turns sucking each one of them. Ivy stuck her fingers in Miri's cunt and I played with her clit and combined with Lex's dick inside me, I couldn't hold on very long.

"Look at you, so fucking filthy," Lex murmured, picking up his pace. "You like pussy in your face while I'm fucking you? Huh?"

I laughed and kept serving my wives.

"What about you, *Weeds?*" Lex laughed. "You like seeing your precious Mister Scott like this?"

"So much," she said with a breathy pant.

"What about my princess?" Lex paused to lean to the side so he could check on Miri. "You like Romeo's cock down your throat?"

She mumbled something that sent vibrations through me, and I almost lost my composure.

"Yeah, you do." Lex hummed and rutted harder, deeper, surging me forward again. "You're all my little dirty spouses, aren't you? All mine. You belong to me." He rambled under his breath, but the pulse of my pounding heart between my ears made it hard to hear him.

His. His, his, his.

The salty tang of sex filled the air, adding to my excitement, euphoria rocketing through me like a drug. Sure, I loved fucking each one of these humans on their own. I even enjoyed it when there were only three of us. But when we all came together like this, when we were all connected, the world could split open and send me careening to hell. I wouldn't care.

The magic inside our molecules, whatever it was that gave us these fairy curses, snapped tight like a rubber band under tension. We became one — one body, one soul, one mind. As soon as the thought hit me, Lex angled his hips in just the right way and pushed me deeper into Miri's mouth.

I exploded.

My muscles tightened. My eyes clenched shut. My whole being erupted down the center as I filled Miri's mouth, my cock jerking and kicking like I'd never had a blowjob before.

Good. Fucking. Lord.

My orgasm *unmade* me, and all I could do was sigh and shiver and pray it never ended.

"Woo," Lex said after bringing me back down to earth. He

spanked me again before carefully pulling out of me. "Wow, what a fucking ride. Who's next?"

But I couldn't think straight. I rolled onto my back and watched as Lex walked to a rustic-style sink to clean himself off. Ivy and Miri kissed, wrestling their tongues like Ivy was trying to get my taste off Miri...or maybe Miri was trying to put what was left of my spend inside Ivy.

It was enough to get me hard again, my abused cock giving a half-hearted thump on my lower belly.

Eventually, Lex came back and broke it up.

"You think I don't want some of that?" Lex grabbed Miri's throat and tilted her chin up so he could shove his tongue in her mouth, lapping at whatever he found. "Fucking delicious." He grinned and gave me a wink before nodding back on the bed. "Lay down so I can fuck you properly, Princess."

She did and he crawled in between her thighs so he could shove inside her, fucking her much more gently than he had to me. Ivy rubbed at Miri's clit until our princess moaned and trembled. Then Weeds ultimately returned to me, getting me hard again before rolling me on top of her so I could make her come the way I'd been doing for years.

On and on it went. We took each other that night for hours. Days. Years. I had no idea how long we were in that bed. It felt like last time, the high, the euphoria, the not being able to get enough of each other or the connection between us. But I didn't black out. I remembered all of it.

Sometime later, hazy and blissed out, I found myself in between Miri's legs, Lex and Ivy behind us, groaning and whispering to each other. I slid inside her, all the way to the root, lowering my face to the crook of her shoulder and pressing my lips in tender kisses on her long neck. She rocked against me, hooking her ankles behind my back, locking her arms around my neck, those honey-brown eyes hooded as they peered up at me.

"Do you remember Malibu?" she whispered. "That drive in my uncle's car?"

I paused, slowing to lift my head and meet her eyes as I nodded. "I remember."

"I never said thank you for that," she said, leaning up to give me a sweet kiss. "So thank you."

I smiled and traced a finger down the tip of her nose. "No thank-yous needed, Juliet. I married you in those woods, too."

"I love you, Romeo." The blinding smile she gave me could have stopped my heart.

"I love you," I said, hoping I returned the generosity.

Yes, my love with Miri would never be what it was with Lex and Ivy. It was different, made of steel and scars instead of fluffy roses or borderline obsession. No less beautiful for its uniqueness. I still couldn't live without it.

"All we have is us." She brushed her mouth against mine, the words barely a breath as they were meant for me and me alone.

"All we have is us," I echoed. "Until the end."

"Until the end."

When I came for the final time, it was in deep groans and guttural releases. I sank myself inside these hedonists, knowing they would be there to catch me when I resurfaced, just as I would always be there for them.

ACT IV

Come, my queen, take hands with me,
And rock the ground whereon these sleepers be.
-Oberon, Act IV, Scene I

23

CARTER

Sometime later, my sore throat and my grumbling stomach woke me. We'd had a long night. Day? Year? I had no concept of time anymore. Centuries could have passed while we took each other, and in the aftermath, I knew only two things: unquenchable thirst and unmatched hunger.

My body ached from the exertion, but I wouldn't change it. We came together, over and over and over again. In that connection, our bond rebuilt itself. I didn't know what would happen when we returned to reality, but I'd make damn sure I kept my promise this time. There would be no running away to LA and never seeing them again. There would be no late nights, trying to contact them. This would be different.

I sat up, swinging my legs over the side of the bed, but a figure at the tent door startled me, and I froze.

Ashley—standing with her hands folded over her stomach and a pleased, smug look on her face. I shoved at the body next to me. Lex groaned and cursed, sitting up with his hair all mussed and that adorable pout on his lips.

"Fucking what?" He squinted up at me with that characteristic sneer.

"Get up, DC." I shoved him again.

"Jesus." He rubbed at his eyes and followed my gaze. When he saw Ashley, he nudged Miri and Ivy on the other side of him.

"Good morning," Ashley said. "I trust your accommodations were…to your satisfaction?"

I cleared my throat and reached for my boxers, tossed on the grass in my frenzy to get them off last night. I yanked them up and stood. "You said you'd come back for us."

"And here I am." Ashley swept her gaze over my spouses, now groaning to themselves and searching for their clothing. "Get dressed. Eat. Then come with me. My lady wishes to have a word."

"She's ready to answer our questions?" Ivy asked, yanking her shirt over her shoulders.

Ashley raised an eyebrow, widening her creepy smile. "The ritual has ended. She's exhausted, but you are her guests. Please. Do not keep her waiting."

Ashley turned to leave, and I met Ivy's hesitant gaze. A conversation with the queen sounded ominous, and the look in Ashley's eyes only raised the hairs on the back of my neck.

This was it. If the queen didn't like us? *Poof.* We'd be dead in seconds.

"It'll be fine," Miri said, slipping her sweater over her head. "Like Ivy said, if they wanted us dead, they would have done it when we got here."

Lex lit a cigarette and ran a hand through his hair. "I'm more afraid of her never letting us go."

Valid.

"Some of the people here aren't fae. I can feel it." Miri took a few steps closer to us, lowering her voice as she spoke. "Smythe told us the fairies treated humans like thralls, that there's a long history between humans and fairies we don't know about."

I finished getting ready, now more anxious about this meeting than hungry, so I grabbed a few pieces of toast to hold me over before we met Ashley outside the tent. She led us through the bodies piled on each other in the meadow, most sleeping, some whispering in hushed tones while the sun rose over the horizon. A misty fog floated in the distance, making the world seem like it had been on fire last night and now sizzled with the embers in the gaining light.

"My lady," Ashley murmured when we reached the platform and climbed the stairs to the tent's opening. Bodies rustled inside before the child appeared, a young blond girl with big brown eyes and rosy pink cheeks. Far away, she had reminded me of Lizzie, but up close, God, it yanked at my heartstrings.

"Hey there," I said, leaning closer to her. "What's your name?"

Intelligence flickered behind her eyes, but she said nothing, just darted her attention between us.

A tall female fairy with ivy vines on both arms appeared next, her long, ashen hair hanging in thick waves down the front of her body. She wore a white robe, which she hugged tight as she looked at us. But it was her eyes that held my attention. Piercing. Incinerating. Like she could murder us with them between blinks. I wasn't entirely sure that she couldn't.

"Ashley," the queen said, staring down at us. "You have brought my guests."

"Yes, my lady," Ashley said with a bow. "May I present Ivette, Alexei, Miriam, and Carter."

"Ahhh." The queen walked to her throne and slowly sat, her movements fluid and graceful, like she'd had thousands of years to practice. They seemed so alien and unnatural.

I wanted to like her. I wanted to trust her. Any hesitation I'd had melted away in response to the soothing energy emanating from her aura. All the fairies had an appeal to them, but she made me want to buckle at the knees so I could pay her homage.

"Yes," she said. "And which one is the recipient of our blessing?"

Ashley nudged Ivy forward.

"Ivette," Ivy said. "Pleased to meet you."

"Are you?" the queen said with a wry smile. "*How* pleased?"

Ivy opened and shut her mouth, seemingly unsure of how to reply. "It's just a saying."

"Hmm." The queen glanced at Lex next. "And this one? Quite beautiful. I adore your markings."

"Thank you." He held his arms out so the queen could look over his tattoos.

Once satisfied, she focused on me and smiled, causing a shiver to race down my spine. I didn't know the intentions behind that grin, and I didn't want to guess. It would probably terrify me either way.

"But here is the real gem," the queen murmured, leaning closer to the child. "What would you do with such a gift?" The child shrugged and shook her head, giggling softly as the queen whispered something I couldn't hear. Then she sighed and rolled her eyes, clearly annoyed already. "Right. Why have you come?"

"Siobhan gave me—gave us—a gift," Ivy said. "One we didn't ask for."

"Well," the queen cut in, "you *must* have asked for it in some way. Fairies are not in the habit of bestowing magic on humans for no reason."

"I think Siobhan favored me," Ivy said. "In any case, the gift has taken its toll."

"How so?" The queen tilted her chin up, hands fisted around the arms of her throne. She seemed defensive as if any gift from a fairy couldn't *possibly* be that bad.

Tread lightly, I wanted to scream.

"We have to be together. Or else—"

"What is wrong with being together?" She raised an eyebrow, her tone bordering on annoyance. "Do you not love each other? Ashley tells me you married in our sacred ruins."

"Yes, but—" Ivy fisted her hands into tight balls.

"You made the sacred vow. It is etched in your hands."

A blush crept up Ivy's neck, into her cheeks, radiating that vibrant X over her pulse. "It is, but—"

"Then I do not see the problem." The queen straightened her shoulders. "You wanted to be together, so now you are together. The consequences of your separation are yours to handle."

"If you could only lift the gift…" Miri started, taking a step forward.

"Just like the English." The queen scoffed and rolled her eyes. "You have been trying to tell my kind what to do for millennia. What makes you think I will listen to you now?"

"We don't want any trouble," I added. "We want our lives to go back to normal."

"Normal?" The queen shook her head and leaned forward, perhaps trying to get on our level. "What is normal? I have lived long enough to know it is nothing. Even if it was, who would want such a boring existence? Better to be happy with what you have than mourn the loss of something that was never yours in the first place."

"Please," Ivy said, putting her hands together while she begged.

The queen waved her fingers at Ashley, flippantly gesturing to take us away.

"They may stay until they are replenished, but then see them home," the queen said. "Be sure you have the ring before they leave."

"Yes, my lady," Ashley said, wrapping an arm around Miri's shoulders to attempt to lead us away.

"Wait," Lex cut in, widening his eyes as panic took control. "*Tell us the truth.*"

A wave of power poured out of him as he said it. Ashley gasped and Ivy froze, looking to the queen to see her reaction.

Why? What is he thinking?

For all the years I'd known Lex, he hadn't gotten comfortable with authority. We made a plan, but if it didn't work in his favor, he did what he wanted. Any idiot would know better than to try to use magic on the queen of fairies.

For a moment, she didn't do anything, just sat there and stared at us. Then she let out a high-pitched, tinny laugh like she thought he was absurd for even attempting it.

"Did you think your fairy gift would work on me, *boy?*" She shook her head and narrowed her eyes into evil slits, clearly apathetic about us now. "I am older than anything you have ever seen. I am the Great Source. All of it. Everything. It lives within me." Her features grew serious and deadly, gaze like a laser about to turn him to dust. "If you attempt to enchant me again, I will rip that pretty head off your shoulders and mount it on my wall so I can kiss those lips every day before I break my fast."

Lex paled as he took a step back.

"Do you understand?"

"Come." Ashley put herself between us and the queen, nudging me away from the platform.

"Get them fed and out of my realm," the queen said, pushing to her feet.

"Yes, my lady." Ashley ushered us back to her tent, wringing her hands and glancing over her shoulder as we walked through the crowd of appalled Faerie residents.

Well, that was a shit show.

"I TOLD you it was a bad time for a visit," Ashley said once we'd returned to her tent. "She's tired from the ritual. If she were better rested, she might have helped you. As it is..."

"Can you just—can you give us some answers? Please?" Ivy sounded desperate. "What is this gift? Why did Siobhan give it to us?"

"It's not really a gift," Ashley explained. "It's an old trick fairies used to play on humans. It's sort of like a love spell. If you don't stay together, you'll hurt until you are. You won't be able to get excited about anyone else."

Rage raced through my veins, and I ground my teeth as my pulse pounded in my head. A trick? How cruel. These assholes played with human lives like they were nothing, like rotten children with ants and a microscope.

"But," Ashley continued, looking back and forth between us, "whatever is going on with you is different."

"What do you mean?" Ivy narrowed her piercing stare at Ashley.

"I thought Siobhan enchanted you and made you perform the sacred vow on hallowed ground. But this?" She focused on Lex with suspicion dancing behind her expression. "What were you trying to do to my lady? Did you think you could make her reveal more than she did?"

Lex pursed his lips and narrowed his eyes on Ashley while he reached into his pocket for his cigarettes. He lit one and inhaled deeply, but he didn't answer her question.

"Yes," Ivy responded, taking a step toward Ashley. "I can see inside people's minds. Miri can make plants grow by touching them. Carter is lucky, *incredibly* lucky."

Ashley took a deep breath and straightened, tilting her chin higher. "Siobhan should not have done that. I've only seen this once before."

"Only once?" I raised my eyebrows. "The myths are filled with fairy curses and gifts. You told us about them yourself the first time we met."

"Yes, those are tales. Legends. My lady commanded that her followers make the vow hundreds of years ago. No more interfering. No gifts. No enchantments. In one night, Siobhan both enchanted you and endowed you with magic. She allowed it to spread to all four of you." Ashley shook her head, rubbing her hands over her face. "Siobhan claims to have the knowing, an instinct about what would happen. She's what's called a banshee." She glanced at each one of us before returning to the folded hands in front of her. "She predicted the king would leave."

"Is that why she did this to us?" Ivy asked. "Did she have a knowing about...about me?"

Ashley sighed. "I don't know, truly. But the only one who can undo this is Siobhan."

"What?" Ivy said. "Why?"

"That's the rules. The caster is the only one who can break it."

"Well, where is she?" Lex asked, flicking ash onto the grass floor. "Let's track the bitch down and make her undo it."

Ashley gave him a nasty look at the curse. "After she was cast out, I lost touch with her. Last I heard, she had joined forces with the king." She sighed and went to the table, slowly lowering herself into a chair so she could take a drink from the chalice. "They used to be together, the queen and the king, for centuries. Eons. As long as I can remember. But very recently, they had a falling out over the child."

"Why?" I asked. "Who's the child?"

"Poppy. She's named after her mother, one of my lady's favorite human consorts. She labored for days trying to bring her into the world, and finally, just as the child tore its way out of her body, she departed this life." Ashley wiped at tears falling down her cheek, her breaking voice indicating how much the elder Poppy must have meant to her. "The queen took the infant as her own; it was one of the last things my lady promised her friend. How could she not?" Ashley shook her head and took a drink of mead. "She's raised Poppy ever since."

"Really?" I raised an eyebrow. "Poppy seems more like a servant girl."

"The child serves at the pleasure of our queen," Ashley said. "As do we all."

I pursed my lips but didn't argue. Poppy didn't know there was another world out there, one with her own kind, one where she could go to school and live however she wanted. If she did, would she still choose this? Would she still hold grapes and pour wine for a fairy queen that kept her kind locked away in this fantasy realm?

"The king doesn't believe in the mingling of humans and fairies," Ashley continued. "If it were up to him, he would have cast all the humans out of Faerie after the last Great War. Humans are destructive and violent. If they found out about this place, they would consume it."

She wasn't wrong. Look at what humans were doing to the planet in their own realm.

"As my queen's lady lay dying, birthing the younger Poppy into the world, my queen tried to revive her. She put her hands on the woman's belly, but whatever happened did not save the dying mother." Ashley looked between us. "Instead, whatever she did passed through the mother into Poppy. And now—" Ashley shook her head, perhaps realizing she'd said too much. "Poppy is special."

"How?"

"Your gifts, *my* gifts, they're elemental. Organic. Poppy's are from space and time." I wanted to ask what Ashley meant by that, but she continued before I could. "Our seer had a vision about Poppy—that she would use this gift to bring peace to the realms and reunite the humans and fairies. Once the king found out about that, about what she could do, he wanted to kill her. In his mind, there doesn't need to be a reunion. He can be terribly superstitious."

"But the queen doesn't believe it?" Ivy asked.

Ashley rolled her eyes. "My queen does not believe all prophecies should be taken literally. The seer's exact words were 'reunite the humans and fairies.' Which humans? Which fairies? All of them? Or only a few?" She raised an eyebrow as she looked between us. "Prophecies are notoriously vague. Besides, Poppy's a little girl. She hasn't done anything wrong. She barely talks. She's the sweetest thing."

My heart melted for Poppy, but at least the queen saw reason. This king sounded like an asshole.

"As you can imagine," Ashley continued, "this caused a rift in their marriage. They've been living separately ever since...which is a problem." She downed her drink and poured herself another one. "One cannot survive without the other. They are equally powerful. Where she is light, he is dark. Hence my lady's irritability. This cannot go on much longer, or we will all suffer for it."

"Where's the king?" Ivy asked. "If he hates humans so much, what's stopping him from going to the other side of the woods and killing us all?"

Ashley took a deep breath as if gearing up for a twisted tale. "A long time ago, he tried. He almost succeeded. It took a powerful fae to banish him back to Faerie, and now he can't get out. Neither of them can, not without a key." Her gaze landed on Ivy, suggesting my wife held the very thing that could allow the king to wreak whatever havoc he wanted.

"The ring," Ivy murmured.

"Exactly," Ashley said with a solemn nod. "This is why I've been hunting you for it. This is why I wanted you to give it back to me. Siobhan knows you have it, and if the king finds out Siobhan knows where it is, he could use it to get out."

"And if he gets out?" I asked, a slice of panic shooting through my sternum.

"Well"—Ashley whistled—"I can't imagine anyone in the human realm would be able to stop him."

"I don't understand. I lost the ring in the woods." Ivy squinted and shook her head. "It was smushed under moss or whatever. Why would Siobhan give it back to me?"

Now it was Ashley's turn to be confused. She furrowed her brows and narrowed her focus on Ivy. "What do you mean?"

"She came to me," Ivy said. "Six months after Midsummer. She told me about the gift and, when I woke up, the ring was in my lap. If she's working for the king, why wouldn't she give the ring to him? Why would she give it back to me?"

Ashley didn't have a good answer. I couldn't think of one either.

"That's why we came to find her," Ivy said. "She owes me an explanation."

"Well, she's gone," Ashley said. This time, her voice sounded cracked and jaded. They were sisters, after all. Siobhan's loss must have hurt. I hadn't seen my sisters in months, and the absence ached more than I'd ever admit.

"No," Ivy said. "No, she was seen not far from here a few days ago."

"What?" That got Ashley's attention, and she snapped her attention Ivy. "How do you know that?"

"That's why we came now," Lex explained. "She was at a gas station a few kilometers outside Killwater."

Ashley launched to her feet, eyes wide and fists clenched. "You're certain of this?"

"I wouldn't have traveled all this way if I didn't think I'd get my answers," Ivy said.

A moment of silence passed between us where the weight of this realization hung like smog. Then Ashley rushed out of the tent. We followed her.

"My lady," Ashley called, ducking and weaving through the crowd. "My lady."

"Yes, Ashley. What is it?" the queen said, coming out of her tent again, twisting her features into annoyance when she saw we were still here.

"Siobhan is here." Ashley held her skirts up so she could run faster. We chased her, my heart pounding at the increasing panic in her tone. "Siobhan...she was..."

She didn't get another word in before everything around us faded to a dark glow like an impenetrable cloud had moved over the sun. When I looked up, big puffy clouds of obsidian twisted through the sky, and a scream ripped through the atmosphere from somewhere behind us. Power settled in my gut, overwhelming and sickening, turning my knees to jelly. My hair stood on end like I'd stuck my finger in an electrical socket, except the entire world was a conductor and the very air could kill me.

"Hide!" a fairy shouted as they rushed by.

"He's back," came another cry. "Hide! Hide!"

Another scream. Another shout.

"Quick! Under the stage," the queen shouted, thrusting Poppy into my arms. "Go!"

24

MIRI

I wasn't sure what was happening until Ivy yanked me under the wooden platform with her. We huddled together near a thick wooden beam while my heart pounded and my hands balled into fists, my body seemingly unable to move.

In front of us, the sea of bodies parted, revealing a tall enigmatic man wearing a black leather trench coat and an opulent breastplate made of a shimmery dark metal. His hair matched his outfit, as did his thick beard, making him impossibly more beautiful than the queen. He emanated a similar magnificence as her, but...darker. More violent and turbulent.

"My love," he said, holding his arms out to either side.

That voice. A crack splintered through a barrier in my memories I hadn't known existed until that moment, my mind shifting and breaking apart only to be put back together again.

I shoved that into a compartment to analyze later, choosing instead to focus on getting out of there. He stepped toward the stage, linking his arms behind his back and setting his black eyes on the queen above us. The floorboards creaked with her movements, moving from one side to the other as she seemingly shifted her weight.

"How lovely it is to see you," he continued. "I trust you spent your Samhain in a manner befitting a queen."

"You know me too well." She tried to mask it, but a stammer in her voice indicated how shaken up she was by his visit. Ashley said their queen was tired and worn out by the ritual. The unexpected arrival of her estranged husband must have been the last thing she wanted. "Please. To what do I owe this great honor?"

He came closer, climbing the stairs to the stage, his boots clinking against the wood in a terrifying rhythm. I didn't know why he couldn't tell that four of his despised humans were hiding under here with the child he wanted to kill. But I held my breath to keep the secret going. One wrong move, one wrong sound, he'd look down and see us. There'd be little we could do to stop him after that.

I grabbed Ivy's hand and squeezed it tight, hoping if he saw us, we could withstand his wrath together.

"I've come to make a deal." The king's voice held such opulence and magic, it washed over me like sugarcoated dew on a spring morning. I wanted to revel in it. I wanted to throw myself at his feet and beg for his leniency, but I knew that was only because of his fairy allure. Whatever it was that gave fairies their strength, it made humans *want* them.

"What deal?" The queen sounded frustrated, rightfully so, but managed to maintain a calm demeanor.

"The child for our peace." The words echoed over the crowd, almost as if he wanted everyone to know about the trade.

The queen made a high-pitched laugh, almost metallic and tinkling like crystal glasses. "What makes you think I'll sacrifice an innocent child for your selfish pride?"

"She's far from innocent." The conviction in the king's tone made me pause and glance over to Poppy in Carter's arms.

What the hell could he mean by that?

"You have no idea the power that resides in that one little

human." The king tsked like she was beneath him, as was this entire charade.

The queen sighed and moved away from him toward her throne, judging by the creak overhead.

"Do I not?" The stage shifted like maybe she sat. "I created her. I gave her life. I know everything about her."

"You perverted her." The king moved closer, and we huddled tighter together, collectively united in our fear of this powerful fairy who supposedly hated us. "You mutated her with our magic. Come, my love. You must see how that is not natural."

"Poppy is extraordinary." The queen cleared her throat. "And she is my child. You and I do not need to agree on this. You only need to live with it."

"Live with it?" The king scoffed like she'd offended him, and my heart rate sped up as I tightened my fingers around Ivy's grip. "How can I live without you? How can you live without me?"

They're dual spirits, Smythe had said.

One can not live without the other, Ashley had reiterated.

"I manage." The queen did not sound convincing. If anything, she seemed heartbroken.

"Come, Diana," the king pleaded, using a name no one had dared mutter up until now. Her real name. The name between them. "Let us reconcile. I see you have already purged your retinue of the filth that once polluted it."

Filth.

He meant us, the disreputable beings hiding under here with the audacity to be born human.

Diana made a sad noise, almost like a sigh. "In all these centuries, Alberich, you have learned nothing."

I tried to pay attention to the grandstanding above me, but a tingling sensation ran down my spine and up the back of my head, and I turned my attention to Ivy. Her eyes went white, and soon, I heard her voice inside my head. I *saw* her inside my head. And Ashley, too, from across the valley.

"I'm using my magic to conceal you, but I can't hold it much longer," Ashley said. *"Take Poppy and go around back. No one will see you. Trust me."*

Trust her? *Trust her?* After all this nonsense, after she'd haunted Ivy for months and given us no help at all? Now, she wanted us to trust her? But what choice did we have?

"Protect Poppy. Protect the ring. Go. Now!"

Ivy didn't waste any more time. She grabbed Lex's hand with the other and dragged us to the back of the stage. We stood, and a part of me worried Ashley had lied, that as soon as we moved, any of the hundreds of Alberich's soldiers would see us. Or maybe, Alberich himself. The power emanated off him in thick clouds and wispy black tendrils that could likely choke the life out of us with barely any effort. I could imagine what horrible things he'd do to us, but he didn't seem fazed. He remained on stage, berating the queen, monologuing to an entranced fairy audience.

I followed Ivy behind the tents, weaving around bodies and tiptoeing to keep the sound of my movements to a minimum. I wasn't sure where we were going, just that we were connected, and Poppy clung to Carter by the neck. My legs trembled, and I couldn't get good traction on the slippery morning grass. Somehow, we climbed the hill to get out of the valley, and once we were far enough away from the fairies, we took off into a run.

I didn't have time to question if Ivy knew the way. I had to get free, back to my reality, back to my kingdom. I didn't belong here. The trees had tried to warn me, but I didn't listen.

The trees always know.

"Where's the child?" someone behind us shouted. "Find the child!"

Uh-oh.

Cover blown.

"Miri!" Lex said, glancing over his shoulder at me, the one with the shortest legs and the least impressive stride. "C'mon!"

I ran harder. Faster. If Ashley told the truth, this asshole couldn't cross over into the human realm. Which meant as soon as we got there, we'd be safe from him.

Dark curls of smoke swirled around me, choking the plant life into decaying dust, disintegrating whatever it found. Their agony echoed through me like ice under my skin, like pinpricks right into my brain. The rottenness surged in my veins and I stumbled, catching myself on my hands and knees with a loud grunt.

"Miri?" Lex's panicked voice forced me to my feet again, helping me to keep going. I just…I had to keep going. Keep breathing and keep running. *Don't look back. Anything except looking back.* I didn't want to know if Death was on my heels. It seemed better to greet the bitch by surprise.

The ruins crept up in the distance, and Ivy beelined for them, corralling the rest of us with her behind the wall, safe inside its crumbling barriers.

"We can't stay here," Lex panted.

I bent over at the waist and put my hands on my knees, gasping for air. This was the most cardio I'd done in years, and my heartbeat became a visceral thump I tasted in the back of my mouth. This, on top of experiencing the king's fury through my gift, made me want to fall over and never get up again.

"We need to get our heads on straight," Ivy said, resting both of her hands on her head while she tried to catch her breath. "We need to figure out where the fuck we're going."

"Ivy's right. We can't go circling the woods for another three hours," Carter said, still holding the silent Poppy in his arms.

The galloping sound of horse hooves loomed closer, and we shut up, backing into one of the dark corners to stay hidden.

"Did you see them?" asked a voice on the other side of the wall.

"No, I lost them in the tree line," another gruff tone replied.

"You definitely saw him with the girl?" The first voice moved toward us, and the sound of him getting off his horse made me take a deep, fearful inhale. "He had her. I'm sure of it."

Footsteps echoed in the night, right up on us now. The jingling of metal on armor bounced off the crumbling stone walls. I backed farther into the darkness, Lex's body hot next to me, Ivy on the other side, and Carter behind us with the child. Alberich's darkness had cast out most of the sunlight, making this corner particularly well-covered. Maybe, with a bit of luck...

"They could have gone anywhere."

The sounds came closer. So...so...close.

I held my breath, terrified that if I let myself exhale, they'd hear it. I prayed I was the only one who could tell how hard my heart beat. One of the guards entered the doorway at the far end, his body angled away from us so he hadn't noticed us yet.

This is it. It's all over now.

"Javier. Norton," someone else hissed. A woman. The guard turned and walked away. "What are you two idiots doing this far away from the village?"

Ivy stiffened and grabbed my arm, widening her eyes as if she recognized the voice.

Siobhan, she mouthed.

"We chased some humans this way," the guard inside said.

"What humans?" Siobhan sounded pissed. "Where are they?" She paused for a reply that didn't come. "Well?"

"We lost them," the other guard added.

"Get your ass back on that horse and follow me to base, or I'll tie you to that tree right now and flog you for desertion. How do you suppose our king would react to that?"

"It isn't desertion," one of them snapped.

"We were chasing someone," the other said. "They had the child."

"I don't care what you thought you were chasing," Siobhan sneered. "Let's go!"

Three sets of horses galloped away, and we waited a long time, much longer than was probably necessary, to finally speak.

"That was Siobhan," Ivy said.

"Did she know we were here?" I asked.

"Yes. She spoke to me." Ivy pointed to her temple. "She told me to take Poppy and get out of here. Go back to our realm and stay there."

"Why is she helping us if she's working for the king?" Carter rubbed at the back of his head, keeping his voice low.

"I don't know," Ivy murmured. "She didn't have time to explain, but I don't think she's switched sides. She told me to protect the child."

Carter hitched Poppy higher on his hip, and she twisted her little hands around his neck, tears streaming down her cheeks.

"Hey," I said, rubbing the back of my finger over her puffy cheek to comfort her. "You okay?"

She pinched her eyes together and tucked herself into Carter's chest. He rubbed his hand over her back, and a part of me fell in love with her then. Her life had been fucked-up by these monsters. She belonged with us. I knew it. I could feel it. The same way I belonged to my spouses and them to me.

"Shhh," Carter said. "It's okay. You're okay now. We'll keep you safe."

"Um." Lex ran his hands through his hair and pursed his lips. "I hate to be the heartless prick here."

"I doubt that," Ivy added.

"We can't take the kid with us." Lex focused his attention on Carter and me.

Ivy sighed and rubbed at the spot on her neck.

"What?" Carter furrowed his brows, seemingly confused.

Lex took a deep breath and straightened his shoulders. "You need to leave her here."

"No fucking way." Carter held her tighter.

"Carter," Lex cut in.

"I'm not leaving her," he said. "And that's it."

"The king will never stop looking for her," Lex said.

I couldn't believe I was hearing this from him, the guy I used to spend my nights planning a family with under the stars. We had wanted lots of children, and he'd never cared if we adopted; he couldn't be this apathetic about her. She obviously needed our help.

"She's human," I said.

"She's none of our business," Lex added.

"She became our business when we got here," I argued.

"And what the fuck are we going to do with her when we get back to reality?" Lex raised his eyebrows, his hands on his hips, big hazel eyes darting between us. "Ivy and I *cannot* show up with a child out of nowhere. Neither can you, Miri." He looked at Carter. "Chicago? You think your brand could take an illegitimate daughter?"

"That's not the fucking point," Carter snapped. "And you know it."

"I'm not saying Lex is right," Ivy said, "but I'm not saying he's wrong."

Carter hung his mouth open as he stared at her, half appalled, half shocked. "Weeds?"

"It's something to think about." Ivy rubbed at the spot on her neck. "Siobhan knows we have her. Right now, she's helping us. But that could change. If it does...If he gets loose, he'll come for us first."

"He'll have to get out of this realm," I said. "You still have the ring. Right?"

Ivy held it up, showing it to us. "But that can't be the only way for him to get out. Millions of years of history exist in this realm. I'm certain there are other keys."

"We can't leave her here to fend for herself," Carter hissed at the same time I said, "I won't leave her here alone."

Silence fell and, for the first time since we were reunited, a canyon widened between us. Now I stood with my hand in Carter's, staring down the loves of my life.

"I don't know how to explain that we should care about a child that needs our help. This isn't up for discussion," Carter sneered. It was the first time I'd heard him talk to Ivy or Lex like that since Midsummer. "The queen gave her to *me* to protect. Not either of you." His jaw hardened, and he shifted focus between the two of them. "And thank God for that. Because if this were *my* child, I'd sooner trust it to a pack of wolves. At least she might get some scraps before they tore her to pieces." Carter gripped my hand tighter. "Now, let's *all* get the fuck out of here before you both say something that makes me hate you."

With the little girl that had captured both of our hearts, he led me out of the ruins.

We walked quietly along the trail, following Ivy and Lex ahead of us. The forest looked as barren as it sounded, the previous signs of life silenced by whatever darkness the king had brought upon them.

That voice.

It gave me chills to remember it. I'd known it from somewhere. It unlocked something in my brain, in my heart, some deeply hidden secret I didn't realize I'd been carrying.

Dark eyes flitted through my mind's eye. But whose? I'd never seen eyes like that before.

"This way," Ivy said, pointing to the distance ahead. "We're almost there."

Both the times we'd done this, I couldn't tell when we'd crossed in and out of Faerie. Of course, the first time I'd been hammered on fairy wine, and the second, I'd been chasing my dead parents. Now, a shimmering force field wavered up ahead, almost like the king's presence had sucked up all the magic that had once kept the barrier invisible. It barely held itself together on whatever energy it could sponge up from the remaining forest.

A galloping sound from behind stopped me as a strange unease bubbled in my chest. Something ancient and powerful gained on us. Old magic. Dark magic. The rotten taste of smoke and despair inched over my tongue and down my throat.

The king.

"Go," I said. "Run!"

Ivy and Lex took off, Carter quick on their heels. My legs pumped as fast as they could, but even then, my feet were anvils. I couldn't stop what was about to happen...I shouldn't. I needed to feel it. I needed to see it, to see...*him.*

Ivy disappeared behind the force field. Lex next. Carter and the child went after them. But this tightening inside made me stop and turn around. The magic took me, holding me in place, locking my knees until they wouldn't move even if I wanted them to. A thrum reverberated in my molecules, rushing in my veins like pure adrenaline. I *willed* the woods around me.

Grow. Grow. Grow. Grow.

Yes, it answered. *Yes, yes, yes.*

It was exhausted from Alberich's dark energy, and it needed time to heal, but this, it could do for me, for us, if I helped. And I could. I fed it my energy, willing the lingering vegetation to burst forth. I pushed everything I had left into it, knowing the woods and I could protect my family. We had to. We were the only ones who could.

I saw him up ahead, galloping in the distance, seated proudly on his horse. If I didn't stop him, he'd get through the boundary with us.

I dropped to my knees and dug my fingertips in the cool dirt, shoving my life force into the earth as hard as I could. A scream tore out of my body like I could drive more of myself into the forest with the exclamation. Hot, sticky liquid dripped down my chin, copper coating my tongue, and I didn't know if it was blood or tears or both, but it didn't matter.

It ripped out of me, everything I had left, like an electrical current or my very own soul.

Together, the woods and I grew a barrier of thistles, thick thorny blood-red patches all the way around Faerie, protecting the barrier in every direction, protecting the human realm from this intruder, this villain.

"Miri!" shouted someone from behind me. It sounded vaguely

familiar, but nothing could stop me. I had to do this. I had to make it as difficult as possible for him to follow us.

"Miri, come on!" said another voice, another person I knew.

"*Miriam*," a deeper tone called from *in front* of me, from the king. "*Little Thistle*. It's lovely to see you again."

That name...*Little Thistle*...It startled me. I jerked my head up and connected with his chaotic, hypnotizing gaze. Recognition blasted through me, punching me right in the gut.

I know him...from the crash.

The thought passed through my mind as a heavy hand landed on my shoulder and yanked me backward, out of Faerie and away from the king.

"Fucking hell, Princess!" Lex's wide, panicked eyes came into view, his hair tussled around his head like a halo. "You're bleeding."

"Is she all right?"

They talked around me, but I could only focus on an obnoxious chattering sound. What was that noise? It needed to stop; it was driving me mad. As I moved my mouth to say so, I realized the chattering was my teeth and the annoying sound was coming from me.

Lex wiped at my chin with the sleeve of his shirt, and it came away bloody.

"Shit," I said. "Am I bleeding?" I clawed at my face. My nose. And my eyes. And my ears.

"What did you do?" Ivy said.

"I stopped him," I muttered, though that didn't answer her question.

"No, Miri," she said, glancing up at something above me. "What...the fuck....did you do?"

I followed her gaze to a ten-foot tall thistle bush with flowers a deep ruby color that matched the liquid on my face. It sprawled for three meters in either direction before disappearing into the ether. Into Faerie. But it was the density of the thorns that made me pause. I'd wanted the king to stay out, and it would be a massive pain to get through them.

Had I trapped them in?

Had I trapped us out?

Could anyone get through it anymore?

"Let him come after us now," I muttered with a silly grin.

As the rest of my energy faded and the world went dark, I had only one thought.

Thistles...the flower of House Stuart.

25

CARTER

The last time I'd stumbled out of these woods, I'd been beat up, exhausted, and bruised from the night before. This time was no exception. We were covered in dirt from the race out of Faerie, and I reeked like sex and wine and sweat.

Poppy hung around my neck like a baby koala, her tiny body so fragile in my arms, I'd thought I'd break her in half with every step I took. Lex carried Miri, who had gone unconscious after building that wall of thistles. The rest of us didn't speak. We walked through town, covered in filth and shock, avoiding the strange looks from the townspeople. When we got to the B&B, Lex waited around back with Miri while Ivy and I went inside to see if Bill had given away our room.

He took one look at us and dropped his newspaper to the ground.

"Bleeding Christ," he said. "I thought you'd gone home."

Ivy didn't answer him. She just held the key up by her index finger. "Is our room still available?"

He looked from her to me and then to Poppy in my arms.

"Who's that?" He nodded at the girl.

"My niece," I answered, my voice sounding strange and foreign even to myself. Perhaps that was the shock, too.

"I don't remember you having a child before." Bill furrowed his brows, staring at her.

"Well, we have a child now," Ivy snapped, her tone more forceful. It brought his attention back to her. "Do you have a room for us or not?"

He paused, the urge to debate flickering behind his gaze. He had questions about the girl, and based on the conversation we'd had with him a few days ago, he must have suspected what she was. But he didn't say anything. He just nodded and gestured to the stairs.

"I was going to give you another two days. If you didn't come back, I planned to send your stuff to the address on your check-in form."

Ivy gave him one of her infamous death stares before forging ahead, but when I passed Bill, he put an arm on my bicep to stop me.

"If that's a fairy child, you'd do well to put it back where you found it before they come for you." There was no mistaking the terror in his eyes, the sheer unwillingness to be a part of whatever fairy scheme we'd hatched and survived.

I narrowed my eyes at him. "Come on, Bill. Does she look like a fairy child?"

He swallowed, his Adam's apple bobbing at the movement. "I don't rightly know what she looks like. But not a person around here will go against the fairies. I'm not looking for trouble, if you take my meaning."

Yeah, loud and clear. If anyone came looking for her, he'd turn us over in a heartbeat. I clapped him on the shoulder with my free hand. "Thanks for the hospitality, my dude."

I followed my wife up the stairs to our room, finding Lex laying Miri out on the far bed once I got inside. I placed Poppy's sleeping form on the couch and covered her with a blanket, deciding to let her rest before I woke her for a bath. She was as muddy and bloody as the rest of us. Maybe I'd get a little food in her, too. I didn't like how thin she was. I could feel each of her bones through that flimsy thing the fairies called a dress.

"Carter," Ivy said, drawing my attention up to them.

Now that we were mostly safe, a hot jab of rage twisted through my gut. They'd wanted to leave her. They'd wanted to leave a *child* alone to face that monster by herself. I didn't know they could be so cruel.

"We need to make a game plan," Ivy said.

"Game plan?" I asked, venom lacing my tone. "Since when do you care?"

"C'mon," she pleaded, softening her stern eyes. "I didn't say we should leave her. Just that we needed to think it through."

"Technically, *I* said we should leave her," Lex whispered, yanking his shirt over his head. "I stand by that."

"You're a heartless prick," I said.

"You're goddamned right," he snarled. "What if you put her in more danger by bringing her here, huh? She's human, but the fairies live differently than we do. Is she going to be able to adapt? Is she even safe on this side of the realm? You don't know."

"The queen wouldn't have given her to me if she didn't think I'd protect her." I crossed my arms, infuriated that he'd leave a child defenseless.

"You were the closest body." Lex rolled his eyes. "The queen would have given her to anyone with a pulse."

That set me off. I didn't know why I felt so protective over Poppy, maybe because she reminded me of Lizzie, but I wouldn't stand for Lex talking about her like that. I launched myself at him, shoulder to his gut, taking him down on the mattress behind him. He growled and elbowed me in the chin, but I punched him in the solar plexus and made him buckle to the side.

"Hey," Ivy hissed, coming to stand at our side. "Knock that shit off right now. We've got more important things to do."

I shoved Lex's shoulder but rolled off him, sitting up at his side.

"It doesn't matter if we should have brought her or not. She's here now." Ivy stood in front of us with her hands on her hips, staring down her nose like a disapproving schoolmarm. She took a deep breath, calming her fury before she spoke again. "We've been gone twelve days. I've got ten voicemails from my academic adviser and fourteen from my mother. Now, we have a child to take care of. What do we do next?"

Neither of us said anything. My chin ached from Lex hitting me, and my pride throbbed from Ivy putting me in my place. I had no good ideas that didn't involve raging at everyone and everything.

"She can't come back with us," Lex said. "Even if we could explain her away as an adopted niece or something, we're too public facing. The shit will raise eyebrows."

"Not to mention what will happen if Alberich ever gets out of Faerie." Ivy sighed and shook her head.

"She needs to be hidden," I agreed. "At least for a little while."

"If he comes looking, he'll come right for us." Ivy rubbed her hands over her eyes, just as exhausted as I was.

"*When* he comes looking," Lex corrected.

"We don't know that," I said. "He'll have to get through Miri's thistles first and then the force field he's supposedly cursed from entering."

"You still have the ring, Ivy?" Lex turned to her, but she opened her mouth and shook her head, patting down her clothes.

"Fuck." She turned her pockets inside out and looked around the room, checking the floor.

"Are you serious?" Lex threw his hands up in the air.

"I had it. I swear I did." She pushed her hair behind her ears. "You saw it at the ruins."

"Did you drop it?" Like he didn't believe her, Lex also patted her down, coming up short.

"How?" Ivy shook her head, astounded and confused. "It was only a short walk from there."

"It doesn't matter," I said. "If he doesn't find the ring, he'll find some other way to get out. Like you said, there have to be other methods, especially if he's got Siobhan."

Lex looked at Poppy and ran his hands through his hair, picking at something brown and cruddy stuck on the strands. "Let's table this. We need showers and sleep."

"Right." Ivy shucked her jeans down to the ground and pulled her shirt over her head. "Ladies first." She pointed at the two of us before heading to the bathroom. "Don't kill each other while I'm gone."

I pursed my lips and refocused on my husband, if I even wanted to call him that. I understood where he was coming from, but I did not agree. My mom used to tell me if someone asked for my help and I refused, that said more about me than it did about them, especially if that person was a child. The silence stretched on forever, the inches between our bodies and hearts turning to miles.

"Do you remember the promise we made in the woods all those years ago?" he finally said, his voice low and gravelly while he spoke. "The one the morning after Midsummer, where we said we would be each other's home, that we would try to make it work."

"Yeah," I murmured.

"I decided that day all of you were mine," he said. "*My* husband, *my* wives, forever."

I thought about the morning he'd taken me in the gym—how he'd owned me, how he'd made me promise to come home and forced me to tell him I was his.

His, his, his.

"I had visions of the four of us at Miri's cottage together," he went on. "Raising our children. Growing old as a family."

I wanted that more than anything in the world, and maybe Lex read this on my face because he slung an arm around my shoulders and pulled me close, touching our foreheads together.

"Hear me now, Chicago." He spoke slowly, his lips moving millimeters away from mine. "I will do whatever I have to do to protect what's mine. *You* are mine. *Miri* is mine. *Ivy* is mine. If it means doing things you don't like, so be it."

He kissed me, hard, deep, and all-consuming. I almost wilted for him, almost sank to my knees and begged him to fuck me to prove it. But I didn't. I curled my fingers into the mattress under me to keep me rooted to the spot.

"Because you're right," he continued. "I am heartless. I am soulless. Someone has to be."

I didn't believe Lex when he said things like that. Yes, he loved us, and he'd only tried to leave Poppy behind because he wanted to protect us, maybe even protect her. But he believed himself to be a decrepit, horrible monster, unworthy of love, all that terrible shit his dad put inside his head. But Lex's heart beat hard and pure, just like the rest of us.

He kissed me again before rising to join our wife in the shower. I watched him saunter away, the gait of a man used to people doing what he wanted. It was an invitation for me to join them, maybe take both of them if I chose.

I sat there and stared at Miri and Poppy, ruminating and brooding. I protected what was mine, too, and the second the queen shoved Poppy into my arms, I felt it between her and I. That little girl belonged to me, now.

Mine to protect.

Mine to raise.

Mine to love.

Because I'd brought her here, to this land of strangers, and I owed it to her.

After Lex and Ivy returned from the shower, I took one myself while they attempted to get Miri clean with a washcloth. Then I woke Poppy and took her to the bathroom, sitting her down on the toilet while I filled the tiny tub with warm water. Ivy came with me, just in case Poppy didn't feel comfortable being alone with me.

"How you feeling?" I kneeled in front of her and Ivy sat on the edge of the tub, her hand playing in the water while it filled.

Poppy curled in on herself, her arms between her knees and a vacant look in her eyes. The thousand-yard stare, like she'd lived a million lives in the span of one night. She looked at me, but she didn't really *see* me.

"Ashley told me your name is Poppy," I said. "Do you like to be called that?"

She gave me the smallest nod before glancing down at her lap. Tears streamed over her cheeks, and she wiped them away, sniffling and wincing.

"My name's Carter," I said. "This is my friend, Ivy."

"I can't go home anymore," Poppy whispered. "Can I?" It was so soft I almost didn't understand her.

"No," I said. "I'm sorry."

Poppy nodded, understanding far too much for her young age.

"How old are you?" Ivy asked.

"Ten," she said. "I think."

Ten? She looked like she couldn't have been more than five.

Barely ten. And she'd lived through the death of her mother and banishment from her home. Now she was in a different realm with people she had no reason to trust, truly alone for the first time in her young life.

"Thank you for saving me," she said.

I couldn't resist anymore. I pulled her into my arms and hugged her. She wrapped her tiny arms around my neck and hugged me back while sobs racked her body. My heart broke for her.

Maybe Lex had been right. Maybe it would have been better to leave her in her own world with her own people.

No. She was a child, a human child. She needed a human adult to care for her. That person was me, at least for right now. I agreed with

Lex that she couldn't come back to the States with us. I didn't know where we'd hide her; I just knew we had to keep her safe.

"Let's get you clean, huh?" Ivy said. "Hold your arms up." Poppy did, and Ivy lifted the soiled white garment over her head, handing it to me afterward. I tossed it in the garbage. No way the dirt stains would come out, and even if they did, ten-year-olds didn't wander around in shifts these days. Ivy helped her into the tub, and she sat, allowing my wife to run a washcloth over her muddy shoulders and tear-streaked cheeks.

"Where's your father, Poppy?" I leaned against the sink, facing them, crossing my arms as I considered our options.

She shrugged. "Don't have one, I guess."

I nodded. "The queen never spoke about him? Or none of the other fairies?"

"No." She shook her head. "Do you think he hurt them? My lady? Ashley and the others?"

Ivy bit her bottom lip and looked up at me, maybe seeking guidance about what to say.

"I don't know." It was the truth; I didn't see any reason to lie.

"It's because of me," she muttered.

"What?" Ivy balked. "No, it's not."

"Yeah, it is." Poppy's eyes filled with tears again, sliding down her cheeks in terrible, tiny blobs. "It's because of what I am. What I can do."

"What do you mean?" I asked.

Poppy covered her face and sobbed again. This time, Ivy pulled her into her lap, soaking wet, and wrapped a towel around her shoulders. My wife hugged her and rocked her until she calmed.

"Poppy," Ivy said. "Listen to me. This is not your fault. The king did this. His actions are his own, okay?"

"If I didn't exist," Poppy whispered, "he wouldn't have come for me. I am the Great Gift, the foretold."

"That's not your fault either," I added. In this realm, prophecies didn't exist outside of fairy tales and fiction. If they did, no one believed them, certainly not enough to rage after a ten-year-old child.

Poppy either didn't believe me or she had gotten tired of arguing because she sank against Ivy's torso and closed her eyes, hugging her like it was the first time Poppy had ever known affection. Then her eyes snapped open, completely white, like that waitress at the coffee shop. Ivy's eyes did the same, the pupil and iris gone. I reached out to shake Ivy, maybe to break this trance, but she grabbed my wrist and dug in her nails.

One second, we were in the bathroom. The next, we were somewhere dark, surrounded by sand. City lights twinkled in the distance, but blinding spotlights burned my retinas up close, and I had to put my hands up to block them out. We were high in the air, standing on a platform.

No, not a platform. A decaying tan statue.

"Eh!" voices shouted from the ground. They screamed in a language I didn't understand, probably telling us to get down from here. And that was when I realized where we were. We stood on top of the Sphinx sculpture in Egypt. I'd never been there before, but even from this angle, there could be no denying what it was.

"Holy shit," I said.

"Are we in Egypt?" Ivy asked, holding Poppy tighter in her arms. "Poppy, what is this?"

The little girl tightened her grip on me, wincing her eyes against the wind, and in the next blink, we were back in the bathroom. Poppy shivered, and Ivy slumped on the side of the tub, closing her eyes as she readjusted to the present. My head fogged, and I had to put a hand out on the wall to steady myself.

"Poppy." Ivy put the girl on the floor in front of her, setting her hands on the child's shoulders so she could get eye-to-eye with her. "Did you take us to the Sphinx?"

She nodded. "That's why he wants me. But I can only go places I've seen before."

"You've been to Egypt?"

"Siobhan has," she said. "She showed me a picture. It's one of the only things I know about this realm."

I met Ivy's gaze, an expression on her face like we were both thinking the same thing. This was a problem. She couldn't go zapping through the human world, appearing and disappearing at will. That would get her locked up or killed. And if the king ever got out, it wouldn't take him long to find the only person on earth who could teleport.

I kneeled in front of Poppy and rubbed my hands over her upper arms, trying to warm her and soothe her. "I need you to make me a promise."

She gave me a small nod.

"Don't tell anyone about this gift," I said, keeping my tone light and casual. I didn't want to scare her. "Lex and Miri are okay, but no one else. You keep it to yourself, and don't show it to anyone."

Poppy pulled her lips between her teeth, looking back and forth between the two of us with wide eyes.

"Just until we know it's safe," I added. "Okay?"

She nodded, and I held up my pinky for her.

"This is the first thing you gotta learn about the human world. Pinky swears are the real deal. You can't break a pinky swear."

"Why?" Poppy said, her voice trembling. "What will happen?"

"Nothing serious," Ivy said. "But that person might not want to do a pinky swear with you again. You'll lose their trust. Understand?"

That seemed to resonate, and Poppy wrapped her finger around mine, giving me another nod.

"Pinky swear," she said.

We got Poppy clean enough for bed and, when we went back to our room, Lex had returned with some clothing options from Bill's lost and found pile. I put her in an oversized hoodie and sweatpants, determined to keep her warm through the night. Then she crawled into my lap and held on to me until she fell asleep again.

"She can teleport," I told Lex once I was certain Poppy was truly out.

"What the fuck did you just say?" He widened his eyes and blinked, perhaps trying to keep up.

"She took us to the top of the Sphinx." Ivy crawled into the empty bed and flipped the covers over her lap.

"Like...the Sphinx in Egypt?" Lex said.

"Yeah," I said.

"Oh." He pretended to be nonchalant. "How was that?"

"Unseasonably warm," I said. "But you know, nothing like ripping through time and space in the middle of the night."

"Fucking hell." Lex pinched the bridge of his nose and sighed.

"It's why they're fighting over her," Ivy explained.

"Ashley told us our magic, the magic Siobhan gifted us, it's elemental." I ran a finger over Poppy's hair, brushing it back from her face. "But hers is from time and space. That's what she meant."

Lex glanced back and forth between us. "She needs us...doesn't she?"

"If the queen is harmed, and the king is hunting her," I started. "Yeah, she needs us a lot."

He took a deep breath, glancing over his shoulder to where Miri was still passed out. "You think she's going to be okay?"

I nodded. "Our Juliet is strong."

"And stubborn." Ivy let out a little laugh.

"Let's talk in the morning," Lex said. "Once we've had a chance to sleep."

Ivy took him up on that, turning out the light next to her bed and hunkering down under the covers. Her soft breathing evened out in seconds, leaving me alone with our husband. This time, something different lurked behind his hazel gaze. Now, some sick version of adoration hit me low in the gut, and if I didn't know any better, I'd say Lex was *regarding* me—sitting here, holding a child in my arms.

It could *almost* be his child.

It could *almost* be his vision.

"Why are you looking at me like that, DC?" I murmured, readjusting Poppy on my chest so her head hit my sternum instead of my pec.

"You look entirely too fuckable," he said, shaking his head. "It isn't fair."

I snorted a laugh.

"I'm telling you this now." Lex shifted his hips in his seat, perhaps readjusting a hardening cock. "If you grow that"—he gestured to all of me—"into a dad bod, I'll never let you out of my bed. You understand me? Chicago, I'll fuck you every morning until you can't walk."

I chuckled harder. "Such things you say."

"You think I don't mean it? Bet me."

I shook my head at his audacity.

"Go on. Bet me."

"No, because then you'll do it out of spite."

He nodded and stood, gesturing to the bed. "Enough. Get some sleep. I'll stand guard for a bit."

"Poppy and I can take the couch."

"I wasn't asking," he said. "Take the child and get in bed with our wife."

"Which one?" I teased.

"I don't care," he said, nudging me along. "Pick one."

Figuring Poppy might feel the most comfortable with Ivy if she woke up before I did, I put her down in the middle of the mattress and scooted in on the other side, tucking the covers around the three of us. Maybe Poppy's presence reached some instinctual maternal part of Ivy because she rolled toward us, wrapped an arm over the girl's tiny torso, and tucked her in close. Poppy let out a contented sigh and relaxed into the touch.

The sight of Ivy cuddling a child to her, the thought of sleeping next to the two of them all night, protecting them with my body and my presence and my warmth, it woke every alpha male caveman instinct I'd ever had. I tried not to melt. I tried not to be a stupid fucking sap. But I was still a sentimental shit, even after everything I'd been through.

They said I'd been protective over Lizzie?

Shit, that hadn't come close to this.

I thought about the picture Lex painted earlier—the cottage in the woods with our children, growing old together.

Come home to us, he'd made me promise. *In the end, it's us.*

I wanted that more than I'd ever wanted anything in the world, including acting, including Hollywood. When I wrapped an arm over both of them and pulled them into me, I swore I'd give it all up to keep this.

Lex's vision had become *my* vision.

Now, Poppy was a part of that, too.

26

MIRI

The memory started the same. I was in the back seat, ducking down on the ground to keep the photographers from taking pictures of me. I didn't like seeing myself in the magazines. I didn't like it when they said things about me.

"Drive faster," my father shouted. His big brown eyes were wild, looking around as he struggled to keep me hidden.

"Gerald," Mum's panicked voice muttered. "We're already going too fast."

"We can lose them, Emma," Da replied. I sank farther and put my hands over my ears, trying to breathe through the hot slice of terror in my chest. I hated the people who chased us. Why couldn't they leave us alone? Why did they have to do this to me? We were normal people like everyone else.

The noise was the part that haunted my nightmares, the sickening crunch of metal on metal as the car hit something hard and impenetrable. The world went topsy-turvy. In my memories, I blacked out and woke up outside the car.

The police had never been able to figure out how I'd done it, and I'd never remembered.

But this time...

This time, I kept my eyes open in the middle of the chaos. Everything circled around me in slow motion. The items from my mother's purse hung in the air like outer space. Her arms and legs were suspended like a roller coaster. I couldn't move, only hang there and marvel at the spectacle of it all.

Then I met a pitch-black gaze set in a face with a dark beard and matching hair. At the time, I didn't know this person, but he reached inside the car while it tumbled to pull me from it. The moment he touched me, time sped up again. He yanked me out and wrapped me in his arms while the death trap whirled away from us, the sounds of my parents' breaking bodies punctuated by metal on asphalt.

He carried me to the side of the road and delicately laid me in the grass. The earth was warm despite the chill in the air, and the sun beamed brighter and hotter on this side of my near-death experience. The sky seemed more blue than ever, the trees more potent, everything just...more.

"What's happening?" I murmured, my voice weak with confusion.

"Shhh," the man said. "It'll be okay. It's all going to be okay now."

"Who are you?" I grabbed at the leather lapels on his black jacket, tugging him closer, keeping him there. "Please. I'm scared. Stay with me."

"Listen to me, Miriam."

How did he know my name?

"You won't remember this for a long time. But one day, you will." He brushed my curls out of my face as he frowned, his soft gaze radiating genuine sincerity. "And when you do, you'll know the time has come to return the favor."

"What favor?" I asked.

"I saved your life," he said. "Now you owe me."

I was so confused. I didn't know what he meant. He saved my life? I hadn't asked him to do that.

"Owe you?" I repeated.

"Yes, *Little Thistle*," he said. "You'll come to owe me quite a bit before we're through."

"Who are you?" I asked again, tears making my eyes burn, my heart racing at the thought that he planned to leave me here alone.

"Rest now." He pressed his warm, soft lips to my temple, and the world went dark around me.

When I came to, I remembered none of my encounter with the man in the black jacket. I lay in the grass ten yards away, staring into the lifeless gaze of my mother, hanging upside down in the car, her head bent at a wrong angle.

I wanted to cry.

I wanted to scream.

I wanted to yank them from the wreck and pray to a cruel, unyielding God to bring them back to life. Just bring them back. But unconsciousness took me again, and when I opened my eyes the next time, I was in a hospital bed with the entire world praying for my safe recovery.

When I woke, I was back in the room at the bed-and-breakfast in Killwater. Ivy and Carter slept across the room with Poppy between them, huddled together in the moonlight, their chests rising and falling in a slow, steady rhythm. Lex was on the couch, his arm bent over his eyes, deep breaths humming from his torso.

What day was it? What time? Where were we?

I checked my phone.

November 13.

I gasped and covered my mouth with my hand so I didn't wake anyone.

Twelve days.

We'd lost twelve days in those woods. Bleeding hell, it was a wonder Ivy and Lex could even sleep. They'd wanted to be back by the fifth at the latest. We'd overshot our landing by more than a week. My brain had gone fuzzy like I'd spent the last twelve days on a bender and sobered up on a stranger's couch in a country I'd never been to before. That wasn't too far from the truth.

I got out of bed and walked across the room, picking up Lex's smokes from the coffee table and lighting one as I went to my perch by the window to overlook the trees. After what had happened, they didn't hum the way they had when we'd gotten here. Instead, their silence deafened me with an aching tinnitus that almost screamed with its quietness.

Had I used all my magic on the thistle bushes? Or was the forest still healing from whatever the king had done to it?

I didn't know, and as I inhaled deeply on the cigarette, I decided I never wanted to know. I never wanted to come back here. I hated this place and all its wretched mystery.

I took another inhale and pinched the bridge of my nose, remembering the dream, the one with the king, the one where he saved me from the car accident and told me I owed him a life for a life. But it wasn't a dream, was it? It felt more like a memory. It *had* to be a memory.

I knew it deep in my gut. That was the truth. That was how I'd made it out of the car alive. That was how I didn't have a scratch on me. All this time, I'd been right. All this time, the world had tried to gaslight me into thinking I'd survived the wreck by circumstance. I must have been awake, they told me. I must have crawled out. I'd insisted I hadn't. I never would have guessed it was because a fairy king saved my life. If he hadn't, I would have been crushed in that tin metal can along with the rest of my family.

And now you owe me one.

You'll come to owe me quite a bit before we're through.

What was that supposed to mean? Owe him what?

A life.

What life? Mine? Why didn't he take it when he had the chance? And more importantly...what would I tell the others?

The thought filled my stomach with sawdust. They already had enough to worry about with Poppy and what to do next. They didn't need this drama. They didn't need to know I might be accidentally in an arrangement with the demented king of the fae.

Was I? Did it count if I'd been a child and hadn't consented? What were the fairy rules around entering into an agreement without the full knowledge of all parties involved? I hadn't asked for him to save me. What choice was there if I was never given one to begin with? He had been cast out of the human realm at the time. How, then, could he have been there to save me?

It wasn't real, my rational brain said, reaching for any straw of doubt, any seed of dissent that could explain this away. *He planted it there when he made eye contact with you. He's manipulating you. It's not real.* I wanted to scream that it felt real. It explained everything I'd never been able to figure out, everything I'd always wondered.

I hated him for it. I hated him for giving me this glimpse, this sneak peek, without explaining himself. But that was the point, wasn't it? If, indeed, he was manipulating me, it was to his benefit to keep me questioning, to make me come to him for answers, to keep me barely satisfied, always hungry. If I were him, it was what I'd do.

I took a deep breath and calmed the rise of panic in my chest. He couldn't cross over into this realm. Not only was he cursed, but I'd also grown the thickest patch of thistle thorn bushes in existence. It would take them eons to get through it.

As long as he didn't find the ring.

We were safe for now.

I expected Lex to hear me get up and move around; he was the closest. But a soft, feminine hand landed on my shoulder before she reached for my cigarette to stab it out. Lost in my thoughts, I'd let it burn down to the filter.

"I'm sorry," she whispered as she sat down facing me, "about Poppy in the woods."

I cleared my throat, remembering she'd taken Lex's side when it came to bringing the child with us.

"You both were right," she said. "Siobhan wanted us to protect her, to bring her here." A pause before she added. "But you know what this means, right?"

I took a deep breath and let it out slowly.

"We're in this," she continued, "for better or worse. Whatever was going on with the queen and the king, we now have the biggest chess piece."

"We've been in this since you did whatever you did with Siobhan," I said, my tone perhaps a little too curt.

"I know," she said, hanging her head, "but Siobhan covered for us when she could have handed us over. We can still break this spell. We have to be patient and play this out."

I wanted to be vengeful. I wanted to blame Ivy for all of this, to put the reasons for our unhappiness on her shoulders, but none of that was true. I'd known what we would find in those woods, and I'd gone anyway. I'd stolen a child and created a physical barrier around the entire fairy realm. I had no idea if it would keep them out, but I'd seen the rage on Alberich's face before Lex yanked me home.

I'd kicked open a hornet's nest.

"Thank you for protecting us." Ivy grabbed my hand, brushing the words of our scars up against each other. "I saw what you did. You're powerful...and incredibly hot."

I cracked out a laugh.

"Even with the bloody eyes and ears and mouth and whatnot."

I giggled harder.

"I love you, Miri," she said, leaning in to kiss me.

"I love you, too," I said against her mouth.

The anxiety in my chest lessened because, even if the king came for us, we had each other. And maybe with a bit of luck, and a bit of truth, and a bit of telepathy, and a bit of mother nature, we could take on whatever he brought with him.

I softened at Ivy's touch. Sure, Carter and I had our star-crossed friendship from California, and Lex had always been my prince of darkness. But I'd met and fallen for Ivy first. She'd come a long way from that naive, innocent teenager I'd seduced on our last night at Mount Oberon. Now, she was a powerhouse, an Amazonian warrior that could read minds and fuck like a goddess.

I may have two husbands, but there was only one woman who held my heart tenderly in her embrace. Our love wasn't like what I had with Carter and Lex, and I never wanted it to be. It was more precious and tender, built on our shared experience of being in the public light. Only I could know what it was like to be her, and only she could know what it was like to be me.

She held me close, massaging the back of my head with her talented fingers, and when I finally broke away, I leaned against her chest to borrow her strength.

"We're in this together," she murmured. "Please don't forget that."

Her words sounded prophetic, like perhaps she was the one that could see the future.

"I won't," I murmured. "I promise."

27

CARTER

The next morning, I woke to the sound of Lex talking to a small, childlike voice that I guessed was Poppy since she wasn't in bed with me anymore.

"Do you like eggs?" he asked.

"Guess so," she said. "Are they the same as in Faerie?"

"I think so. We'll check," he said. "And pancakes. I bet you like pancakes, too."

"What are pancakes?"

"They didn't have pancakes in Faerie either?" He blew out a disbelieving whistle. I didn't have to look at him to know he was shaking his head. "You've been missing out, kid."

"We liked to eat roasted boar and salted fish for breakfast." She said it like she ached for that very same thing.

Fucking. Yuck.

"Sure," Lex said, his tone dripping with the same disgust I felt. "If you're into that sort of thing. But when I was ten, I liked French toast the best."

"When Lex was ten," Ivy said, rolling over to prop herself up

245

against the headboard, "he used to sneak his eggs under the table to his dog."

Lex gasped and held a finger to his lips, glancing down at Poppy with a smile. "You see? Ivy can't be trusted with secrets."

"Don't worry, I still haven't told your au pair." Ivy shot him a grin and winked.

"What's that?" Poppy asked, glancing between us. "Au pair?"

"It's someone who takes care of you," I said.

"Like you?" She raised her eyebrows, expectation dripping from every syllable. The question hung between us because we hadn't officially discussed this yet. "Are you going to take care of me now?" She seemed unsure and hesitant. Who could blame her? We'd brought her here with no plan and no idea of what to do next.

"No matter what, Poppy," I said, swinging my feet to the side so I could stand and walk closer. "We'll always make sure you're safe. Okay?"

She nodded and frowned. It wasn't the answer she was looking for, but it was the only one I could give her. I agreed with Lex and Ivy. She couldn't come back with us to the States. If she did, she had to stay hidden. She had to stay with someone unconnected to any of us, somewhere Alberich wouldn't think to look if...*when*...he came searching.

"Thank you," she said again, her voice small and hushed.

"Don't mention it." Lex chucked her chin with his fist, giving her his classic charismatic wink.

The whole scene warmed my heart, and I again hated the fact we couldn't bring her home. We'd spent the last two years apart, but being together again reminded me why we were given this gift to begin with. *We* were soul mates, all of us. *We* were each other's home. We'd promised so long ago that it seemed like lifetimes had passed since then.

Were we really so different from those college students in the woods? I looked down at the scars on my hand and reminded myself it hadn't even been half a decade. We'd made a vow that night, and we had the proof etched into our skins. We were already committed to each other, and in the end, it was the four of us.

I had to believe that. I had to believe Lex's vision would come true because if I didn't, I'd be sucked down into misery and I simply would not have that. We would end up together or so fucking help me...

"Breakfast's here." Miri came into the room carrying a tray of coffee and a few plates of food.

My stomach growled. Loudly.

"Carter's *always* hungry," Lex said to Poppy.

"That's right," I said, rubbing at my belly while I hovered over Miri's shoulder. "A never-ending pit. Whatcha got, Juliet?"

"Let the girl pick first, Romeo," she said, shielding the tray with her body.

Poppy looked over the items on the plate but ultimately decided on an apple and sat down.

"That's it?" Lex said. "Here, try this." He handed her a cinnamon roll, but she shook her head and clutched the apple tighter.

"No thanks. Just this."

"All right," he said. "Your loss. More for Carter."

That made her smile, at least.

Miri nodded to the alcove, gesturing for the rest of us to come with her so we could have a private conversation.

"You stay here and eat," Lex said to Poppy, rubbing a hand over her messy hair. "We need to have a grown-up talk, okay?"

Poppy sighed, scribbling a pen over a piece of loose-leaf paper. "Okay."

"We can't stay here," Miri said once we were in a circle far enough away from Poppy. "Bill is already asking when we're headed out."

We told Miri about Poppy's teleportation ability, how she'd taken Ivy and me on a wild carpet ride last night only to return with a tale of gifts from time and space.

"She's one of us," Miri said, her hands covering her mouth in shock. "She needs us. She belongs with us."

"Are you volunteering to take her back to grandmother's house?" Lex raised an eyebrow.

"Well, no." Miri furrowed her brows.

"Exactly." Lex sighed.

"We need to figure out what to do next," I said. "We can't go home with her, but we can't stay here."

"Should we check on Smythe?" Ivy said.

"Smythe?" Lex asked.

"He lived in Faerie for how long?" she said. "He might know who her father is. He might know where to hide her."

Lex cleared his throat. "Yeah, or he might steal her to sell to the highest bidder." All our gazes snapped to him. "They kicked him out, remember? What would he do to get back in? Abduct the Great Gift and barter her to the king, perhaps?"

Ivy scratched her fingers over her X and clenched her features. "Well, I don't have any other ideas."

"I do." Lex licked his lips. "Last night, I made a few calls." He scrubbed his palms over his face, stalling.

"Out with it," I said.

"My uncle Dmitri."

I tried to swallow my reaction. Dmitri Romanov was the brother of the emperor of Russia and a powerful man in his own right, even before the country became a parliament. He was corrupt, sure. But from what I understood, he loved his nephew. Blood was the most important thing to a man in his position, and he'd doted upon Lex his entire life. Lex's mother used to say Marcus had been born a Fairfax, but Lex was Romanov blood through and through. I'd never asked him what that meant, but I could have guessed.

"Will that work?" Miri asked.

"I don't see why it wouldn't," Ivy agreed. "Would it be safe?"

"I think so, and if we go down the rabbit hole far enough," Lex continued, "she'd be completely removed from all of us, me included."

I didn't like the thought of Poppy in Russia alone with more strangers. Perhaps it was a risk to put so much distance between us. But what else were we going to do? The only people I could call were my family, and they'd be in just as much danger as she was if Alberich came to this realm.

I blew out a breath, the weight on my heart damn near a ton.

"Let's do it," Poppy said, snapping all our heads in her direction. "Russia, you say? Sounds nice. If your family is as kind as you, I'm sure I'll be safe."

I looked back at Lex, who glanced between the four of us. After my conversation with her in the bathroom last night, I knew there was more going on with Poppy. She may be ten years old physically, but mentally, she seemed as old as us. Time worked differently in the land of the fae. A night or two had been twelve days. How old was Poppy *really?*

Ten years in Faerie could be the equivalent of sixty here in the human realm. Did that mean that Poppy's mind was like a sixty-year-old? I didn't have the qualifications to answer that.

"Well?" Lex looked at me, followed by Miri and Ivy, like they were awaiting my permission to go forward with the plan.

"Let's go to Russia," I said.

"No," Lex said. *"I'll* take her to Russia."

I narrowed my eyes on him, digging in my heels. I trusted Lex; I did. But after his speech about protecting us last night, I wasn't about to leave her alone with him, either. I didn't think he'd do anything to hurt her, but I needed to know for sure. "I'm not leaving her until I know she's safe."

Lex's hazel gaze darted between mine before he ultimately relented and nodded. "As you wish."

ACT V

The best in this kind are but shadows,
and the worst are no worse if imagination amend them.
-Theseus, Act V, Scene 1

28

CARTER

RUSSIA

Saying goodbye to Ivy and Miri this time didn't wreck my heart like it did two years ago, probably because it wouldn't be long before I saw them again. I couldn't stay away; terrible things would happen if I did. We made plans to get together for Christmas next month, and even if it would take some massaging my schedule, I'd do whatever I could to make it happen.

Poppy, on the other hand, needed to disappear. Unlike my spouses, I truly didn't know when or if I'd see her again. I'd only met the child two days ago, but my fate had become as intrinsically linked to hers as it was to the others.

She kicked her feet over the seat of the charter plane Lex rented, resting her chin on her crossed arms as she watched the clouds go by out the window. She seemed lost in thought, biting her bottom lip between her teeth. Lex sat opposite us, his attention on his laptop as he caught up on school.

It had been a rough couple of days.

Hearing ghosts in the woods. Having sex in Faerie. Meeting a fairy queen only to have her ambushed by the fairy king. And now, we had a gifted child in our care.

What a fucked-up tale. Who would believe it? I barely could, and I'd lived it.

If Poppy was curious about anything she saw, she didn't mention it. She hardly said anything, which I figured was appropriate considering what she'd been through, what we'd all been through.

I tugged on a blond pigtail, and she looked at me.

"Flying is so long and boring," she said. "Why can't you show me a picture of where we're going and I'll take us?"

I laughed. "Remember our promise? No one can know. You need to stop using it so much."

She rolled her big doe eyes like I was an idiot. For only being ten, she'd read me like a book.

"I need to tell you something," I said.

"Okay." She seemed unsure.

"I'm really lucky," I said. "I never lose a game of cards. I once gambled twenty bucks and made over a million dollars in three hours."

She pulled her lips in between her teeth and looked down to the ground between us.

"Lex over there," I said. "He can make anyone tell him the truth. I mean anyone."

"Really?" She raised her eyebrows.

"Miri can make plants grow with her hands."

"Like the thistles," Poppy said, seeming to understand.

I nodded. "And Ivy can get inside anyone's head, know what they're thinking, talk to them."

She sighed and rubbed her tiny hands over her face.

"You're not alone," I said, trying not to overwhelm her. "We're special. No one else on earth is like us. At least, not that I know of."

"Which is why you need to keep it to yourself," Lex said. "My family, they're good people. They'll look after you. But they don't know about this."

"No one knows," I said.

"Okay," she said, exasperated. "I already pinky swore."

I snorted and wrapped my arm over her shoulders, pulling her closer to me, relishing the connection for as long as I had it left.

We stepped off the plane to a bitterly cold wind that pierced my wool jacket, flurries of snow floating in the air. Even in the middle of November, it was a true Russian winter morning. An older gentleman wearing a calf-length peacoat greeted us from in front of a limo. Two men flanked him on either side, their hands linked together in front of them. Another person stood immediately to his right, holding up an umbrella. Everything about him gave off a *don't-fuck-with-me* vibe, and I wondered if he was mob or government.

Would it have made a difference?

Lex warned me his uncle Dmitri was a brutal man, but loyal. Dmitri was his mother's brother, and blood meant everything in Russia. It had saved them after the fall of the Empire, and it had shuttled Lex's great-great-grandmother, Anastasia, and her little brother out of the country before they could be executed with the rest of their family. They'd risen up a few years later and taken back their birthright, reinstating a parliament with an honorific monarchy, kind of like England.

But Russia had always been more open about its corruption, and even if the Stuarts were no better than the Romanovs, the British royal family had shoved their heads in the sand about that bad PR ages ago. It didn't matter if Uncle Dmitri ran the mob or the royal household. They likely were one and the same here in the Motherland.

"Alexeeeiiii," Dmitri called, holding out his arms to either side. He looked exactly how one might imagine for a Russian mobster—thick gold chains hanging from his neck, big matching rings on his tattooed fingers, a tailored suit, and unblemished loafers. Eastern European aristocracy at its finest.

"*Djadja*," Lex said, embracing his uncle in a tight hug.

They spoke to each other in boisterous tones I didn't understand, undercut with laughs and claps on the shoulder. Dmitri pointed to me and Poppy.

"My friend, Carter," Lex said. "Like a brother to me. And his...
niece, Poppy."

"Niece?" Dmitri said, raising an eyebrow.

"Yeah," Lex said. "Niece."

Dmitri nodded, understanding dawning on him. "This is the
one?"

"This is the one," Lex agreed.

I held Poppy's hand tighter, and she ducked behind my leg when
Dmitri squatted to get a better look at her.

"She's skinny," Dmitri said. "She won't last the winter."

"Guess *Tjotja* will have to fatten her up, huh?" Lex teased,
shooting a wink in our direction.

"You know she will," Dmitri said. "I can't get that woman out of
the kitchen. She was born with flour on her nose." He muttered
something to himself in Russian that made everyone else laugh. One
of the guards opened the door to the limo, and Dmitri ducked to
climb inside. Lex looked back at us and nodded, gesturing for us to
get in with him.

Poppy sat tucked into my side, clutching a stuffed animal bear
Miri had purchased for her in Dublin. Lex and Dmitri talked to each
other in Russian, and based on the names Lex threw out, I assumed
they were catching up on family.

"You okay?" I asked Poppy, tugging on her jacket to grab her
attention.

She nodded, eyes glued to the white scenery outside. Winter was
well on its way in Moscow, and the farther we got out of the city, the
more barren the landscape became. I, too, found myself fascinated
by the sights. I'd never been here before.

After about an hour, the car finally stopped in front of a huge log
cabin estate with a maroon slate roof. It sat tucked into the woods,
like it was always meant to be a part of nature, like you could blink
and miss it if you drove past it on the highway. The bodyguard
opened the door for us and an older woman wearing an apron
barreled out of the house with her arms spread wide.

"Alexei, *malysh*," she said. "Come here. Come here."

Lex embraced his aunt and introduced us. Once Vera's eyes landed on Poppy, the anxious tension in my gut lifted. She had a glowing warm aura that gave off "momma bear" vibes. Nothing would come for her den of cubs while Vera stood watch. She muttered something in Russian before switching to English.

"Look at you." She put her hands on her hips and raised an eyebrow. "Do you like lemon bars?"

Poppy shrugged.

"Well, let's find out, huh?" She nodded toward her house and gestured for us to follow. We went, and I tried to keep my shit on straight at the decadence of this place. The foyer opened into a large great room on one side and a parlor on the other. Up ahead, the hallway led into a dining room, where I could only see half of the long table before it disappeared behind the wall. The chandelier overhead screamed opulence, somehow more shimmering and shiny than the one at Miri's Malibu dream house.

Vera shoved sugary sweet decadence in our direction and my amazement at their house disappeared in favor of watching Poppy's face light up as she took one. She licked her lips and smiled, sucking the lemon bits off her fingers.

"That was delicious, thank you," she said.

"There is more, my dear," Vera said. "Come. Come." Poppy followed her down the hallway and into the dining room, but Dmitri waved his fingers to beckon us down a long, dark corridor to our right. He pushed open a door on the left, a study judging by the enormous desk by the window and the two sofas facing each other in front of it. He walked to the dumbwaiter in the far corner so he could pour three shots of vodka before handing one to each of us and holding his up in the air.

"Zdrarovye!" he said. Lex and I echoed the sentiment and tipped them over our heads. I shivered as it burned down my throat, warming my belly, but it was the best vodka I'd ever had. Fresh from the source, or whatever.

"Tell me," Dmitri said, lowering into a big recliner next to one of the couches. "Where did this child come from?"

"Her family abandoned her." Lex sat on the couch next to his uncle as he spoke. "Carter's all she has left."

Dmitri nodded and reached for a cigar, clipping the end before offering it to Lex. He did the same to another and handed it to me. Cigars usually made me want to vomit, but I couldn't politely refuse. I didn't want to piss off Uncle Dmitri before we'd secured his help. When he lit it, I puffed on it and swallowed down my reflex, pretending not to be bothered.

"You are a fancy TV star, yeah?" Dmitri lit his cigar and leaned back in the seat. "Why isn't she going home with you?"

"Her family was in big to some asshole calling himself King Alberich," Lex explained before I could say anything.

Dmitri rolled his eyes, muttering something in Russian that sounded demeaning. "Every day, a new idiot comes up with something ridiculous to call himself. King Alberich." He made a noise of disgust. "Figures."

"We need to keep her safe," Lex said, "and hidden until we can deal with him."

Dmitri rolled the cigar between his index finger and his thumb. "Deal with him, how?"

"We're still working on that," I cut in.

Dmitri bit the end of his cigar and inhaled on it before saying something in Russian that made Lex's attention snap up, something meant for me not to understand. Lex flashed his uncle a devilish, charming grin and winked, answering in the same language, purposely excluding me.

Dmitri gazed back and forth between us before he laughed and clapped his knee, leaning forward so he could choke and wheeze even harder. I narrowed my eyes and opened my mouth to question what was going on, but Lex shook his head to stop me.

"I'll hide her as long as I can," Dmitri said, wiping at his eyes, finally calming. "She will be safe with me. You have my word. No harm will come to her under my watch."

"Thank you, *Djadja*," Lex said. "Please let me know how I can repay you."

"Bahhhhh," Dmitri said, waving him away. "We're family. Blood is more important than debt, yeah?" He tapped his cigar and looked back at us. "Now...tell me. Are you still dating that beautiful English princess?"

Lex laughed, and the conversation drifted to other things, my initial discomfort easing. Dmitri and Vera seemed like kind people, even if Lex assured me they were George and Evelyn Washington without the need to hide their evil deeds from a public that adored them. The public already knew (or suspected) the Romanovs were dirty.

When I found Poppy playing dolls with one of Lex's cousins, I lost the rest of my opposition. I believed Dmitri when he gave me his word she'd be safe. And I believed Vera had that spark that meant she'd mother anything that needed it, whether they wanted her nurturing or not.

Poppy needed it in a big way.

"You doing okay?" I asked her when Lex wanted to take our stuff to our rooms.

She nodded and smiled, snacking on some cheese and crackers, returning to her game with her new friend. I followed my husband through the mansion, hoping to catch a shower before dinner.

WE STAYED there for a few days while Poppy settled in to make sure she was comfortable. Dmitri obtained an American passport for her with a new name, Penelope Smith, just in case she needed to run at a moment's notice. He gave her a room next to Lex's cousin, Ursula, and during those few days, Poppy came to life.

Sure, she had a long road ahead of her and every day, she'd have to live in fear Alberich might show up. But she knew what to do if that happened. We'd made a game plan.

"You have the picture of Ivy's house in DC," I told her, giving her the burner phone and showing her how to pull up the photos. "Go there immediately, okay?"

"Thank you for this, Carter," she said with a nod, grabbing my hand with her miniature one. God, she was so small, so little. She shouldn't have been able to understand as much as she did. She shouldn't have seen all that she had. "Thank you for keeping me safe."

"I promise I always will," I told her, holding up my pinky finger. "Pinky swear."

She laughed and squeezed it. "Pinky swear."

What warmed me the most, what replayed in my mind before I fell asleep, was the way Lex had bonded with her. I found them whispering to each other in dark corners, laughing and giggling.

"She thinks I didn't want her," Lex said when I asked, pinching a cigarette between his fingers and running the other hand through his hair. "And she's right. Now I'm trying to show her that maybe I was wrong."

Fuck, my heart melted for him. If I didn't love him before, I'd fall for him all over again. But Lex reminded me homosexuality was illegal in Russia, and if we were found out, his uncle would toss me and Poppy on the first flight home. He'd likely beat Lex to hell for besmirching the family name in his own house. Either way, we were careful with our PDA.

About a week after we arrived, I received word from my agent that one of my auditions had been pushed up and, if I wanted to do it, I had to come home soon.

"How you feeling, kiddo?" I asked Poppy on our walk in the woods behind their estate. She had never seen snow before, so after outfitting her with an appropriate suit to keep her warm, I showed her what the stuff was all about. Snowballs. Snowmen. Snow forts.

All of it. But she seemed content to wander and try to catch the flakes on her tongue.

"I'm better," she said.

"Do you like it here?" I shoved my hands in my pockets, bracing myself against the bitter chill in the air.

"Oh, yes," she said. "Very much. Vera is nice, and Dmitri seemed scary at first, but he's a big softy like Lex."

I stiffened. He only *seemed* like a big softy to her. I'd heard the rumors, and I didn't need to ask to know that most of them were probably true. But Poppy was part of the family now. Vera had seen to that. Dmitri treated her the same way he treated any of their other children.

"Would you be okay hiding here for a while?"

She didn't answer at first, but then she nodded and pursed her lips. "I can come to Ivy's house whenever I want?"

I squatted down to be at eye level with her. "You should try to stay here if you can. It's safer."

She nodded.

"But yes," I answered, "Ivy's house. My house. I gave you the addresses. You have the photos."

"Does this mean you're leaving?" She stared up at me with big, curious eyes, reminding me so much of Lizzie.

I sighed and adjusted her jacket, wrapping it tighter around her neck. "Yeah. I have to work."

She took a deep breath, resigning herself to this next chapter of her life. "Okay."

"I wish you could come with me," I said, standing again. "And one day, you will. When it's safe."

She grabbed my hand while we walked. "When will that be?"

"I don't know," I said. "But one day."

"Do you think I'll ever be able to get back to Faerie? Back to my lady?" She squinted up at me, perhaps hoping I'd be able to tell her she could.

"I hope so." That was the best I could offer.

Ursula came out of the woods and threw a snowball at Poppy's chest, beaming her right in the shoulder. Poppy gasped and then burst into giggles, chasing after her new friend.

"Ursula! Poppy!" Vera called from beyond the tree line. She followed with something in Russian that I suspected asked them to come back for lunch. They both ran laughing in that direction. I turned to follow, but a big body hit me from the right and took me down to the ground with a loud grunt.

The smell hit me next.

Lex.

I wrestled with him, pushing his shoulders so I was on top. He countered, and we crested a hill, rolling in the snow until we stopped in the valley at the bottom, me on top of Lex, his legs bent on either side of my hips. His cock dug into my pelvis, already hard despite the cold, and I shivered with anticipation.

I pinned his arms above his head, chuckling low and deep in my throat as he thrashed against me. We'd both gotten bigger with age, but I worked out for a living. My job was to look powerful for the camera. I outweighed him by at least thirty pounds of muscle.

"Well, well, well," I said. "What do we have here?"

"Don't gloat just because you're a stupid fucking meathead now."

I laughed, dragging my nose along the side of his face to take another long inhale of my favorite man. The air was cool and the snow around my legs started to melt, but I didn't care. All I could feel was my heart pounding, the heat from his body so fucking close to mine.

It had been a week since I'd touched him, a week since that night in Faerie. I didn't know if it was the curse or the forbidden nature of it, but I wanted him more than I ever had. My skin ached for his touch. My tongue yearned for his cock. Whenever I caught him staring at me in that seductive Lex way, it took all my willpower not to drop to my knees and open my mouth in blatant expectation.

But now I had him alone in the woods. All to myself.

What's a boy to do?

Everyone else was eating lunch. Our absence would be noted, but they'd suspect Lex was showing me the grounds on our last day here. And oh...how right they were.

"A meathead you want to rail your tight little ass," I whispered, biting his earlobe between my teeth. My cock twitched when he trembled and tried to hide it. I'd always been able to break Lex to pieces, and that kind of power boosted a guy's ego.

"I'd rather you swallow my dick," he said, leaning up so he could swipe his warm, wet tongue across my bottom lip. The touch rattled all the way down in my toes, and my balls clenched.

Fuck, I'd always have it bad for him. One touch. One kiss. One look. I was his, and that would never change.

"You never did know when to stop running your mouth," I said. "Here you are, trapped under someone who could flip you over and pound you into the snow, and you still can't shut the fuck up."

I rolled my hips into him, grinding my dick against his between our pants.

"More threats?" he said. "Tsk. Tsk. Tsk. Do you know who I am in this country? I could tie you up and flog you in front of a live audience. No one would bat an eye."

"Oh." I let out a sardonic chuckle. "Don't tempt me with a good time."

"Good thing we're friends, right?" he continued, biting my bottom lip between his teeth. God damn it, he was so hot.

"Friends? We've never been friends, DC." I rolled my hips again, causing a deep groan to tumble out of his chest, inflating my sense of pride. "Not when I've only ever wanted to fuck you. Not when that's all you've ever wanted, too."

He laughed, trying to tease me and get in my head. "Why do you think I give a damn about you? I know how this story ends. You'll go back to Hollywood and forget about me again. Forget about *her*."

This might have started as play, but those words edged too close to the truth to be fake. I heard a sliver of doubt in his tone.

"Is that what you think?" I hissed, my temper starting to rise. "That I forgot about you? That I forgot about her?"

"Why should I trust a damn word you say?" He was trying to rile me up. He liked angry sex the best, and he especially liked it with me.

He wanted it like that? Fine.

I'd fuck that blue-blood smirk right into this goddamn blizzard. I didn't give a damn who saw us.

"Why should you trust me? Because I love you, Lex," I said. "I loved you first. I've always loved you."

He opened his mouth to argue, but I pressed my lips to his to *finally* silence him. *God,* they felt so good. I melted against him, moaning as my cock sought his, rubbing against it, urging it to respond. His fists dug into my jacket, yanking me to him tighter, and when I broke the kiss, he panted to try to catch his breath.

"Chicago," he started to say.

"Enough, DC." I sat back and flipped him around so he was on his belly, his knees under his hips, ass up in front of me.

I wrapped my fingers over his mouth to keep him quiet and whispered, "Warm my hand up for me." I tugged his pants down just enough so his ass was exposed. "So when I finally let you fuck my fist, your cock doesn't freeze off." He chuckled and the hot air of his breath surged between my fingers.

Then I dug in his pocket to find the lube. Because, of course, he tackled me with the sole purpose of fucking me out here in these quiet woods. He'd planned this. Though, I was sure my fucking him was not how he saw this going. Most of the time, I bottomed for Lex. But every now and then, Lex needed the reminder I, *too,* could take care of him. And that he, *too,* needed a good fucking to put him back in his place. I was all too eager to oblige.

I squeezed lube in his ass and worked my finger inside him. One finger became two, and soon, he was bucking back on me, mewling against my palm.

Fuck. Yeah.

To see Lex at his most vulnerable gave me the biggest hard-on in the world. Yeah, I loved being with Ivy, and fucking Miri was amazing. But Lex?

Jesus. Fucking. Christ.

Slipping inside him was always a reunion of souls, a hot, tight reminder that we were a match made in the stars. I couldn't wait any longer. I unzipped my pants and lined my cock up at his entrance, slowly easing the tip inside.

Fuuucck, he was so perfect. He relaxed into me, sagging into the contact, like it felt better for him than it did for me. I understood the feeling. When Lex fucked me, my legs shook for hours afterward.

"Good goddamned hell," he grumbled, his words muffled by my fingers.

"Shhh," I whispered next to his ear, my body pressed against his. "Wouldn't want *Djadja* overhearing his *malysh* getting railed like a filthy whore, would we?"

Lex let out a sick, twisted noise, and I buried myself deeper inside of him, hitting that spot that drove him wild. I froze and rolled my hips, and he trembled. That made *me* shiver, too.

"I love you, Lex," I whispered. "I've always loved you, and no matter what you do or what you say, that won't change. I can't forget you. Don't you know that by now?" I pressed my forehead to the back of his hair, inhaling his scent deep in my lungs, wishing I could bottle it up and carry it around with me so I could smell it whenever I wanted.

He made a sound kind of like a sob, and he collapsed under me, his whole body going limp at the confession. Maybe he'd come already. Maybe he was realizing how deep my feelings for him truly went. Either way, I needed him to remember it.

I pushed up on my knees behind him, one hand pressing his head into the snow, the other pinning his shoulders down. I took him harder and deeper, marking him, claiming him as deeply as he'd ever claimed me.

"Years and miles may separate us," I said. "But you're mine. Understand? Always."

I thrust harder now, deeper, curling my fist in his hair. My cock swelled inside of him, my climax hitting me right between the eyes, splintering down my spine and into my legs.

"Fuck," I moaned, spilling deep inside him, my orgasm rocketing through my veins. I stayed like that, letting my dick have its way, not knowing when it'd get another chance.

This moment is pure euphoria. I could live in it forever.

Eventually, I eased out of him, taking special care to run my hands over his spine before giving his ass a quick pat. I pulled his pants up so when I flipped him around, he didn't have his bare ass on the snow. Because I planned to suck his cock just like he wanted, and when he came in my throat, I wanted him to be comfortable.

See? I'm a gentleman, too.

He pouted and his cheeks blushed, making him look like the sex-soaked hedonist I'd always known. I freed his cock, and his lips parted to say something probably shitty and degrading, but this was my scene. This was my show. So I covered his mouth again and pushed him to lie flat, leaning down to get to work.

I teased him by licking the tip, making him groan and let out a deep exhale. When I sucked him the way he liked, licking and flicking the spot just under his head, I had to shove a forearm in his gut to keep him still. He tried to grab for my hair, but I circled his wrists and pinned him down again. When I finally let him come, it was with my fingers down his throat, my lips wrapped around his dick, and my name on his tongue.

I absolutely lived to unravel him.

When we were done, I rolled to the side and threw an arm over my eyes, breathing down the dopamine rush, panting into the frigid air.

"Christmas," he finally said, his voice gravelly like he'd swallowed a sandblaster. "Promise me Christmas."

I looked at him, taking a deep inhale before nodding. "I think I can swing it."

He shook his head and rubbed his hands over his face. "I have a secret I need to tell you."

"Oh?" I raised an eyebrow. "Go on."

"You know I love Miri," he said, rolling on his side so he could face me. "And Ivy and me...well...it's complicated, but I do love her."

I snorted. After all these years, I was happy he could finally admit it.

"But you..." He shook his head, finding and lighting two cigarettes, one for each of us. "There's something about you, Chicago." His voice dropped so he could whisper the next bit so low that only I could hear it.

It seemed sweet, right? To be craved by someone you loved, someone you also craved. But his face grew more somber when he realized I was being too romantic about it.

He rubbed a hand over his hair, brushing it out of his face. "Those two years I didn't see you felt like I'd quit smoking cold turkey. And now that I fell off the wagon—" His eyes widened, and he inhaled his cigarette, blowing it out in a thick puff of gray smoke. "I *can't* go another two years, Carter. I'll fucking lose my mind."

"I promise, DC," I said, leaning in to kiss him.

"Whatever this magic is," he said. "It's affecting me in really fucked-up ways. Carter, I could *feel* you getting closer. I knew when you were in DC. I don't know *how* I knew, but I did." It flickered behind his eyes, the first real bite of fear. Up until now, he'd hardly flinched. Running from a fairy king? No big deal to Lex fucking Fairfax. Cursed by a trickster fae? Rolls right off the Russian prince's back.

But for one brief second, he looked like a little boy, small and terrified. It made him seem fallible for the first time since I'd known him.

And that scared the living shit out of me.

"Christmas," I said again, reassuring him. "I promise."

29

MIRI
LONDON

Ivy had an eight-hour layover at Heathrow that she extended to twenty-four hours. She had to return to the States, but she could do some homework from the UK, enough to get her up to speed. The rest she'd finish when she could. From the plane, security snuck us into the limo waiting for me. Even though the windows were tinted, Ivy ducked down to stay hidden, just in case.

Photographers swarmed the car on either side, circling us in all directions, shouting questions about where I'd been and if there was any truth to the rumors about me and Reginald, prince of Monaco. I rolled my eyes, remembering the nonsense I'd escaped when this whole thing started—the dinner with the prince and the donations for Danae. I'd caught up on the plane ride, sent a few emails, and agreed to several events so I could squeeze more money out of the right people, but I'd practically forgotten about my upcoming nuptials.

Bollocks.

I was supposed to go to Monaco sometime soon. I was supposed to deliberate his proposal. I was supposed to be the Duchess of Aberdeen. I'd gone on this fantastic magical journey only to arrive right back where I'd started with an entirely new perspective on the whole thing. Me included.

I'd seen terrible things—a queen made humble by her own husband, a child that could teleport halfway around the world and back, a completely new realm full of creatures that were only supposed to exist in fairy tales. I'd learned the truth about my connection to my spouses and what the implications were of the vows we'd made that night in ruins.

I remembered.

I remembered Alberich saving me from the wreck.

Yes, Little Thistle, you'll come to owe me quite a bit before we're through.

I shoved it down inside of me, relegating it to a part of my mind that I could lock and forget about. The point was, in the span of a few days (or what felt like a few days to me), I'd become a completely different person and the rest of the world had stayed much the same.

Once my driver felt confident we'd lost the paparazzi, Ivy sat up and shook her head, heaving a deep sigh and muttering something about vultures.

"You used to say it was the price we paid to live the life we did," I said.

"My *mother* used to say that," she corrected, smiling from next to me. "I'm not so sure I agree with her anymore."

"Uh-oh," I said. "That sounds like rebellion."

She shrugged. "Maybe it's time for me to be rebellious."

Oh, I liked this side of Ivy. Perhaps a little too much. Maybe she read that in my gaze because she winked and leaned in to kiss me, but my phone vibrated and drew my attention to my lap.

Gran.

"Shite," I said. When my phone finally regained signal, I'd had three missed calls from her and thirty from Sandra. If Grandmother had bothered to call me *three* times, and I hadn't answered, I was in immense trouble. This was now call number four. I picked it up, my hand shaking, my voice more anxious than I'd liked. "Hello, Gran."

"Hello, Gran?" A brief, appalled silence before, "Darling, where have you been?"

"Would you believe I lost my charger?" I lied. "I went on a trip to Ireland, to that college where I did the intensive. You remember the place, surely."

"I wish you'd let someone know," she said. "I almost deployed the royal guard to find you."

"Gran." I sighed. "I'm twenty-four years old. I'm allowed to vacation when I want."

She clicked her teeth, a noise that echoed her disapproval. I was her granddaughter and her subject. One did not simply *tell* the queen what to do, but it got Ivy's attention, and she raised an eyebrow at me.

"Now, listen to me, my dear," Gran said, but my attention drifted to my wife, my one and only wife, as she kneeled in front of me. I zeroed in on her hand going to the switch for the partition, sliding the tinted glass up so my driver couldn't see back here.

It set my heart racing.

What is she planning?

Stupid question, of course. The look in her eyes and the flick of her tongue across her bottom lip told me what she wanted. Heaven damn me, but I wanted it, too.

I should have been paying attention to whatever the queen of England babbled on about. I should have been the respectful, responsible granddaughter and listened. But I only mumbled an unintelligible *uh-huh* at appropriate breaks in the conversation and followed that piercing gray stare as it slid down my body.

She coasted her palms up either side of my legs, tucking under the hem of my floral patterned skirt. My pussy clenched, and my clit throbbed in time with my heart as she twisted her fingers in the fabric of my tights, right at the crotch. Then she yanked, splitting them up the middle.

I gasped and jumped. It was one of the hottest things anyone had ever done to me, made even more so because I was on the phone with the queen while *THE* daughter of the American Revolution went down on me in the back of my limo.

"Miriam, darling? Are you okay?" Gran asked.

"Uh-huh."

"Okay." She didn't sound convinced, but she continued.

Ivy disappeared under my skirt and pushed my satin panties to the side, sliding her tongue against my skin in a decadent display of pure euphoria.

I hissed in a breath and rolled against the touch, rewarded with a small chuckle and her arms over my hips, pinning me in place.

"What was that?" Gran asked, bringing my attention back to the phone call.

"Nothing," I sputtered. "Stubbed my toe."

Ivy laughed again, and the vibration rattled through me at our connection. I arched into her, my free hand going to her soft hair. She grabbed my wrist and held it down, staring up at me with that spark of mischief in her eye that had originally attracted me to her. I loved her so very much, and this impulsive creativity was only the start of the reasons why. Ivy sucked at my swollen nub and licked me until a breathy sigh poured out of my throat. Pleasure skated across my skin, warm and ecstatic, and I never wanted to come back to reality.

"Miriam!" My grandmother was near hysterics.

"Yes?" I said, my attention diverted again.

"Reginald has asked when he can see you again."

"I don't know," I said. "Gran, I'm feeling a bit flu-ish. I'll call you later." Without waiting for a response, I hung up. It was likely the most unceremonious goodbye she'd ever received, and I'd pay for it later.

Ivy pushed two fingers inside me, slowly allowing me to accommodate them before she did that thing with her tongue that made me fall apart. I clamped my thighs around her head, but she giggled and held them open with her elbows, tipping me over the edge, bringing me back down to earth.

I panted and hummed a sick sadistic noise as I planned my

revenge for this Yankee brat who took what she wanted without care for the repercussions.

"Fucking hell," she said, wiping at her chin with the back of her hand, leaning the side of her head against my knee. "I love making you come on my face."

"You owe me a pair of tights."

"Bill me," she said with a scoff.

I wanted my retribution right then and there, so I used my body weight to push her onto her back on the limo floor, devouring her mouth with mine. She tasted like sex and me and her, the perfect mix to drive me wild. I wanted to see her fall apart. I wanted to make her as wild as she'd made me. I grabbed the button on her trousers and flicked it open.

"Princess Miriam," she whispered. "How naughty you've become."

I laughed and bit her bottom lip, sliding my hand down her trousers, finding her wet and ready for me. "You love me this way."

She started to reply, but I swallowed down her moan when I pushed my fingers inside her and rubbed at her clit with my palm, focusing on her contorted features as her pleasure ramped up. Ivy had always been very selective about who she let inside her body, so to be given the privilege of this intimacy almost made me come again from the thought alone.

What a silly little queer I'd grown up to be. I watched as Ivy fell apart around my fingers, a delicate pink flush creeping up her neck and into her cheeks. Ginger hair stuck to her face as her breathy moans urged me on. I loved fucking Ivy, even more when she let me have control like this. Most of the time, when we were together, she took the lead. She liked being in control of me, but oh, to have her bucking against my palm, to bury my fingers deep inside her, it reminded me of the first time. She'd been so naive and innocent in that dorm room, and I'd been the deviant princess who stole her innocence. No one could ever take that away from me.

When she rolled her hips against me, I worked her faster, deeper, inhaling her moans and sucking her neck just the way she liked. I licked over that succulent X and held her through her climax, smiling when my fingers came away from her wet and sticky. I licked them clean and kissed her again, delighting in her disheveled smile.

"Stay with me tonight," she whispered against my lips, breathing down her climax. I loved her when she was relaxed and euphoric, her mind free of that frantic race it normally contained. Like this, she was vulnerable, sweet, and unguarded. Like this, I could see the girl I'd met in a dorm room in Virginia all those years ago.

"I can't," I whispered back.

"Sure you can," she said, kissing the tip of my nose. We were still on the floor of the limo, her arms wrapped around me, my head on her chest, right above her heartbeat, so familiar and soothing and steady. "You've already insulted her by hanging up on her. What's a few more hours?"

I sighed and laughed, curling into her. "I shouldn't."

"But not won't," she whispered. "C'mon. I've had to share you with Lucifer this whole time." That made me look up at her where I met that steel gaze, flickering with something sinful. "Let's have a girls' night. Like we used to."

"You need to be sure," I said. "One wrong move, our affair is on the front page of *The Puck*. Nowhere is safe."

"I'll sneak you into my room," she said. "I booked the presidential suite on Lex's credit card."

I snickered, everything in me wanting to give in to her, wanting to give in to this sweet temptation. A night alone? With my wife? In a big hotel room? Well, not even the end of the world could sway me from that.

"Okay, darling." I pushed up to kiss her, and her moan of approval sunk deep down inside of me.

I spent the rest of that night making her moan.

Sometime later...much, much later...after I let her strip me bare and lick whichever parts pleased her most, we lay in the king-size bed on our stomachs, facing each other. Naked from the waist up, I let my eyes trail over her freckled ivory skin. Such beautiful skin. I wanted to spend all night connecting the dots, seeing what constellations I could make.

We talked about everything. Poppy. Lex. Carter. My grandmother and her mother and the upcoming wedding.

"She'll expect it before I run for Congress," Ivy said. "Sometime in the next year."

I could no longer act like it didn't hurt, and I bit my bottom lip as I imagined what it would be like when it finally happened. When the two loves of my life stood in front of the whole world and pronounced their love for each other. I'd have to pretend to be happy, even as it spread like rot inside every part of my heart.

"It doesn't change anything." She grabbed my hand, bringing my knuckles to her lips for a tender kiss. "We still married each other in those woods."

I snorted. "Yeah, and now we even have a child to take care of."

She pulled one side of her mouth into a smile. "How are you feeling? After the thistles?"

"Fine," I said. But my secret weighed on me. I didn't tell anyone about my memory or what Alberich said. Part of me wanted to spill it right then and there. Ivy would understand. Ivy might even know what to do. Of the four of us, I'd loved her first. We were best friends, lovers, girlfriends, soul mates. She understood me in ways no one else ever could.

But Alberich's words rattled through me again.

Little Thistle, you'll come to owe me quite a bit before we're through.

It sounded so…intimate. The nickname. The promise of a debt to be paid. What did he know that I didn't? How was he able to be at the car accident? He was supposed to have been locked up in Faerie. Cursed! Unable to come to the realm of man. If he did, his first act was *supposed* to have been the complete annihilation of my species, not rescuing little ole me from a tumbling car wreck.

Perhaps I imagined the whole thing. Perhaps I made it up — a dream, an invention of my subconscious to deal with what I'd seen and done.

"Are you okay?" Ivy danced a finger over my shoulder and down the center of my spine. I shivered at the touch, scooting closer to her so I could use her body for warmth.

"Of course," I said. "Why wouldn't I be?"

"This trip was intense," she said. "It's okay to be messed-up about it. I am."

"Honestly, darling," I said, "I survived growing up royal. I can handle a deposed king's temper tantrum."

She tried to smile, but concern radiated out of her gaze. "Miri, you stopped him dead in his tracks."

Little Thistle, his voice hissed through my head again.

"We got lucky," I said. "I wouldn't have been able to do it without the rest of you." I knew that in my soul. They each gave me strength, and from that, I'd been able to surprise myself.

Ivy raised a skeptical eyebrow, but that was her. Her mind was always working, always calculating the next risk, always planning four steps ahead.

I should tell her. The words were right there on the tip of my tongue.

But...I stopped myself.

I promised her honesty. I promised her the truth. But I didn't even know what this was yet. Until I did, I wanted to keep it to myself.

Ivy left the next morning in a tearful goodbye with promises of Christmas on her lips. I'd do everything in my power to make it happen. Then with my tail firmly between my legs, I dragged myself to Kensington where Sandra waited for me with her arms crossed and an eyebrow halfway up her forehead.

"She's been expecting you," she said.

"Yeah, I'll bet she has," I murmured.

Technically, my grandfather was the regent. He was the one who had inherited the throne from his father, and so on. But they'd been married since they were fifteen and had long ago decided to split up the duties in a manner befitting 1942. She would handle the family, the house, and the matronly tasks. In turn, he would handle the Commonwealth. It was what had made the English crown work for many centuries.

My stomach twisted as we made our way to my grandmother's sitting room, my hand trembling on the railing as I climbed the carpeted stairs, the scent of Ivy's perfume lingering in my nose.

I can do this.

Be strong.

I wasn't the same person I was when I went running out of here.

I know that.

When we reached the door, the attendant knocked twice and waited for Gran to ring her bell before opening the entry and walking inside.

"Her Royal Highness, the Princess Miriam, duchess of Aberdeen—"

"Get in here this instant." My grandmother cut him off, quite out of character for a woman of her stature and grace. My knees shook as I walked inside. She sat in her favorite lavender chair with one of her Corgis across her lap, stroking a wrinkled hand between its ears. "Where have you been?"

I opened my mouth to reply, but she shook her head to silence me. Her question was rhetorical. Knowing her, she had implanted a tracking chip in the back of my brain when I was a child. She knew where I was without my needing to say so.

Her attendants left us alone together, the door closing with a deafening *snick.*

"So long as you are Duchess of Aberdeen, you will never hang up on me again."

Fair enough. Even if she wasn't the queen of England, it was still a rude thing to do to someone.

"Apologies, Gran," I said. "I was in the middle of something."

She pursed her thin, dry lips and placed her dog on the floor before reaching for the tea on the table next to her. Then those haunting eyes raked over me, looking for imperfections, looking for cracks she could use to her advantage. But I'd been extra careful to dress myself appropriately this morning—calf-length dress, sensible kitten heels, wool blazer. I looked like a modest member of the royal court.

"You left before an event to go to Washington, DC and spend several weeks with Ivy Washington and Alexei Fairfax."

I cleared my throat and linked my hands behind my back. No sense in denying it. She already knew.

"Why?" she asked.

"They're old friends from college," I said. "I missed them dearly, and Ivy needed my help."

"With?" Gran raised her eyebrows, expecting a proper response.

"That's none of your concern."

She didn't like that answer. Deafening silence hung between us while she sipped her tea, a clear sign of her disapproval.

"You're my granddaughter by blood, my daughter by law." She tried to soften her tone despite the words dripping with disappointment. "Everything about you is my concern."

"I'm twenty-four, Grandmother," I said. "Well past the age of adulthood. You gave me a duchy before I was married."

"Because I wanted you to bloom," she said, clearly exasperated by my insolence. "Not cause more scandal."

"No one saw me." I'd made absolutely sure of that.

She took a deep breath and let it out with a sigh. "What to do with you, Miriam? What to do, indeed?"

"I know," I said. "An independent woman is such a dangerous creature." I stomped on thin ice at this point, waving a red flag in the bull's face and daring it to impale me on its thick horns.

She shot her stern gaze to me. "Do you think this is about independence?"

"This is about you having different expectations for your granddaughters than you have for your grandsons."

"Of course, I have different expectations for you." She pushed to her feet, and despite the fact I had at least five inches on her, she dwarfed me. "*They* have different expectations for you."

She meant *them*—out there, the world, England, the public I'd sworn to serve. I snapped my mouth shut because she was right. I'd known this my whole life. It was the same reason Lex could sleep around in his adolescence and I'd been called a whore for doing the same.

She brushed a piece of my hair behind my ear with her cold, bony fingers, attempting to be maternal for the first time in my life. "I've already lost a son and daughter," she said, almost tenderly, her eyes softening for a moment as she mentioned my parents. "I won't lose you, too."

"I'd like to have my own space," I forced myself to say. "An apartment. A few blocks away. Close, but far enough to live my life."

It landed like a dead fish at her feet. Her expression hardened again as she dropped her hands to her side. She gave me no reaction, but that was the worst one. It meant my request wouldn't even be considered, much less granted. If anything, now that I'd mentioned it, she might tighten her grip.

"We'll see," she finally said. "For now, prove to me you want to be a member of this family and update me on your progress with Danae Enterprises."

Shocked and outraged that there wouldn't even be a *discussion* about my living elsewhere, I forced myself to say some words about the Prince of Monaco's donation and how we needed to secure more funding to make a dent.

"I'd like to see you get America involved," she said. "They're one of the biggest polluters on the planet, but they have a liberal government right now. See what you can do."

See what I can do? As if it was as easy as that.

I nodded and said something like, "Of course, Grandmother."

"Anything else?"

I shook my head and left when she dismissed me, wandering the cold, isolated walls of Kensington Palace back to my apartment on the third floor. It was the same hallways, the same portraits, the same people bustling about, but it all seemed so...*comical* compared to what I'd lived through.

I'd made a fairy vow in a different realm that etched itself on my palm, binding me to three other people for the rest of my life. I'd stopped a fairy king from enacting his maniacal plan. I'd grown *kilometers* of thistles in seconds, using nothing but my bare hands.

Look at these naïve, ignorant people.

They had no idea the chaos that would be headed this way. My grandmother thought that what some wanker said on the front page of a magazine was the most important thing about me. How... *ridiculous.*

It made me laugh, and the more I thought about it, the more idiotic it seemed. I could cover this whole world in ivy, choke the life out of everything in it. And she thought keeping me trapped in this castle would keep me safe?

Ohhh...how little you know me, Grandmother.

On the other hand, staying here would keep *them* safe. If Alberich came looking for me, the first place he'd check would be here. He brought the queen to heel with very little effort. What would he make of my aging grandparents? My cousins? My uncles and our hundreds of employees?

Yes, I had to stay, I agreed. But not for my protection, and certainly not because my grandmother thought it was the best for my reputation. If Alberich came, I'd have to protect them. If Alberich came, I'd be the only protection they had.

So, begrudgingly, I went back to my apartment, determined to fall in line.

30

CARTER

NOW

"Wait, what's this?" the talking head said, catching my attention as I hung up. "I'm being told now that Ivy and Lex are missing. No one can find them in the marital suites."

I shot to my feet, alarm ricocheting down my spine.

Son of a bitch.

My phone rang again.

Weeds.

I picked it up, about to ask her what the hell was going on, but a heavy weight hit me in the gut. Power and magic. Twisted. Evil.

The king.

I'd only ever felt this once before—in Faerie two years ago when we were hiding under the stage. That heady electricity twisted through the air, making the hair on my arms stand on end, coating my tongue like battery acid.

Shit. I brought the phone to my ear.

"Carter, he's here." Ivy sobbed, the sounds of rustling fabric in the background distracting me.

"Where are you?" I needed to get to them. We were stronger together, the four of us.

"We're in Mount Vernon," she said.

"Is he still in London?" Lex asked in the background.

"Yeah," I said. "But I can be in DC soon." I scrambled into action, grabbing my jacket and stuffing my wallet into my back pocket. I was on a publicity tour for season four of *Fractured Crowns,* but I could be in DC in less than six hours. I left my clothes, figuring I'd have my assistant pack them and send them to me. "I'll call Miri." I'd just talked to her a few moments ago. She'd answer if I tried again.

I ignored Ivy's sob, hating how things were between us now, hating that things had gotten so incredibly fucked up.

"Have you talked to her?" Lex asked.

"Yeah." I couldn't tell them Miri's secret, at least not over the phone, not like this. "It's complicated."

"Be careful," Ivy said.

"Of course, Weeds," I said. "I love you."

"I love you," came her somber reply.

I opened the door to my hotel suite and went to hang up, but the two people on the other side made me pause. I lowered my arm, the call still connected, and dropped the phone to the floor at my feet.

"Lizzie?" My gaze ran the length of my little sister. At sixteen, she stood five-ten with the same long, lanky limbs we'd both inherited from our father. She had curly blond hair that poofed around her head, what I imagined my hair would do if I let it get that long.

Then I looked at Poppy next to her. She'd been here two years now, enough to grow into the body of a twelve-year-old. But we all knew a much older mind hid behind those eyes, even though she did her best to conceal it. "Poppy? What are you doing?"

"I'm sorry, Carter." Poppy's red-rimmed gaze met mine as tears slid down her cheeks. "I'm sorry for what I have to do."

"What?" I narrowed my eyes on her, confusion and apprehension snaking down my spine in a sickening shiver. "Lizzie, what's she—"

But Lizzie looked terrible, pale with blushed, wet cheeks. She'd been crying, and she had an expression in her wide, terrified eyes like she'd seen a massacre and the shock was too much to talk about.

"What the fuck is going on?" The rage and fury in my voice startled me as I clenched my hands into fists.

"I have to do this, Carter," Poppy said. "I know you don't understand now. But you will. I promise."

"Do what?" My stomach churned as reality caught up to me. There could only be one reason the king had come to this realm, and it was for her. Had he already caught up with her? Had he already screwed with her mind? "Poppy, tell me what's going on. I can help you. Is it the king? Has he threatened you?"

"No, it's not the king." Poppy gripped Lizzie's hand tighter. "I just thought you should say goodbye."

"Goodbye?" Rancid horror coated the fear in my gut, sending sizzling vibrations through my veins. "What do you mean goodbye?"

"I love you, Carter," Poppy said, glancing up at Lizzie. "She's been entranced or else she would tell you she loves you, too. She'll miss you. We both will."

"Poppy, no." I started toward her, trying to grab her. "Wait. Poppy. Stop!"

But it was too late.

Just before my hand reached Poppy's shoulder, they both disappeared.

To be continued in Book Three: Solstice

WANT MORE?

Thank you for reading *Samhain,* and if you enjoyed it, please consider leaving a review on Goodreads, Amazon, and/or anywhere else you get your books. Not only do they help other readers, but the algorithm uses reviews to promote and categorize the book.

The next book in the series, *Solstice,* releases on November 26, 2024. Book four, *Beltane,* will go live March 25, 2025.

If you want more while you wait, I have a novella featuring Siobhan, Finn, and Donnelly. It's a 13k short that takes place before *Midsummer*. It gives a taste of what's to come and what the king and queen of fairies are actually like.

If you're interested, please follow this link: https://books.jenadoyle.com/WeWildThings

Thanks again. Keep reading for a sneak peak at *Solstice.*

SOLSTICE
...TO DIE UPON THE HAND
I LOVED SO WELL
JENA DOYLE

SOLSTICE BLURB

<u>Lex</u>

Even though the wedding event of a lifetime is looming over us, Ivy and I still hate each other. But I don't want a marriage full of spite and resentment. I want Ivy to want me, and the more I try, the harder that gets.

When my spouses and I left Ireland the last time, we tried to prevent any unwanted consequences from following us home, but that proved to be more difficult than it should have been.

With our bad life choices hunting us down, I don't have time to fight a fairy war that has nothing to do with us...even if it crosses over into the human realm.

<u>Ivy</u>

Lex is up to something, and I suspect he's keeping secrets from me again. But I don't have time to dive deeper into his mind.

Congress is stressful, my mother is making her own plans for my wedding, and Miri is more closed off than ever.

I just need to get through these next few months without any fairy tale nonsense following us home from Ireland. But even my best laid plans go to waste, especially with the fairies involved.

SOLSTICE
PROLOGUE

LEX

Now

It was a sham wedding.

Everyone knew it.

I knew it. Ivy knew it.

Four years of faking it, and here we were, staring down a night that would live in infamy for all the wrong reasons. The public wanted the glitz and the glam. They wanted the star-studded event with the free booze and the photo ops. But that wasn't us anymore. That hadn't been us for a long time. Not since Ireland. Not since Samhain and the changeling child, Poppy, and the mess in the woods with the king and the queen two years ago.

We'd be lucky to make it out of this alive.

We'd be lucky if this so-called wedding didn't end in bloodshed.

"You look pissed," Ivy's brother, Jon, said, fixing my tie. Like his sister, he had steel-gray eyes and thick ginger hair. We'd been friends since we were little, and though he reminded me of my bullheaded

289

wife, he'd become an adopted brother to me over the years. "You need to fix your scowl before photo time."

Fuck.

Today, the crease between my eyebrows had more to do with the shit about to go wrong than my resting bitch face. I lit a cigarette and took a deep inhale, relishing the nicotine buzz as I looked in the mirror. The clothes were right. The hair was right. Everything about today had been planned down to the fucking minute.

But I itched for reasons I couldn't tell anyone.

Am I really going to go through with this?

Twenty-six years, all leading up to this moment.

I looked out the window at the crowd gathering below—fifteen hundred of America's finest sycophants, here to suck the life out of what little remained of my soul. I'd grown up around them, so I could handle the pressure. But after what happened to Ivy and Miri, after how the world had reacted, these blue-blood fuckers didn't deserve to share the happiest fucking day of my life with me.

This is going to draw him out. This is a bright, shiny beacon.

Everyone I'd ever known and loved was here, well...*almost* every-one. But this was my plan, wasn't it? I cracked my neck and took another draw on my cigarette.

This is the stupidest thing I've ever done on a long list of stupid.

Ivy had been right. What the hell was I thinking?

Visions of Samhain danced in my head—thick fogs of smoke, a dark, maniacal laugh, thistle bushes twenty feet tall. Getting out of Faerie had been hell both times, and I didn't want to bring that chaos here.

Too late. All of it. All of this. Just...*too late.*

Someone knocked on the door, and my mother appeared when it opened, followed by my father.

"*Malysh! Malysh!*" She walked closer with her arms out, tears in her eyes, and cupped my face, leaning in to give me a kiss that didn't touch my cheek. "You look so handsome. Such a beautiful day. So long in the making."

"Yes, yes," said my father, the current president of the United States, swirling a glass of whiskey in his hand and forcing a smile. "You're doing the right thing, Alexei."

He kept his attention on the guests outside, the sounds of the pre-wedding music echoing from the string band.

It was all so fucking pretentious, this circus and the way my mother blubbered over me, as if I chose this, as if it were my decision. She'd broken a promise to me years ago, one I hadn't forgotten about, one I could never forgive her for.

"I know you weren't thrilled about this at the beginning." Father shifted his gaze to me. "But my ratings are through the roof. Despite the scandal, people still love you both."

Despite the scandal.

There it was again, that judgmental look in his eyes, the one that reminded me the wrong son had died nearly a decade ago.

Standing here today, I'd drown you in the Boston Bay myself if it meant I'd get my son back.

He'd told me that once, but even that was my fault because I'd *made* him confess. It was the only way I'd ever gotten the truth out of him.

I sighed and shook my head. *If only Marcus were here.* If only Marcus were the one to marry Ivy instead. If only Marcus had been the one in Ireland, the one at those ruins, gifted with the ability to make anyone tell the truth.

Despite the scandal.

What would Marcus have done if he were me? What would have happened if the golden child had been cursed by fairies and doomed to live a life he didn't choose?

It doesn't fucking matter.

Marcus was dead, and I inherited this mess. Even if my father continued to be disappointed I'd lived, neither of us could change that. I stabbed out my cigarette and immediately lit another one.

"Alexei," my mother said. "I wish you would stop that filthy habit."

"We're all wishing a lot of things right now." I drew a deep, soothing inhale.

My father let out a disappointed sigh and scowled. "You'll never change, will you?"

I shot my gaze to his, horrible things threatening to spill over my lips.

"Still that same petulant boy," he continued. "Angry at the world for no good reason."

No good reason.

"Is that what you think?" I blew out smoke. "That I'm angry for no reason?"

"You decided a long time ago you weren't going to be happy, and you've been living to spite me ever since."

I cleared my throat. Well, it wouldn't have been my wedding day if my father hadn't found some way to rip out my guts and eat them in front of me. He had no fucking clue what waited for us out there. He had no idea what monsters lurked in the trees, biding their time for the right opportunity to strike.

This was so fucking trivial, so fucking unimportant. I had a thousand other things to worry about—an evil fairy king, reuniting my family, making sure this realm stayed safe. And this? This is what addles the mind of the president of the United States?

I tried not to laugh. "Thanks for the pep talk."

"We're almost ready for you," Marcia, the wedding planner, said, sticking her head into the room.

"We'll see you downstairs." My mother gave me another tearful kiss as my father turned to walk away, barely an acknowledgment for his surviving son.

After they were gone, Jon winced and then sighed. "If it helps, I'm certain things went about as well with my parents in the bridal suite."

I started to laugh, but as the sound came out of my mouth, a heaviness settled in my gut. Power shifted in the air, magic coalescing on my tongue. It reminded me of...

No. Not yet. It's not time.

I need to find Ivy.

I raced across the suite to open the door, but Ivy's sister, Kit, grabbed the handles from the other side and swung them open. She startled back a few steps when she came face-to-face with me.

"Lex, I need your help." She shifted her icy blue eyes from me to Jon and back again. "It's Ivy."

Then she took off down the hallway.

Acknowledgments

Dear Reader,

We are halfway through the story. When I first set out to do an adaptation of *Midsummer Night's Dream,* I knew two things: I needed the four lovers to actually be lovers and I wanted them to have a chance to defend themselves. Lex and Ivy took over *Midsummer.* Their voices were so loud in my head that Carter and Miri were drowned out. This time, I wanted to do my knight and my princess justice because both are valuable in their own right.

The next two books will feature all four POVS. Prepare yourself for more fairy shenanigans, queer love, and twisty plot turns. Poppy is more than she seems. The king did some fucked up shit to the queen. And we're finally going to find out what happened at Lex and Ivy's wedding.

I owe a lot of people thanks with this story:

To my faithful and loving beta readers — Maggie Sims, Leslie Grace, Jenn Britt, Shannon, and Sarah. You continue to have faith in me and push me to better things. Thank you for being my cheerleaders.

To my partner, Adam — I couldn't do it without you. I love you to pieces.

To my editors, Misha and Kim - A million thanks and my undying gratitude for your wisdom and support.

To my ARC readers — Thank you for taking a chance on me and reading whatever I put into the world.

To my shadow work friends — Amethyst, Nae, Willow, Becca,

and everyone who supports my mental health. You have saved me in more ways than you know. If it weren't for your support, I don't know if I ever would have been around to publish this. Thank you, with so much love.

To you, dear Reader — Thank you for supporting me and giving this queer poly love story a shot.

And finally to the voices that made up Shakespeare, especially those that history forgot — I don't believe Shakespeare was one illiterate man from Stratford-upon-Avon. If I have one tin-hat conspiracy theory, it's that the Shakespeare plays were written by a group of people, most notably Edward de Vere, 16th Earl of Oxford, Emilia Bassano, Charles Marlowe, and Ben Johnson. This explains why they catered to the rich and the poor, to the gays and the straights, to the gender fluid, the Christians, and the Jewish people. They are rife with contradictions about feminism, marriage, and royalty. I could get on a soapbox about this topic, but suffice it to say, I aimed to do these authors justice with my adaptation. Here's to all the queers that history forgot. I see you, and I love you.

Cheers!

Jena

Also by Jena Doyle

<u>MIDSUMMER</u>

We Wild Things (Prequel Novella)

Midsummer

Samhain

Solstice

Beltane

<u>STEEL ROSES MC</u>

They Called Him Saint (Prequel Novella)

Crimson Chaos

Savage Saint

Oleander Oaths

Mischief Mayhem

Ruthless Reign

<u>ROYAL BASTARDS MC: HELENA, MT</u>

Blood and Whiskey